Finding Me

Also by Darnella Ford

Naked Love

Published by Dafina Books

Finding Me

Darnella Ford

KENSINGTON PUBLISHING CORP.
www.kensingtonbooks.com

I dedicate this book to the divine essence that lives within me, who has loved me into life, lifetime after lifetime, after lifetime after life; and to my beautiful teacher, Ramtha the Enlightened One.

You are more than bone
Blood
Mass
And flesh.
You are so much more than skin.

Chapter 1

Identical

It was the late spring of 1983, and I was a pee pot.

I was addicted to peeing in the bed.

I did it every night, without fail.

I would wake up midstream, but by then it was already too late. The deed was done, and I would lie there, shivering.

Not again.

Why couldn't I wake up before I peed?

Was that too much to ask?

Pee.

Pee.

And more pee.

The sheets would fill to capacity with the strong, pungent liquid spilling warmth from my bottom, which quickly turned cold, but that wasn't the bad part, just the unpleasant element. The bad part was that the acid of the pee had eaten through the flimsy mattress of the top bunk, burning a hole straight through it. Literally, it ate it right up. When I took off the sheet, the springs were exposed, and gigantic brown stains howled disapproval from one end to the other.

This was especially bad news for my identical twin, Aerial, because we slept in bunk beds. I had the top bunk, and she had the bottom. Every time I peed in the bed, it would leak through the springs and drip on her face. This happened so much that I would tease Aerial and call her a pee-pee face.

I offered on more than one occasion to switch bunks with her, but she refused each time, stating as the basis for her refusal, "The top bunk stinks—smells just like pee!"

"So does the bottom bunk," I reminded her. "It's seen just as much pee as the top bunk."

"Yeah, right!" she snapped with a twisted expression.

Aerial was a beautiful girl, but when she poked out her lips and rolled her eyes into the back of her head like that, those good looks flew straight out the window.

"That face you make ain't cute," I always told her.

"And neither is bed-wetting," she'd always remind me.

In infancy, bed-wetting was an acceptable form of self-expression, but once I grew out of diapers, it wasn't cute anymore. It's just not a cool thing to do when you're in the sixth grade.

I went to sleep dry.

Woke up wet.

Every night.

No exceptions.

Dry.

Wet.

Dry.

By the way, I should probably tell you my name, since you already know some pretty embarrassing stuff about me.

My name is Blaze LeDoux James. I am eleven years old, but I am a long way from being average. I am gifted by way of intelligence. Now, nobody has officially confirmed my "gift" of being unusually smart for my age, so you may ask the question, "Who said I was gifted?"

I said it.

And why did I say it? 'Cause in the end, the things we say about ourselves are the only things that end up being true. We are self-created. Now you can see firsthand why I call myself gifted.

I live in Shreveport, Louisiana, across the street from a garbage dump. Truth is, my whole block stinks to high heaven, not just my bunk bed.

We live at 216 Turnpike Street in "economy housing," or something like that. It just means the houses are darned near free, because our backyard and front-yard views are of city trash. It seems like the house is almost turned around sideways on the street. Rent is real cheap, 'cause we live behind the railroad tracks, and every hour the walls shake from the railcar passing through.

All of the houses on this street are small, run-down shacks, and the neighbors are shady—not because they're covered by trees but because they do crooked things.

Our next-door neighbor calls himself "Reverend Mike," but he ain't no more a preacher than you or me. He stands on the corner selling fake jewelry and gold teeth to anyone who wants to get a good deal for cheap. But the only thing I say is *buyer beware*. It has been rumored on the street that Reverend Mike's jewelry turns both the skin and the teeth pea green. Not very attractive at all.

Four doors down from our dump and directly across the street lives Miss Felicity Hardaway. Rumor has it she's the best barber in all of Shreveport, Louisiana. She owns her own little barbershop close to downtown called Cutting Up. It's always packed, because not only is Miss Felicity really good, but also the fellows are partial to her good looks.

According to the little perverted neighborhood boys, they use a term called stacked to describe her 'cause of the way her body is built. Miss Felicity's breasts and hips are extra large, and the boys go nuts for her. She's always prancing around half-naked in the neighborhood, wearing these itsy-bitsy booty shorts, smacking gum and smoking one cigarette after the next. She talks with the volume turned up on high, and we can always hear her telephone conversations, which are mostly cackling laughter, because the sound trickles out of her living room and down the driveway, spilling out into the street.

I oftentimes find myself staring out of the big picture window that sits in our living room, waiting on Miss Felicity to come home. There's something downright mesmerizing about her that brings me here.

"Why you always staring at that woman?" Aerial would ask.

"'Cause she's different," I'd say.

"You don't even know her," Aerial would insist.

"Yeah," I'd agree, "but I'd like to."

"You think you might like to be fast like that when you grow up?" she'd ask me. And I would look at her and roll my eyes, and stick out my tongue at her.

Miss Felicity Hardaway is well-known in the neighborhood because she's good for blasting her radio all night, till the early morning hours. Most of the fellows overlook it, 'cause most of them have crushes on her. The women in the neighborhood are good and sick of Miss Felicity. Good and sick. Mama is not a big fan either; she's never said anything bad about Miss Hardaway, but we can just tell she doesn't like her. Maybe 'cause our daddy, Mr. Rufus, is always trying to sneak a peek out the window when Mama ain't looking, but that's impossible, 'cause Mama's always looking.

Always.

"What you think she's like?" I asked Aerial every afternoon when we'd pass Miss Felicity's house on the way home from school.

"Seems something like a movie star to me," she would always say.

"You think she's prettier than Mama?" I would ask.

"No way," said Aerial.

"I do sometimes . . ."

"Bite your tongue, Blaze James," she'd say. "Nobody's prettier than Mama."

"You think she's crooked?" I'd ask.

"*Everybody* on this block is crooked," Aerial would say. And because of that, everybody on the block owned a gun; people here don't respect private property.

They'll knock on your door in the middle of a bold afternoon, pull out a cheap handgun, and kindly scoot you over to the side while they help themselves to everything from a cup of sugar in the kitchen to your television set in the bedroom.

I've seen three robberies in broad daylight with my own eyes. It didn't faze me much, but Aerial always freaked out. Both were commonplace in my neighborhood—the theft *and* Aerial's oversensitivity to life.

I didn't take too much seriously and was able to shake off a lot, but Aerial didn't seem to have that ability. It appeared to me that she was a bleeding heart to everybody's cause. She was the sensitive one for sure, and overly darned caring in my opinion. She was always trying to bring home stray animals and feed homeless people, oftentimes giving her own lunch away on the way to school each day.

"Why do you always give your lunch away?" I'd ask her.

"They're hungry, Blaze."

"Well," I said, "how hungry *you* gonna be without lunch?"

"I'll be just fine," she'd affirm.

And, of course, she would be just fine, because I'd always end up sharing half of my lunch with her, and she would eat it with a smile, look into my eyes, and ask, "Doesn't it make you feel good, Blaze? Helping the homeless?"

"No," I'd say, pouting as we sat beneath the same sap tree on the school playground sharing my measly lunch each day. "What would make me feel good is having the other half of my lunch!"

And Aerial would smile.

"But don't you feel good helping?" she'd ask.

"No!"

"Yes, you do!"

"No, I don't!"

"Yes, you do," she'd keep saying until I made this pitiful expression, and she would look at my dramatic face and burst into laughter. She would laugh so hard, I couldn't help but eventually break down and laugh, too, even though I was mad about splitting my lunch straight down the middle.

Still I would laugh.

I laughed because maybe it was funny.

Aerial's laughter was contagious, and it would sneak up from behind and catch hold of me.

It was *real* like that.

Tangible-like.

"Stop making me laugh!" I would command her. "Stop it!"

"You know you love helping the homeless," she would tease, tickling me.

"Do not!"

"Do too! You got a good heart underneath all that stuff," she'd say to me.

"What stuff?" I would ask.

"Your stuff."

"Well, what stuff is that?" I'd insist on knowing.

"Just stuff," she would always insist back.

"I never know what you're talking about," I told her. "You're always talking in code. This stuff. That stuff."

"It's not this stuff or that stuff," she'd insist. "It's *your* stuff."

Whatever.

Our sibling bickering always ended with the same grand finale—Aerial's s*mile*. It was "the smile of life," a river of gold and to see it was to be in awe of God itself.

Aerial and I were identical in appearance, identical beyond telling each other apart, both wearing the same beautiful shade of brown, both with long, flowing hair as thick as horse manes, both with the faces of Gods, both direct descendants of black/French ancestry.

We were really pretty girls.

God made us perfect.

Strangers knew it. Our parents knew it. Even blind people could tell we were pretty. Somehow, they could sense it. And we knew it, too, and every time we looked at each other, we really did see ourselves.

On a deeper level, I was the one with the regular smile, an everyday kind of smile. It was beautiful, but it wasn't *magical*. And if you looked at both of us at the same time, honest to God you couldn't tell us apart till you looked at the smile; then it became obvious who was the truly *beautiful* one.

Like I said, we were both really pretty . . . but Aerial . . . Aerial was a different kind of pretty. I knew it, but it was no big deal, because most people got caught up in the stupid stuff, like our skin and our hair, or maybe they got stuck on the fact that we were just about identical; but those who had the good sense to look past all that could always see us *and* tell us apart.

Always.

Aerial had something I couldn't touch. She had a shine that could not be duplicated, even by me, her twin.

Her soul passed mine up.

Way up.

I don't know how to explain it any better than that, and never in a million years would the average person know the truth that I accepted the moment we joined souls in twin-hood: *Aerial would always outshine me.*

Always.

And I was okay with that.

I knew it.

And she knew it.

It was an agreement we made at birth.

She would shine and I would bask in the glow of her reflection. I would be the real smart one, and she would be the real magical one.

That was our deal.

I can't convey it in bigger words than that. It pretty much says everything on its own. Like I said, we were both mighty fine-looking girls, but Aerial, Aerial, Aerial, *would be the one to shine.*

Chapter 2

"What Makes You Special?"

Mr. Rufus and Aliyah James were the two grown people who lived in our house and paid stuff like rent and bought stuff like food. We had the same last name and even shared similar facial features and expressions. Actually, we were the children of our mother and saw very little evidence of any relations to the notorious drunk Rufus James, who stated his paternal claim so boldly on our birth certificates.

In short, our mother was a high school beauty queen who traded in her crown in the twelfth grade for motherhood and two shifts as a waitress at the local dump . . . I mean diner.

Rufus was ten years her senior, a tenth-grade dropout and kind of on the lazy side. A wanderer of the neighborhood, he worked odd jobs here and there, maybe. He knew everybody, but nobody really knew him, including us, the identical seed of a misunderstood sperm shot.

From time to time, Aerial and I would see ourselves in them, but it was fast and fleeting, the view.

Most of the time, we watched from the sidelines in awe of their stupidity. *Stupid* may not sound like a nice word, but for the life of me, I don't know what else to call it.

That's how they behaved most days.

In your language, Rufus and Aliyah would be what is termed

parents. But we only called them that for lack of a more suitable noun, because in our twin language we often referred to them as *nincompoops*.

"Do you think the nincompoops are home yet?" I would ask Aerial each day as we walked home from school.

"God, I hope not," she would respond.

Sigh.

Sigh.

She didn't want them there, because wherever they were, chaos would follow.

Drama.

Tension.

Arguing.

You name it.

A case of the crazies would grab hold of them. Maybe it was because Rufus drank hard liquor as if it were grape Kool-Aid. And when he actually did go to work, he did so for a factory across the river. He was a fill-in janitor. When the regular cleanup crew was out, Rufus would fill in. Or better yet, "fill up," because he hated work but loved the booze and the women. At least that's what the walls whispered in the late-night hours. Actually, the walls don't whisper at all; they kinda shout, scream, and cry at 2:00 A.M. when nobody's looking—but they're always listening.

"Word is you and Etta got something going!" Mama would yell.

"Who's Etta?" Rufus would slur.

"Etta's the tramp you been seeing behind my back!"

"I don't know no Etta!" he'd insist.

"Etta sure knows you," Mama would accuse.

"Who knows me?"

"Etta knows you!"

"Who's Etta?" Rufus would ask again.

"The tramp you seeing behind my back!"

"I don't know no Etta, heifer!"

"Well, Etta sure knows you . . ."

And back and forth it would go like a bad comedy or a song gone way wrong. It was like a dying dog that you prayed somebody would put down so the rest of the litter could sleep.

"Sweet God in heaven, I wish the nincompoops would go to sleep!" Aerial would declare, forcing a pillow over her head to drown out the background noise of their ignorance.

Sleep was wishful thinking.

Sleep was something that white kids with real daddies got on school nights—not broke, disadvantaged black kids who lived across from city dumps with drunk pappies who filled up on cube steak and Jim Beam.

Sleep?

What was that?

"You don't love me," Mama would whine. "Do you?"

He never answered.

"You love me, Rufus James? You love me?"

Silence.

"Goddammit," she'd scream. "Don't you love me? I work two jobs to take care of you, and I gave you two kids out of my own body!"

"And?" he'd respond, like what she was talking about wasn't a big, huge deal.

"And don't you love me for it, Rufus James? Don't you love me for it?" And this is where he would bust up laughing. It was always right *here* that Crazy Rufus would laugh on cue.

"Why you so special?" he'd ask Mama. "Why you think you so doggone special?" Now, funny thing is, she never had an answer, except to say, "I work two shifts at my job and had two kids out of my *own* body for you."

"So what?" he'd say. "What makes you special?"

"I spit out two kids at one time for you," she'd say with a righteous twang in her Southern drawl. "And they look just like each other."

"Yeah," Rufus would say. "They so busy looking like each other, they ain't got time to look like me. I'm supposed to be the daddy. . . ."

"Where I'm from, two kids born at one time that look just

like each other is called a *miracle*, 'cause it don't happen that much," Mama would boast.

"Where I'm from, two kids born at one time is called a *burden*, 'cause they eat you out of house and home!" Rufus would bark.

"Ain't no more expensive than your old liquor and bad gambling debts," Mama'd say.

"It don't matter, no mind," Rufus would say. "You still ain't said *nothing* about why you supposed to be so special."

And here is where it always went dead.

Dead air.

Mama went silent like somebody had yanked out her vocal cords or something. Truth is, sometimes I wanted to knock on the door and say, "Big whoop-de-do . . . can't you come up with a better answer than that?"

I even wanted to ask her, *What makes you special, Mama?*

What makes you special?

What makes you shine like a light?

And what makes you matter?

I figured this out a long time ago, maybe back when me and Aerial was still sharing a sack on my mother's insides, and that's why I came out so doggone smart. You gotta know the answers to those kinds of questions. At some point, we all gotta know what makes us matter.

But Rufus and Mama's conversation never went very far. In fact, it would end with the sound of Rufus moaning, groaning, and saying things that wouldn't be very ladylike for me to repeat in mixed company. I guess *that's* what made Mama special. Yeah, that's what made Mama special.

Mama spends a lot of time in downtown Shreveport where she "pulls doubles" almost every day, in her own words. Her double shifts pay the rent, buys food, and settles Rufus's liquor tab at the end of the week. Now, why she needed him was some kind of confusing to both me and Aerial, because neither one of us was sold on his contribution to the family. They were legally married, so it seemed like a forever kind of doom, in my opinion.

Some kind of romance.

Never you mind, I'll just stay single till my toenails curl up and fall off.

When Rufus ain't drinking, sleeping, fighting, cursing or breathing heavy through the walls, he's really kind of ordinary, but Mama, now, she's beautiful.

I believe that back in her day, she was even more beautiful than both Aerial and I put together, but Rufus beat the pretty out of her. At least that was what Aerial says, and I believe mostly everything Aerial says.

We might seem a little detached from these people, but it's normal. We're only distant from our parents, because we're so close to each other. Well, because of that and also because they're crazy.

Aerial and I don't need anybody else. We got each other, and most days, with the exception of a single breath that separates us, we are each other.

We are each other.

We *are* each other.

Chapter 3

All of Nothing

Life changed in one night for Aerial and me, and it would never go back again.

Never.

Ever.

Ever go back again.

It was one of those kinds of nights where you wish you could blink and wish it all away. But we couldn't.

Never.

Ever.

Ever could we wish it all away.

It was like one of those movies where all you did was take a pee break, run to the snack counter for a bag of popcorn and a drink, and by the time you got back to your seat, it was like you were in a whole different movie.

It was like, *Well, what the heck just happened?*

Excuse my poor choice of words, because I know eleven-year-olds aren't supposed to swear, but sometimes you gotta make an exception.

Like now.

Like life did to us.

It made an exception.

Somewhere between the beginning and the middle, it all just

went to shit. Excuse my grammar, but *shit* is a word I learned from Rufus.

"This is some bullshit!" was his favorite saying. "This is a bull-shit job!" or "The white man is full of bullshit!" And, of course, my all-time favorite: "This bed-wetting is some straight-up bullshit!"

Funny thing is, this night was like any other.

Black.

Humid.

And damp . . . because I had just peed in the bed *again.*

Damn.

That was one of Rufus's words, too, and it was all I could say in recollection of a "good talking to" that he had just given me in the middle of our raggedy living room floor before I went to bed that night.

"Blaze James, if you wet that bed again, I will beat your little narrow, yellow ass come morning!" he yelled.

"I don't pee in the bed no more, sir," I replied dutifully. After all, I had a moral obligation to save my little narrow, yellow ass from a beating, didn't I?

Tall and scrawny, with a lopsided mini-afro and bad skin, Rufus leaned forward, meeting me eye-to-eye. "You think I don't know?" he said in my ear.

"Know what, Mr. Rufus?" I questioned.

We never called him *Daddy*, Aerial or myself. It seemed kind of overrated that word, especially for a man like Mr. Rufus. I kind of figured that *Daddy* was a nice white man with a steady job and a couple suits and ties in his closet. Yeah, *Daddy* was a white man for sure, with matching shoes and a steady paycheck. *Daddy* damn sure didn't take public transportation, and I highly doubt Daddy passed out every night with Wild Turkey on his breath.

A real daddy had one of those funny haircuts and maybe was even going bald in the middle of his big white head. Daddy was an American hero . . . or maybe he was something simple like a dentist or an ice-cream man.

Rufus didn't mind being called Rufus, as long as we put the *Mr.* in front of it.

"You is a piss ass, wet the bed every night!" he shouted.

My eyes swelled with fear. "Not every night," I said in my defense.

"Room smells worse than the dump outside . . ."

I lowered my head, ashamed.

"Why is you too lazy to get up and use the toilet like grown folks do?"

"I ain't lazy, Mr. Rufus," I said in a low voice.

"What you say there, Miss Piss Ass?"

"She *ain't* lazy," said Aerial with her arms crossed, standing boldly in the corner of the room.

"What you say over there, girl?" he asked, his wild eyes scanning the corner of the room where Aerial stood.

"She ain't lazy," she repeated, more firmly.

"Well she somethin'!" he shouted back. "That bed comes up wet every morning."

"She's just fine," said Aerial.

"What is you now, some kind of authority on bed-wetting?" he asked Aerial with a wicked laugh, holding some hard liquor down by his side. We could tell he had already been drinking most of the afternoon. He stunk to high heaven and walked with a sway, because his balance was off.

"I guess you the piss authority," he said to Aerial with smoke in his voice, "and you *is* the piss maker!" he said, turning to me.

"And what do you be, Mr. Rufus?" Aerial asked, eyes ablaze with fire.

"I be the king of this here house," he said, nodding. "I am the *last* word on everything around here! Everything you see is mine! That means I'm the boss."

"But how can you be the boss of anything when you ain't paid for *nothing*?" asked Aerial.

Oh, Mr. Rufus didn't take too kindly to that kind of question-and-answer. His wild eyes shot across the room, with his arms stretched out, trying to hold his balance.

"Get outta here!" He scowled at Aerial. "You just trouble . . . the both of you . . . just trouble."

We quickly retreated to our bedroom and shut the door tightly behind us. We sat down on Aerial's bunk bed and held each other's hands.

"Mr. Rufus sure is crazy," I said.

"Indeed," said Aerial before turning to me with a real serious face, pointing to the top bunk. "Don't you pee in that bed tonight," she warned.

I looked down.

There were *no* guarantees.

"Mr. Rufus is crazy enough to string you up alive," she said. "He'll beat you till you can't stand up."

I looked down again.

I knew she was right.

It had happened before.

We both had scars that nobody saw; some were on our backside, but most were on our inside.

"You go to the pot right now!" said Aerial. "And don't you drink another drop till morning!"

"But I already drank three glasses of Kool-Aid," I said.

"Then you better pray the Sweet Virgin Mary wake you up tonight to go pee," she warned.

"What if the Sweet Virgin Mary oversleeps?" I asked.

"Then you better ask Jesus to post up right outside this door, 'cause Mr. Rufus ain't going for no more wet sheets!"

Aerial kissed me on the cheek, climbed into her bunk, and pulled the covers over her head. I just sat there like a gnat on a log, looking at her still body as she drifted off.

"Aerial?" I asked beats later.

"What?" she answered, groggy.

"You think God knows where we live?" I asked.

"God knows everything."

"You think God might come in the case of an emergency, if I pee in the bed by accident tonight?"

"God knows you by name," said Aerial, "and you're gonna be just fine."

Suddenly, there was a loud banging sound against our bedroom wall that made Aerial sit straight up and me come right out of my skin.

"He's sloppy drunk tonight." said Aerial, "Sloppy drunk. If you wet that bed by mistake, you best climb out that window over there and dry those sheets by morning."

"How do I dry sheets outside?" I asked, dumbfounded.

"Swing 'em in the wind," she said. "It's warm enough outside."

"When is Mama coming home?" I asked with a big sigh.

"Probably around two A.M.—just like she always does," said Aerial.

I climbed into the top bunk and sat up for a long time, scared to go to sleep for fear that I might wet the bed. I just sat and listened to Rufus, banging around in the other room, drinking and singing. Well, I wouldn't actually call what he was doing *singing;* It sounded more like howling and barking. I couldn't tell if he was serenading a woman or turning into a werewolf.

"Aerial?" I whispered. "Aerial."

Like petrified wood, she was as stiff as a dead man. Aerial could sleep through anything. The only thing I was able to sleep through was bed-wetting.

Kiss Delilah's black ass.

That was one of Rufus's famous phrases. I had no idea who Delilah was, but it sure was funny when he said it.

That night, somewhere around midnight, I fell asleep, nodding straight off while sitting up. Next thing I knew, it was 1:31 A.M. and I woke up soaking wet.

Doggone.

I knew I had to dry these sheets, but I only had twenty-nine minutes to do it. Mama would be home at 2:00 A.M. sharp, and she and Rufus would argue till about 3:00 A.M. as usual, and then funny noises would leak through the walls by about 3:15 A.M. Our lives were scripted like that, and every night we got the same show.

Rain or sun.

Sun or shade.

We got the same show.

Late spring nights were warm, but I was in need of a spring

heat wave to dry up all of this pee. I was twenty-nine minutes away from a late-night beating or an early morning miracle, and only God knew which one it was going to be. Holy hell, the Virgin Mary must have overslept.

I focused my dimly lit eyes toward the other side of the bedroom. It seemed like a world away, the window. What was I supposed to do—squeeze my backside through the tiny opening, drag this pee-pee sheet, and go hang it out in the night air like some kind of oversized flag?

What will the neighbors think?

"Who cares?" I told myself. "None of them are home right now anyways. They're all out robbing banks and holding up liquor stores."

"Aerial," I whispered, trying to wake her up to come help me. "Aerial . . . Aerial . . ."

No answer.

She was either asleep, dead, or both. Either way, I was on my own, me and these doggone sheets.

I got down out of the bed, scooted over to the window, and climbed out with two twin sheets in hand. Our window faced the backyard, but so did Rufus and Mama's window, so I was trying to dry the sheets real quietlike, because if Mr. Rufus heard me out here, the story would end here, because I doubt I'd be around to finish it.

I had twenty-seven minutes, and the night air was gentle and mild, too mild to dry a sheet no matter how badly I wanted it. I stood in the middle of the yard swinging, waving, and fanning, but mostly praying—praying that the Holy Mother of God or somebody close to her was going to rescue me.

I fell to my knees and started to cry. "Dear God, I need a miracle, 'cause I don't want another beating on my backside from Mr. Rufus. . . ."

Before another word was uttered from my eleven-year-old tongue, the world as I knew it *ended*. In the twinkle of an eye, there was a gigantic explosion from the inside of the house, and my prayer went from a humble sob to a violent scream. I stood up, my entire body brightened by the inferno that engulfed the house.

"Aerial!" I screamed. "Aerial! Aerial! Aerial!"

I tried to run toward the house, but the heat from the fire prevented me from getting too close.

"Aerial!" I screamed at the top of my lungs.

Aerial!

Aerial!

From where I stood, there was no more Aerial or Rufus. From where I stood, nothing stood anymore, and the brittle lumber from the old house started to fall in on itself, and the whole thing began to collapse to the ground. I fell to my knees horrified, burying my body into the earth's soil as my tears dug into the ground.

Sirens had already started going off. Somebody had called somebody who had called for help. The neighbors, those who weren't out stealing, started coming out of their houses, aghast by the smoke, flames, and fire.

I could barely breathe, watching it all.

"Aerial," I sobbed, head lowered.

Within moments, Aerial burst through the bedroom window, set ablaze with fire, running toward me. It was like a movie, not real.

Not real at all.

Her scream shot through me, cutting me like a bad paper cut. It wasn't human, her scream. It was animal. Maybe it was half human, half animal, half death and half holding on to life; half something and all of nothing.

I jumped up, grabbing my pee-pee sheet, and ran toward her. I threw my body on top of her, which helped to drown out the flames.

I don't remember much after that, because by that time, grown people came and took over the nightmare. All I remember was that Aerial was lying still on the ground, dead for all I knew. The sheets were burned through and through, cemented on the ground, smoldering, smoking.

Mama had just pulled up in her old, raggedy pickup truck. I could hear her screaming as neighbors tried to comfort, console, and restrain her from running into the burning house. These were people we had seen every day for years but never really knew. We weren't the most social family on the block, maybe because we were ashamed of the acts of our house's inhabitants.

What would we say to our neighbors?

We're that crazy bunch of heathens who you hear every night till three, four o'clock in the morning.

Yeah, right.

Well, embarrassed or not, this is what our neighbors would awaken to tonight, exchanging the sound of their own lullaby for the deafening echo of our nightmare.

Mama's scream sounded like Aerial's.

Half human.

Half animal.

Half death, holding on to life.

Half something.

And all of *nothing*.

By the time the sun rose, we were a front-page headline in the *Shreveport Daily News:* DEADLY GAS EXPLOSION IN SHREVE-PORT HOME LEAVES ONE DEAD, ONE BADLY BURNED.

Rufus James was dead at thirty-eight.

Aliyah James was widowed at twenty-eight.

Aerial James, eleven years of age, was sent to a Baton Rouge Burn Center for recovery. And the Blaze James I knew would never be the same again, because the mother-loving ground opened up when I wasn't looking and swallowed the James family whole.

I don't remember the break of dawn that day, after the fire had been put out and the stench of burnt skin, black smoke, and death filled our block.

I don't remember how the coroner got Mr. Rufus's body out of the house, and I surely don't remember Aerial being trans-ported by helicopter to Baton Rouge for treatment.

I was a living, breathing ghost in a human body. You could see me, but I wasn't really there, so I am hard-pressed to give you details. There are some things that are just too surreal to recount, and trust that any words I would translate by way of this page wouldn't be even *close* to capturing the real deal.

In the commotion of it all, Mama was whisked away in the helicopter with Aerial, and I was entrusted to the guardianship of our infamous neighbor, Miss Felicity Hardaway. That's right, Miss Felicity Hardaway. But that was supposed to be for only a little while, just till my grandmother could get to Shreveport from Pasadena, California, where she had moved after retiring from the post office last year.

It wasn't like we had a blueprint for how this whole thing was going to go down.

Mama was screaming.

Aerial was lying on the ground.

Rufus was zipped up in a body bag and carted out.

Mama was trying to board the helicopter and see what was left of Aerial. And somewhere in the crowd, in the midst of all the confusion and terror, Miss Felicity Hardaway emerged from the crowd, grabbed me by the scruff of the neck, and shouted to Mama, "You go ahead! I'll take this one!"

This one?

This one?

"Yeah," said Mama in a daze. "There is another one, right . . . they were twins."

"Mama . . . ," I whispered, knowing that she was half out of her own mind, delirious with grief.

"Yes! Yes!" she said, shocked to see me. "The other one," she mumbled. "There is another one. . . ."

It was like her brain had a short in it, and she forgot she had two kids. How could she forget there were two of us? Did we look so much alike that, in a moment of crisis, we blended into one? I couldn't be offended, could I? After all, she had just lost Mr. Rufus, even if he was as raggedy as the day is long, and one of her only *two* children swung in the balance between life and death.

Miss Felicity promised to call Mama at the burn center and let her know where her "other one" would be posted up. It wasn't a formal type of arrangement, and Felicity Hardaway didn't have a babysitting diploma on hand for Mama to verify her qualifications. She offered. Mama accepted. And that was pretty much it. Little did I know that life would change *again* in that moment, in the finite space between Felicity's "You go ahead" and "I'll take this one."

Chapter 4

What Feels Real

By daybreak, I had lost a home, a father, maybe even a twin, but life drops one side and then lifts another. In two shakes of a tail feather, I had a new home, a family, and some kind of mother figure with full hips and breasts. Granted, she was nothing to write home about in the maternal department, but it was a ready-made and thrown-together hog's-mix-kind-of-living situation, and in the end, it did beat sleeping outside.

I didn't know Felicity Hardaway at all before this day. I had only been fascinated with her all of my life. We had not so much as exchanged a sound between us or a head nod, handshake, friendly wave, nothing. Aerial and I had seen Felicity all the time on our way home from school out on her front lawn watering the grass, wearing very few clothes.

She was like the rest of the neighborhood, a little shady to the naked eye. It seemed like she always had a little *something* going on, legal or illegal; we couldn't really call it. She was much taller than me and Aerial, but that wasn't saying much, because we were all of about five feet, maybe.

Nobody did what Miss Felicity could do. She was the best in town at cutting boys hair for a living. The men who did that for a living were put to shame by a woman who could outcut them any day of the week. She did mighty fine work and had a fine reputation for cleaning up even the scruffiest of folks on the outside. Even Mr. Rufus had gone to see Miss Felicity a time or two, and he came home looking kind of human on those days, and even smelled nice too.

Felicity had short blond hair, with one side a little longer than the other. She had really pretty skin, like cocoa butter, but it worked darned good when she laid it against her yellow hair. She had two big green eyes. They were the kind of green that made black people stop and ask, "Them your real eyes?" *Well, who else's eyes they gonna be? She's wearing 'em, ain't she?*

Felicity was the curviest kind of woman I'd ever seen. Her hips and legs ran for days, like the Nile River. She had huge breasts that sat up on her chest like they was trying to order a plate of hot grits or something. Her breasts had huge nipples, and you could kind of see them through her shirt. Her nipples were so round and pronounced, they looked like they could have been little islands, surrounded by a mass of ocean breasts. And she had a booty that shook so hard when she walked by, it kinda felt like the earth was quaking.

Felicity Hardaway was something for sure, and all of the men in the neighborhood LOVED her. They would drive by her house, blowing and honking, waving, smiling, and grinning, those with teeth and those without. She was the queen of ghetto beauty and made living in a slum seem effortless, almost like everybody did it.

She made it look easy, like we all lived in the slums by choice instead of by force. She had this bold walk, this larger-than-life stand that seemed to suggest, *I live here because I like it!*

She was confidence in motion, and that's what I really liked about her. She was so different from Mama, who was weak and fragile and so unsure of herself, defeated and passive, always waiting on Mr. Rufus to tell her what makes her special, what makes her matter. He never told her nothing, and since he didn't tell her nothing, she didn't know nothing. Mama didn't know if she was coming or going, staying behind or had already gone ahead, but not Miss Felicity Hardaway; she was the original know-it-all-about-it-all.

When we arrived on the doorstep of Felicity's two-room shack, which was situated four doors down from where our house used to be, I was not surprised to find that the interior walls of her house were painted pink and green, bold like her.

"Come on in here, girl," said Felicity, prodding and slightly poking me on the backside to hurry me along. "This little place ain't much too look at, and it's only a temporary spot for me, but least it's an honest place to lay your head down."

Once inside, she shut the door, which seemed like a little bit of relief to get away from the crowd, but not really, because her house smelled just like the outside, burnt up. I could still hear the sound of a helicopter hovering overhead. The reality of it all was starting to set in, and I could feel myself leaving that numb place in exchange for one with feeling.

It was starting to hurt.

"This here is the Love Palace," Felicity said. "How old is you, girl?"

"Eleven years old," I said boldly, "and with a birthday three months away, I'm getting ready to be twelve."

"Is you now?" she asked, her head snapped back.

"Yes, I am," I said proudly.

"Hmmm," she said, tossing her blond hair to the side with the smack of her hand. "I see . . ."

She crossed in front of me, staring me up and down, eyeing me like I had stole something out of her house when she wasn't looking. "I promised your mama I was going to look after you," she said. "I always keep my promises."

"Yes, ma'am," I responded dutifully.

"And don't call me no 'ma'am,'" she said, kicking off her shoes, flopping her big ol' booty into an oversized chair. "I'm a young lady myself, only twenty-six years old."

"Okay, ma'am," I said, but quickly corrected myself, "I mean . . . Miss Felicity."

"Well, sit down over there somewhere," she said, pointing to a pink and green love seat as she pulled out a cigarette. "This here is a grown folk's house."

"Okay," I replied humbly.

"Ain't no kids over here," said Miss Felicity, "so what I do in this house is grown folk's business."

I nodded.

"I call it grown folk's shit," she said emphatically.

I repeated it for confirmation, "Grown folk's shit."

"That's it," she said, nodding her head, laughing. "Grown folk's shit."

"Is that another word for illegal?" I asked, childlike, but not so much with childish intentions, 'cause I was thinking she was as crooked as the Montana sky, Miss Felicity Hardaway.

Her eyes widened, and she looked a little taken aback. "That's some funny shit," she said.

I laughed, too, a little bit but not a lot. I thought if I got to laughing too hard, she might haul off and whack me a good one.

She stood up, took another good, long look at me, took a hit off the cigarette, and then blew the smoke right in my face.

I coughed.

"You is a lightweight," she said.

Gasping, I asked, "What do you mean?"

"This is a grown folk's house," she said again. "I smoke Marlboro's and reefer, and drink Wild Turkey on the weekends."

"My daddy used to drink Wild Turkey," I responded without thought. And on the edge of those words, the house got quiet. I guess 'cause we both knew that my daddy was newly dead.

"I'm sorry 'bout your daddy," she said before turning away. I had a hard time responding to her sympathy.

"I don't feel as sorry as I should," I said, the words spilling on the floor, and where they came from I just didn't know.

Felicity stopped and turned to look at me. "There's no such thing as *should* when it comes to a feeling, I guess."

"I probably should be a little more sad," I suggested, in my own defense. "My mama's pretty cut up about it."

"Was you fucking him?" she asked, straight out. She didn't blink, apologize, or wait for a good time to retract the whole darn thing.

My eyes widened to the size of a casserole bowl, and I covered my open mouth.

"Was you fucking him?" she asked again.

I could NOT believe it!

Who was this Felicity Hardaway?

I was embarrassed, because I do believe she was waiting on an answer. "No," I stuttered.

"Then you don't have to feel *shit*, except for what feels real to you," she said.

Wow, I thought. That was the smartest thing I had ever heard anyone on earth say. *I don't have to feel shit, except for what feels real to me.* My mama would never be that smart if she lived for a million years.

Miss Felicity walked into the kitchen and started riffling through the cabinets. Slowly, I approached and stood just outside the kitchen. "Miss Felicity," I said. "I'm only eleven years old."

"So?" she asked, grabbing some bowls from an overhead cupboard.

"So, I'm too young to . . ." I stopped.

"Too young to what?" she asked.

"Be . . . you know . . . ?"

"To be fucking?" she asked.

Geez, she was straight out.

I nodded, lowering my head.

"It depends on who you asking," she said casually, mixing batter in a bowl.

"What's that mean?" I asked.

"Eleven ain't too young to know what it feels like to have some dick shoved up your ass," she said like it wasn't nothing at all.

Kiss Delilah's black behind, I thought. *This woman is about as raw as it gets. She must never go to church on Sunday!*

"I was sure enough fucking at eleven," she said, battering bread for French toast.

I didn't know what in blazing hell to say after Miss Felicity said that. What is the next natural line of conversation after words like that fall off somebody's tongue?

"Uuuuuhhhh," was about as far as I could go.

"Every night," she said.

She lit the stove, and all I could do was stare at the flame.

"Every night?" I asked, my face curled up into a frown.

"Every night," she confirmed. "Go wash your hands down the hall there, girl, and sit down here at the table so I can feed you."

I stepped away from the table and made my way down the hall in a mesmerized daze. I don't even remember washing my hands, just knew that I must have because when I returned to the table, they were wet.

"Sit," she said, scooping up a nice piece of French toast and placing it real proper like on my plate. "What?" she asked, looking at me with sharp eyes as I pretended not to look at her or even remotely remember what she had just said. "You wanna know about me, don't you, girl?" she asked, pulling another cigarette from her purse and sitting down at the table next to me.

I nodded slowly. Maybe I did, maybe I didn't, but all I really wanted to know was who was she "doing the do" with at eleven years old? Seems awfully young to be that kind of active, even for a fast-ass like Miss Felicity Hardaway.

"I can read your inquisitive little mind," she said, puffing the cigarette and blowing the smoke in my face again. "You ain't never met nobody like me, have you, girl?" she asked.

I shook my head. I guess *Hell no* would have been an inappropriate response. And she laughed out loud, as if she had read my mind.

"Hell no!" she said.

And I jumped with fear. *Could she really read my mind? Uh-oh,* I thought. *If she can, then she's gonna see that I wanna know . . .*

"Who fucked me?" she asked with a grin.

Too late.

She already saw.

My eyes dropped off to the table and hit the floor.

"Well," she said, leaning back in her seat, exposing her hefty-sized chest, and piercing me with the most captivating green eyes I'd ever laid my own brown eyes on. "It wasn't really that I was fucking somebody; more that it was somebody fucking me . . ."

I bit my lip, just a pinch, and that's when Miss Felicity leaned in to me and whispered quietly into my ear, "It was my daddy."

I choked on the toast, and she pulled back and just looked at me long and hard before blowing a big puff of smoke in my face. "When Daddy died, I was thirteen years old," she said with no emotion. "I was the only person at the sorry bastard's funeral who didn't shed a tear."

She got up from the table, and I just sat there like a mummy. "Don't you get it yet, girl? You ain't got to feel SHIT, except what feels real to *you*."

I was shocked and too numb, horrified to speak.

What could I possibly say?

Nothing.

So I ate the balance of my food in silence. After breakfast, Miss Hardaway showed me to my very own bedroom. It was just across the hallway from hers.

"This here is my guest room," she said with a smile. "It's for guests . . . so I guess on that basis you qualify."

She opened the door and I looked inside. It was a simple little room with a twin bed pressed against the wall and a wooden dresser off to the side. It had green and pink walls like the rest of the house and green and pink curtains. Like I said, real simple.

"Are green and pink your favorite colors?" I asked.

"I suppose," she said.

"This is a real nice room here, Miss Felicity," I said. "Thank you for letting me stay."

"It ain't no big deal," she said. "You ain't gonna be here that long; your mama be coming for you soon . . . probably by the end of the week."

I nodded.

Miss Felicity brought a bath towel and set it on the bed. I stood in the middle of the room, not really knowing what to do or where to go.

"I know you got some real deep stuff going on with your insides . . . with your family and all . . ."

I looked deeply into her green eyes, and it looked like she was fumbling over herself trying to find the right words. "I ain't no minister or counselor," she said, shuffling from side to side. "Ain't got no fancy degree . . . only went to the ninth grade and dropped out of school when my daddy died . . ."

"Sorry," I said.

"It ain't no big deal, girl," she said. "It was time for me to move on."

"At thirteen?"

"I had already lived a whole lifetime in thirteen years. See, that's the biggest difference between me and you."

"What?" I asked slowly.

"You probably like most people I know," she said with certainty. "You probably going to live one good time, then up and die. But me, I ain't never gonna die."

"Everybody dies someday, Miss Felicity . . ."

"Bite your tongue," she said, cutting me off at the knees. "Only those who don't know no better."

"You think my daddy didn't know no better?"

"Obviously not—he's dead, ain't he?"

I laughed. "I ain't never met nobody like you, Miss Felicity. I don't know what to make of the stuff that comes out of your mouth."

"Pay me no mind, girl," she said. "All I want you to know is that if you need a friend, you can come here and knock on this here door," she said, pointing across the hall to her own bedroom, "and if I ain't drinking, smoking, getting high, or entertaining company, I'll let you in."

I laughed again, and Miss Felicity laughed, too, as she looked real hard into my eyes. "You ain't nothing ordinary, is you, girl?"

"Ain't nobody ever told me that before," I said quietly, fading into myself.

"Well, you ain't. You got some kind of fire in you, and I like it. The way I see it, there's only one problem between me and you, girl."

"What?" I asked, my eyes wide with curiosity.

"I don't know your name."

"Blaze," I said, smiling.

Miss Felicity made some kind of sound, then smiled and walked out of the room. Funny thing is, after Miss Felicity left, I realized I had been in her house about half an hour, and I felt more at home in her house in thirty minutes than I did in my own house after a whole lifetime. I guess that says about enough, now, doesn't it?

Chapter 5

"Knick Knack, Patty Whack"

It had been seven days and counting since the house blew up, and I did not shed a single tear at the funeral for Mr. Rufus James. Miss Felicity had dressed me up real nice and fixed my hair like I was some kind of movie star before dropping me off at the church that morning for Mr. Rufus's service. Quietly, I filed in and sat among the dead in the front row beside Ms. Aliyah James, widow of Mr. Rufus James.

When Mama saw me, she smiled, extended a hand, and pulled me close to her, offering a fragile hug. It wasn't like a real hug. It was one of those kind of hugs that I had watched on television where two white ladies, who were both wearing too much makeup, fake kissed each other's cheeks from side to side.

"Come sit, darling," said Mama.

Darling???

What the hell.

Oh, it's showtime, huh?

Mama wore a long black dress and an attractive strand of fake pearls. I knew they were fake, because she only made minimum wage, plus meager tips. So I ask you, how much real stuff can you buy on a few hundred dollars a month, especially when you have two growing kids and a lazy man to take care of?

Mama wore a big black hat tilted to the side and the saddest face you ever wanted to see. As far as being the grief-stricken widow, she really played the part. As a matter of fact, she always played the part.

Weak.

Sad.

And pitiful.

Aliyah James didn't have no fire, and that used to drive me half out of my mind. She was a yes-man for Mr. Rufus, and whatever Mr. Rufus said was "the gospel, gospel truth." Mr. Rufus didn't know nothing about the gospel . . . shoot, he couldn't even read, so what was he going to tell anybody? I wanted to see some fire in Aliyah Damn James! Hell, my mama gave me the name of Blaze, but I wanted to give it back to her, just so she could have some fire.

Light it up, Mama! Light it up!

I wanted to see flame in my mama like Felicity Hardaway had. Yeah, I wanted to see *that* kind of fire.

Sass it up, Mama! Sass it up!

Don't you go holding your head down for NO man.

What makes you matter, Mama?

What makes you matter?

Sometimes when I looked at my mother, despite all of her pain and pitiful nature, I knew she was one of the most beautiful women I had ever seen in my life. Like a cardboard cutout, it was my humble thought that she could have done a *lot* better for herself than that broke-down corpse in a casket, sitting over there in the corner. And as people poured into this little Southern Baptist church in the sopping rain, all I really wanted to do was go and be with my twin, Aerial James.

"When is Aerial getting out of the hospital?" I whispered into my mother's ear during the service, interrupting a great spell of grief that was trying to take her over.

She shot me a wicked eye. "Show some respect to your father," she snapped under her breath.

"How is Aerial, Mama?" I asked, waiting for an answer. Her condition had been kept top secret by Mama. Sometimes, I thought she might be dead and they just didn't want to tell me. Mama's lips were closed so tight, I thought they had Superglue inside of them.

I was Aerial's twin. I deserved to know, but every time Miss Felicity and I would call Mama, she would just say, "Pray that the Good Lord does a miracle for my baby . . ."

Well, what exactly does that mean?

"Is she still breathing, Mama?" I would ask.

"Yes," she would answer quietly.

"Then that's our miracle," I'd say. "When's Aerial coming home?"

"Only the Good Lord knows," was her customary response. So, I was just trying to see if the Good Lord knew yet. I wasn't trying to interrupt Mr. Rufus's memorial service, but I hadn't even seen an inch of Aliyah James since the accident happened up till the morning we poured into the church. I was still staying with Miss Felicity, and Mama was living at the burn center with Aerial.

My highfalutin grandmother, Ms. Dixie Mae Brown, came straightaway from Pasadena, California, but she bypassed Shreveport all together and went directly to Baton Rouge to be with Aerial and Mama. The original plan was for Ms. Dixie to come fetch me and take me to Baton Rouge, but that didn't happen. Not sure why, just knew it didn't happen.

"Baby," said Mama three days after the accident, "I'ma need you to stay with Miss Felicity for a little while longer while Mama takes care of Aerial."

"Where's Ms. Dixie held up?" I asked her.

"Ms. Dixie's here in Baton Rouge," said Mama. "She's renting a hotel for us so that I can stay here with Aerial in the daytime and still have some place to lay my head at night."

"Well . . . what about my head?" I asked.

"Miss Felicity's got pillows, right?" she asked.

"Yeah."

"Then you got a place to lay your head. I'll be coming to get you soon," she always said at the end of every phone call.

"When is soon, Mama?" I would ask.

"Soon . . . soon," she'd always say. "I gotta go, baby."

Ms. Dixie didn't come to Mr. Rufus's service. Truth is, she never really liked him anyway, so she opted to stay with Aerial at the burn center.

After the service, Mama and I rode to the cemetery in what had to be the most raggedy so-called limo I had ever seen. It was smoking and squealing, howling and screeching. The hearse that carried Mr. Rufus was as raggedy as the limo. A couple of times, the back door unlatched and I thought Mr. Rufus was going to spill out of the back and come sliding out of that cheap box we were burying him in.

"This is some kind of raggedy-ass car," I said.

"What did you say, Blaze James?" Mama asked, taking notice of the bad word that slipped out by accident.

"This here car is raggedy," I said again in a more polite presentation.

"You best watch your dirty little mouth or I'll have to wash it out for you with a whole bar of fresh, new soap," she threatened.

I didn't respond, just looked out the window and wondered what time lunch was going to be served today.

We dropped Mr. Rufus off at the cemetery and had a gravesite burial. It was here that Mama showed out. She threw herself on Mr. Rufus's casket and started crying out to Jesus, the Virgin Mother Mary, Buddha, Allah, Krishna, and then a whole lot of less famous people like LeRoy and ReRe and Tookie Love. While Mama did a whole lot of whooping and hollering, I stood in the background, as usual, and allowed her to have the stage. After all, she was the one who had been "fucking him," in Miss Hardaway's words, not mine.

All of the people at the funeral were strangers to me, though a lot of them had the last name of James. They were extended family, but I would say real extended, because I never saw most of them, even on holidays. I didn't have family or friends; I had Aerial. Mama didn't have family or friends; she had Mr. Rufus.

As Mama fell out and did whatever kind of voodoo rain dance she was doing, my eyes *and* my mind tried to find something else to focus on. That's when I looked behind the sea of poverty-stricken family members, ex-prisoners, rehabilitating drug addicts, and welfare mommies and saw Miss Felicity Hardaway at the opposite end of the cemetery. She was standing beside a tall tree, carrying a big wide umbrella and wearing a long black coat and a black miniskirt, with shiny black boots that ran all the way up over her knees.

"Miss Felicity," I whispered. "Miss Felicity is here . . ." Seeing her in this moment was like seeing a black angel, surrounded by light. I glanced over at Mama, who was still calling the many names of Jesus, and felt a little embarrassed that we were related. Miss Felicity would have never allowed herself to "act up" like this, in public or in private. I couldn't see her doing no voodoo dance around her pink and green love seat.

After the gravesite service and all the well-wishes, hugs, pats on the back, tears, tissues, and crying out to God and Save the Whales and Dear Sweet Jesus or whatever else had been said on this day, it was *finally* done!

I stood in the middle of the rain with one steady eye on Miss Felicity to make sure she wasn't going nowhere no time soon. And it was in the middle of a downpour that Mama bent down, grabbed my cheeks between her cold hands, kissed me on the forehead, and said, "I gotta go, Blaze."

She handed me two black dolls that looked just alike. They were little dolls, nothing more than a few inches high with fancy dresses, pretty brown faces, and shiny black hair. I took them in my hand and held on tight, staring at them.

"Twins," said Mama, looking at the dolls. "Just like you and Aerial." Mama turned, looked at Miss Hardaway, and nodded. Miss Hardaway nodded, too, and then Mama turned her attention back to me and knelt down on the wet ground. "Now, you mind Miss Hardaway."

"Yes, ma'am," I said, eyes lowered. "When is Aerial coming home?" I asked.

"You keep up on your studies," she said, straightening the collar on my dress, avoiding an answer altogether.

"When is Aerial coming home?" I asked again.

"I don't want you missing no reading assignments this month," she said, fumbling with my bangs and the curls that Miss Felicity had put in my head.

"I said . . . when is Aerial James coming home?"

Mama looked down and took a deep, deep breath, followed by a long, long sigh. "Aerial's got a long way to go before she's able to . . ." said Mama; then the words dropped off at the end.

"How long?" I asked.

"She was burned real bad, Blaze," said Mama. "Real, real bad."

"Is she in pain?"

"Something awful," Mama said without hesitation.

"Then take me to her," I demanded. "She needs me." Mama didn't say nothing. "I said take me to her!" I repeated with more force. "She been asking for me?" I asked Mama. "She been asking?"

Mama slowly shook her head.

No.

"That's a lie!" I said. "Aerial always asks for me, and you know it!" Tears fell from Mama's eyes, but I was immune to her tears by now. She had cried too many of them in the past for them to count anymore. "Aerial's not talking much right now, Blaze," said Mama. "She's in and out . . . but mostly out."

"Well, tell her to wake up," I said, starting to tremble. "Tell her I said so . . . tell her Blaze James said so!"

Mama just stood there and wept, and I don't know why, but I wanted to knee her in the chest, punch her in the stomach.

Toughen up, old broad!

Toughen up!

You's gotta be a grown-up now!

Your raggedy man just bit the dust; it's all on you!

All on you!

That's what I wanted to say with all my might, but I held back on my opinion for the sake of good grace. "Why you keeping her from me?" I screamed.

Toughen up, old broad!

Between Mr. Rufus's gravesite burial and all my demands, it was just too much for her. Mama was melting like a wax doll under a flame. I could see that her little bee brain was overloaded. Maybe I shoulda been more nice about it, but I didn't appreciate how she and Dixie Mae just moved me off to the side, like some kind of stale piece of cheese.

"Go with Miss Hardaway," she said, pointing in Miss Hardaway's direction. "It's all I can do to keep myself from having a nervous breakdown, It's just too much now, you hear! Go with Miss Hardaway!"

"Take me to Aerial!" I commanded my mother. "Take me to her, you hear me! You hear me, Mama!" I thought if Mr. Rufus pushed Mama around, so could I. She listened to him good enough, but now that he was dead, she would have to find somebody else to listen to, and it may as well be me.

"Miss Hardaway!" screamed Mama, turning around in circles. "Miss Hardaway! Miss Hardaway!" Next thing I knew, the crowd of people had descended upon us, pulling me apart from Aliyah James. Maybe I had taken a swing on her, but I don't remember for sure. I remember the crowd separating us and Miss Hardaway snatching me up, straight into the air, feet off the ground, dangling me off her side like some kind of knick-knack, patty whack, give Blaze a bone.

Miss Hardaway stomped straight off the cemetery grounds and back to her car, carrying me all the way, flopping at her side like an almost-dead chicken. I remember the sky opening up in that moment, and the downpour turned into something like a flood. I remember the ground turning to mud and slosh and seeing Miss Hardaway's hooker-type boots get muddier and muddier.

I remember the bloodshot eyes of all Rufus's beat-down relatives as they stared into my eyes as Miss Hardaway carried me off the field, defeated. And nobody said nothing. They were the biggest bunch of losers I ever did see. They didn't even say good-bye. But then again, maybe they did. Maybe they did.

Chapter 6

Compassion

Within the hour, I was back at Miss Felicity's house, sitting at the kitchen table, and staring at her black, shiny, thigh-hugging boots. They were sitting in the corner, against the front door, and not looking so shiny anymore. They were covered in splats of mud, with caked-on dirt at the bottom of the heels. I just sat at the table, looking at the boots, unable to take my eyes off them.

"Them boots look a lot like life," I said to Miss Felicity, who didn't utter a sound. She was busy boiling hot milk on the kitchen stove and paying me no mind at all. "Gets a little muddy sometimes, doesn't it?" I asked.

Miss Felicity shot a sharp glance my way. "Why you give your mama such a hard time today?" she asked me.

"Maybe she deserves a hard time," I said with my eyes dug into the floor. Something about Miss Felicity's words made me hot with anger.

"Sometimes when people seem a little weak, it's okay to be nice to them," she said. "I think they call that *compassion*. I read that once on the back of a box of hot chocolate."

"I ain't never read nothing about compassion on a box of hot chocolate," I said.

"Goddammit, Blaze," snapped Miss Felicity. "She buried her husband today!"

Her words silenced me in an instant. Miss Hardaway wasn't one to beat on the bush or around it. She always went straight for the vein.

"He wasn't worth much more than the box they buried him in; don't you know that?" I asked, my eyes looking straight into hers.

"Yeah, I know," she said. "But he was worth something to her."

"That's 'cause she's kind of dumb," I said.

Miss Felicity laughed. "That's your mama, Blaze. She had you out of her own body."

"I've heard that before," I said, rolling my eyes.

"And she's just about the prettiest lady I ever did lay eyes on," said Miss Felicity, setting down a cup of nice hot chocolate on the table in front of me.

"Thank you," I said, snatching up the cup eagerly.

Miss Felicity sat down beside me and opened a bag of big white marshmallows.

"Sometimes," she said, "you gotta give people a little bit of room."

"For what?" I asked.

She paused, then took two huge, white, fluffy marshmallows and dropped them into my cup of hot chocolate. "To be human."

"I don't appreciate her leaving me behind, Miss Felicity," I said with a pout. "I matter . . . I matter a whole lot . . . and she just waltzed on down the street like I don't matter at all."

"She didn't leave you behind, girl," said Miss Felicity. "She left you with me."

"They keeping me from Aerial, and I don't take too kindly to that. She's my twin.

"Aerial's hurt, Blaze . . ."

"Then who better to heal her than me?" I asked straight out, and she knew I was right, 'cause she couldn't answer me back.

And she never would.

She never would.

Chapter 7

Argentina

I woke up in the middle of the night to Miss Felicity shaking me. She had a firm grip on my forearms, almost pulling them loose and out of the sockets. My head was thrown back and forth, back and forth.

"Wake up!" screamed Miss Felicity. "Wake up! Wake up!"

By the time I came to, I was in a daze and the previous moments a blur. "What? What?"

"You was screaming something awful!" said Miss Felicity. "I thought something had happened to you."

"Oh," I said, still groggy. "I musta been dreamin . . ."

"You musta been having a nightmare."

Miss Hardaway sat down on the bed, felt something wet, sat back up, and started feeling around on the mattress. "What is this?" she asked.

Uh-oh. Bed wetter in the house.

"Sometimes I wet the bed," I said timidly. "But I don't do it on purpose."

"You outgrown diapers, right?" she asked.

"Yeah," I said.

"Well, you too old for this shit," she said, going into the other room, grabbing a set of sheets, and returning with them under her arm.

"Go on and get in the tub." Ashamed, I lifted myself from

the bed and marched straight toward the bathroom, in search of salvation. Before I got all the way to the bathroom, I stopped and turned to Miss Felicity. "It ain't bad . . ."

"It ain't good neither," said Miss Felicity as she ripped off one set of sheets in exchange for another. "What's a big girl like you look like peeing in the mother-loving bed?"

"Everything ain't what it looks like," I said.

"What?"

"Everything ain't what it looks like," I repeated. "That night . . ." I began slowly before dropping into silence. Miss Felicity looked at my face and knew I was trying to say something, so she stopped talking and judging. She had to stop judging so she could hear what I was saying.

"What night, girl?"

"That Mr. Rufus was killed and Aerial was burned . . . I was outside trying to dry wet sheets. If I hadn't peed in the bed that night, don't you know there's a real good chance that I'd be dead right now?"

Disarmed, Miss Felicity looked at me with a blank expression. It would be yet another time that her vocal cords were stunned into silence.

The next night was Saturday, and I had been with Miss Felicity Hardaway for fourteen days straight. Mama was good for a call every two days or so, but I didn't see her anymore after Rufus's service, and she always sounded the same on the phone, like she was far, far away.

"How's Aerial?" I would always ask, and always I got the same reply. "She's steady . . ."

Steady?

What does that mean?

"How's school going?" she would ask, changing subjects mid-air. "Steady," I would always respond with no more of an explanation than that. I assumed that she knew what that meant.

Well, it was neither here nor there, because our conversations never really went anywhere, and I always felt a little jumbled when I hung up the phone after talking with her. It was kind of how I felt on this particular night, in my temporary living situation with Miss Felicity Hardaway.

Jumbled.

Miss Felicity was getting restless and, in her own words, "needed a little something to take the edge off." I assumed she meant Wild Turkey. Later that night, I discovered how wrong I was. She had been extra cranky all day long, prodding, pushing, and hounding me: "Hurry up with the dishes. I got company coming tonight!" And later that afternoon, "Hurry up and clean the bathtub. I got company coming tonight!" And early that evening, "Hurry up and eat your dinner. I got company coming tonight!"

"Gee Whiz, who's coming tonight, the Queen of England?" I asked her, trying to chug down a bowl of hot soup and half a sandwich.

"Don't be no smart-ass," she snapped, snatching up my dinner dishes before I could finish my last couple teaspoons of soup. "I don't like no smart-ass kids."

"Sorry," I mumbled.

"Go get yourself a bath and clean up before the company gets here."

"Okay," I said.

"Brush your teeth real good, and clean behind your ears."

"Okay," I said, scampering off into the bathroom.

"And scrub your knees and elbows!" I could hear through the walls as I stood face-to-face with myself in the mirror.

"And your ankles!"

"My ankles?" I whispered to myself.

As I ran a nice, hot bath, I couldn't help but wonder about who in the holy hell was coming over here tonight. Miss Felicity was making a big ol' deal out of it; must be one of her men friends or something like a boyfriend. That's the only time that a girl usually acts weird like that.

"And put on a couple puffs of that good-smelling cologne sitting there on the sink when you're done scrubbing up!"

"Cologne?" I asked.

"Yes!" she shouted from the other side of the door.

Miss Felicity has lost her marbles.

Before I could even get out of the tub, I heard somebody knocking at the door. I didn't see Miss Felicity run to the door like she was in a race, but then again, I didn't have to; I could hear the clacking of her high-heeled shoes as she raced toward the front door. I thought for a minute that she was going to be like the cartoons and just plow right through the door and keep going—that's how fast she was running, in my opinion.

She sure sounds desperate enough, I thought. *This must be the prettiest man in town, coming over here tonight.*

From the tub, I heard mumbling and low laughter.

Uh-oh, they must be talking dirty. That's grown folk's shit, I thought.

I could hear Miss Felicity's voice change, go up a whole range or two. She sounded like a sweet little daisy flower or something real delicate, not like the cactus bush with a bunch of thorns on it, which is what she sounded like just three minutes ago.

Miss Felicity must have really liked this boy, 'cause from the minute the door opened till I got out of the tub, dried off, dressed, and cleaned behind my ears, all she did was laugh and cackle.

Oh boy.

I looked in the mirror and was convinced that I had "prettied up" enough to show my face in public and still be held respectable by all.

I smiled.

And, of course, I smelled good, too, and I had the cleanest set of ankles in all of Shreveport. What more could a pretty boy want?

I opened the door and slowly wound down the hall to the living room, where Miss Felicity sat on her green and pink sofa with one of the prettiest *girls* I ever did see.

Girl?

Where's the boy you been flirting with all night? I wanted to ask but didn't, 'cause Miss Felicity and this pretty girl were sitting on her loud couch drinking and smoking, and I could tell by the eye she gave me when I entered the room that she wasn't in the mood for any lip from me.

"Come in here, Blaze," commanded Miss Felicity. And I responded, slowly inching my way to her close quarters. "This here is Blaze James," she said, introducing me to her friend.

"Bella . . . beautiful," said her friend in a thick accent. She had long black hair that shined like silk and big black eyes and long lashes.

"Thanks," I said slowly.

"She is pretty, ain't she?" said Miss Felicity. "Blaze, this is Rosario from Argentina."

"Wow . . . you live in Argentina?" I asked, impressed.

"You know Argentina?" she asked, brows raised.

"No, but it sounds like it's far enough away."

They both laughed.

"It's far enough."

"How did you come to be in Shreveport?" I asked. "It's the last place on earth anybody would come on purpose."

They laughed again.

"I came to see my friend," she said, looking at Miss Felicity with a twinkle-type light in her eye.

"You live here or you just visiting?" I asked.

"Get off all these questions, Blaze," warned Miss Felicity, and they both started to laugh. "You gonna give Miss Rosario a headache."

"Sorry," I said with a bite.

"Oh, let her be," said Rosario to Miss Felicity.

Yeah, I thought to myself. *Let me be.* It didn't take long for me to figure what kind of night it was going to be by the display on the coffee table, which included a bottle of Wild Turkey, several packs of cigarettes, and two reefer joints rolled up, lying right out in the open. Mr. Rufus used to smoke the little funny-smelling cigarettes, too, but he would try to pretend to hide them from me and Aerial, even though we knew what it was.

"I'ma go to bed," I said.

"At seven o'clock?" asked Miss Felicity, looking at the clock on the wall.

"I'm beat," I said.

"Have a good rest," said Rosario.

"Good night," I mumbled, and off to the bedroom I went, where I shut the door and got into bed.

Boy, I sure did miss Aerial. I had never really known what lonely felt like till Aerial got hurt. We had always had each other, were breath of each other's breath, and that's what we were, twin souls sharing a lifetime. I loved Aerial with all my heart, and being without her didn't make good logic to me at all. It was like chocolate being separated from the color brown, or a zebra being kept from its stripes. It was like serving Kool-Aid without sugar—why bother? Boy, did I miss Aerial James. I looked out the window and into the night sky, staring at all the stars and thinking about my twin. "God knows you by name, Aerial James, and you're gonna be just fine."

I fell asleep early that night, and it would be the last so-called normal night of my life. I would say that life was already anything but normal, but believe it or not, it was about to get even weirder.

Chapter 8

Something Altogether Different . . .

I woke up later that night to sounds. With my current vocabulary, I don't know the best way to describe the sounds, so I won't even try. I will, however, tell you what I saw, and then maybe you can use your own imagination to come up with some "sounds" that make sense to you. None of it made sense to me, at least, not in the beginning.

It was somewhere around 9:30 later that night, and I had decided to go to the bathroom so I wouldn't get caught peeing in the bed, with company here and all.

My room was very dark, but I could see light shooting from beneath the door. The house smelled of liquor, cigarettes, and "good times." I opened the door and headed for the bathroom, which was only next door, but the peculiar sounds over the hot, night air called my attention elsewhere, namely to the living room where I was headed for an investigation of the night's goings-on.

When I hit the living room, my eyes bugged out and my jaw dropped to the floor so fast, I thought it had surely smashed against the hardwood and gave me away for being there.

Oh, Sweet Virgin Mother Mary, I couldn't believe what my eyes were showing me! Miss Felicity Hardaway and Rosario of Argentina were naked, with the exception of their high-heeled shoes, and they were crawling all over each other like crabs at the beach. Miss Felicity had huge breasts that were almost resting on her stomach and were flopping from one side to the other. Her legs were split wide open, and she lay on her back, showing all of her business to the neighbors. Well, maybe not the neighbors, maybe just Rosario from Argentina, who was down on all fours, butt naked, with her big booty raised high up in the air and her breasts, which were even bigger than Miss Felicity's, bouncing off Miss Felicity's knees. Rosario of Argentina was licking on Miss Felicity's business, and Miss Felicity was the one who was making all those unusual sounds.

I watched Miss Rosario's head go up and down, while Miss Felicity squeezed the back of Rosario's head so hard that I thought the top part was going to come unattached from the bottom part.

"I want you to come!" said Rosario.

"I'm comin', baby, I'm coming," moaned Miss Felicity.

"I want you to come like you never came before," said the lady from Argentina.

Well, hell, where was they supposed to be going?

What was happening here? I mean, I wasn't no baby or boo-boo the fool; I knew that boys and girls kissed and maybe rubbed up against each other for something to do every now and again, but this was altogether something different. This was something on a whole nother level. This was something that I should probably write to my congressman and ask about. This was something that needed some type of explanation, and if they hadn't been so caught up in what they had going on right now, I might have just stepped dead center of that living room, with my hands boldly on my hips, and asked, "Now, what do you call this particular situation right here?" And what brought all this on? In other words, how does something like this get started in the first place? I mean, really. At what point does a girl say to her very best girlfriend in the whole wide world, "Excuse me, but can you kindly take off all your clothes, lay on your back, and open your legs real wide so I can lick all over your personal business?"

How does that come into being? I just really, really wanted to know.

"I'm coooommmmiiinnnggggg!" screamed Miss Felicity, interrupting my thought and bringing me back into full focus of the moment. Miss Felicity raised her butt up in the air, and I thought she was going to fly straight up off the ground. She started shaking all over, kind of like the old ladies did at church when they caught the holy spirit, but I doubt the old ladies at church were doing anything close to what was going on here in Miss Felicity's living room. After Miss Felicity stopped shaking, Rosario climbed right on top of her, and then they did a little something else that threw me for a loopy loop. They kissed each other on the mouth and then started sucking each other's tongues and rubbing all over each other like they were playing with a heap of Play-Doh. They were breathing real heavy, sweating and carrying on and pulling on each other's breasts and taking turns sucking each other's nipples.

Sweet Virgin Mary!

This might be too much for my eyes to see.

It didn't matter none, because what happened next was just about enough to knock an eleven-year-old's knees straight out from underneath her backside.

Miss Felicity strapped on this long stick to her front part and sat on top of Rosario from Argentina and shoved this stick up inside of her.

I almost squealed when I saw it, and I covered my mouth and ran back to my bedroom and shut the door.

I stood in the dark room, in silence, numb. What just happened out there? What was all that about, and is that what Miss Felicity called "grown folk's shit"? It was like seeing two confused animals in the animal kingdom mating on the wrong side of the fence. It was weird seeing Miss Felicity in *that* way. I don't know what way you'd call it, but it was definitely a way I didn't understand.

I felt weird.

I felt like I had seen something by accident that I wasn't supposed to see, and there I stood, taking it all in, like someone who had sneaked into the theater without paying for a ticket. It might have even been fun watching what I didn't really understand, but at the same time, I wanted to hate Miss Felicity for being a freak show in high-heeled shoes. Never in a million years would I have guessed that out of all the boys who were wild about Miss Felicity, she'd be keeping the company of women right here in her own living room. With all the boys in the neighborhood to choose from, why Miss Felicity would lick a lady like a lollipop was too big a question for me to answer on my own. But who was going to make themselves available for a conversation?

I doubted anybody in Shreveport would know about such a thing. This was a God-fearing place, after all, at least on Sundays; even the criminals showed up to church on Sundays. Now, they might rob you blind and beat you in the head with a baseball bat on Monday, but come Sunday, they were God-fearing soldiers in the House of the Lord. And Miss Felicity Hardaway, oh boy, she was going straight to hell for sure. I thought the drinking, smoking, and swearing were bad enough, but that wasn't nothing compared to sucking on her very best friend's personal business, if you know what I mean.

I always thought God gave us a little leeway to make a mistake or two, but *little* mistakes, you know—like peeing in the bed, or holding a gun to your neighbor's head while helping yourself to all their stuff, or drinking yourself stupid. But big stuff, like sucking on your very best girlfriend's personal business, whew! I didn't even want to stand too close to Miss Felicity, 'cause the ground might open up and swallow her big, hairy booty right where she stood.

That's right . . .

Right where she stood.

Chapter 9

Crack-Ass Early

The next morning wasn't nothing too pretty. I woke up bright and early and eased my way down the hall where Miss Felicity and Miss Argentina lay passed out on the living room floor. They were both covered by a blanket and looked close to dead. The living room was a mess, with empty liquor bottles and heaps of ashes sprawled all over the floor and on top of the green and pink couch pillows. I shook my head.

What a pitiful sight.

I made my way into the kitchen where I started toasting some frozen waffles. I burned the first batch in the toaster, then tried another set of two. I burned that batch too.

Pity.

I moved on to a pile of bacon that was in the fridge. I lit up the gas stove and started cooking. It smelled pretty good till that started burning, too. I took the bacon off the stove, but by that time, the kitchen was filled with smoke. I tried to fan it out, but not before it disturbed Sleeping Beauty and her new girl-friend.

"What are you doing?" asked Miss Felicity, standing at the entryway to the kitchen, looking a wretched mess. It was pretty easy to see that she was not in the best of moods. Her eyes were crinkled up and red. One side of her hair was standing on end, and the other side was smashed to her head. She was wearing a terry-cloth robe and a pair of pajama bottoms. Plaid, I think they were.

Oh, I felt like saying, *don't dress yourself on my account.*

"What are you doing?" she asked again, a little more perturbed than she was the first time she asked.

"Making breakfast," I said humbly, eyes widened. She walked very, very slowly into the kitchen and leaned over the stove and the toaster, inspecting the damage. She looked like the walking dead. "You don't look so good," I said.

"No shit, Sherlock," she said, reaching for a cigarette and lighting it. My eyes automatically glanced to the clock. It was 5:30 A.M.

"What are you looking at?" she asked.

I shook my head.

"I don't give a shit if you think it's too early for me to have a cigarette," she said, looking at the clock with a twisted face. "And what are you doing up so goddamned early on a Sunday morning?"

"I thought I'd make you and your friend some breakfast, and maybe we could go to church," I said.

And with that, she softened a bit, but not much. "I'm not really in a church mood today," she said with another puff on the cigarette. "Not that I'm *ever* in a church mood."

"Looks like the Lord could be of some good use around here," I said, summing it up pretty good before exiting the kitchen altogether.

"What is that supposed to mean?" she called out from the kitchen, but I didn't bother to answer. I was about good and done with Miss Felicity Hardaway; what was once a cool lady, was turning out to be a pain in my good butt cheek.

I went into the bedroom, shut the door, and got back in bed. Two minutes later, here comes Dragon Lady, who didn't even bother knocking, just came right on in. Guess she didn't have to knock; it was her house after all, not mine.

I lay back on the bed, not even looking at her.

"Listen," she started. "I don't mean to be a bitch on wheels, but this whole kid thing takes some getting used to. And frankly,

I'm not used to looking after nobody for this long; hell, I can barely look after myself for this long."

"So take me to my mama if I'm too much for you to handle!"

"I told you I don't like no smart-ass kids," she snapped, cutting me off at the knees. "You remember when you first came here and I told you this was a grown folk's house, and I do grown folk's shit . . ."

I nodded but still refused eye contact with her.

"Well, sleeping late on Sundays is grown folk's shit, and I don't like getting up crack ass early on a Sunday morning before the damn rooster even crows!"

I didn't respond.

"Sorry if that shatters your little eleven-year-old world, but that's not how we do things around here! Grown folks sleep in on motherfucking Sunday morning, and they smoke at the butt-ass crack of dawn if they damn well please," she said without apology, then slammed the door, but not before throwing it open again to say one more thing. "And they cuss like sailors, just 'cause they mothafucking can—'cause they GROWN!"

The door slammed again, and something snapped in me when Miss Felicity slammed that door for the second time. It was something about her slamming that door, mixed up with Aerial being hurt, Mr. Rufus being dead, Mama being gone, and Miss Felicity taking a strange liking to women that just about sent me off the deep end.

I wanted to get out of this here bed and smack the dizzy sense into Miss Felicity. I decided to pay her back for hurting my feelings. I would make her feel real stupid in front of her little girlfriend, Miss Argentina.

Who did she think I was?

I wasn't a nobody.

I mattered.

I mattered a whole lot.

She'd see.

Chapter 10

Lady Lickers

The real morning came about one o'clock in the afternoon that same day, because that's when those two "lady lickers" finally got up. Actually, I was excited that they were finally woke, 'cause I was fixing to give these two broads the show of a lifetime. I waited till they got situated in the kitchen at the breakfast table; then I grabbed the two little brown dolls Mama had given me that day in the cemetery at Mr. Rufus's funeral. I made my way to the dining room table where they both sat.

Miss Felicity was drinking a beer and smoking a cigarette. She kept one eye on her booze and the other eye on me. Miss Argentina was buried so deep in the local newspaper, she didn't even notice that I had appeared.

I didn't say nothing to Miss Felicity Hardaway, and she didn't say nothing to me. I went to the fridge, poured me a glass of orange juice, and sat down right alongside both of them.

Miss Felicity just kept puffing on her cigarette, staring at me and waiting. She was waiting like she knew a good show was coming. Oh and she was right—*it was.*

I took a swig of my juice, then pulled out those two dolls and hiked up both of their dresses. Miss Felicity's brow raised as she watched and waited.

"I think you're mighty pretty," I said as the voice of one doll to another, with a heavy Southern accent. "And so are you," I said as the other doll's voice.

"Why don't you come over and play with me tonight?" asked doll one.

"Sure," said doll two.

"What do you think you might like to play?" asked doll one.

By this time, Miss Argentina had poked her head from around the side of the newspaper and was looking dead at me, while Miss Felicity monitored me under the hard glare of a steady eye.

"I might like to play under your dress," said doll two. Just then, Miss Argentina choked on a bit of coffee she had just drank, and Miss Felicity cut a set of nervous eyes her way.

"What might you like to play under my dress?" asked doll one.

"I might like to play a friendly game of lickety lick," I said.

Miss Argentina almost spit out her coffee by accident, sitting the coffee cup down hard on the table.

"Lickety lick?" asked doll one.

"Yes," said doll two. "Lay on your back and open up your legs, and I'm going to crawl in between them and go to town on your personal business."

Miss Felicity stood up with her mouth open and eyes wide, but nothing was coming out. She didn't know what to say, so I just kept going.

"And then," said doll two to doll one, "I will strap on a popsicle, turn you around, and ram it up your backside!"

"Oh my God!" screamed Miss Argentina.

"You little pervert girl!" screamed Miss Felicity, snatching me up from the table and pulling me by my right ear toward the back bedroom.

Miss Argentina sat at the table, staring at me like some kind of freak-a-zoid as Miss Felicity led me away. I didn't like how she was looking at me, so I stuck my tongue out at her, and Miss Felicity popped me on the back of the head when she saw it. We ended up in the back bedroom where a fistfight nearly broke out between Felicity Hardaway and me. "Are you crazy, little girl?" she screamed. "What are you trying to do, embarrass me in front of my company?" I crossed my arms over my chest and just looked at her without budging. "What is wrong with you, you little freak show!" screamed Miss Felicity.

I didn't answer or flinch, just stared at her.

"What?" screamed Miss Felicity. "What?"

No answer.

No flinch.

Just hard anger and a long stare. "So you saw me with Rosario," said Miss Felicity. "Big deal."

"It's a big deal for me. I'm eleven years old!"

"You coulda fooled me!" said Miss Felicity sarcastically.

"And what I just seen could have messed me up for life!" I shouted.

"You were already messed up for life!" she said callously.

"I used to like you, Miss Felicity Hardaway," I said with a force in my words, "but now I can see I was just giving my 'likability' away for no good reason. You ain't worth being liked by me!"

"And who are you anyway?" she asked bitterly, turning to exit the bedroom. "What makes you so goddamned special, kid?"

"My name is Blaze LeDoux James. I am an identical twin, which means to a buffoon like you that I am very, very *rare*. I am as beautiful as the black night sky or as golden as the sun rising in the east. And what makes me so goddamned special is as simple as a mathematical equation—I was born, therefore I matter!"

On that note, Miss Felicity exited the room and slammed the door. She had damage control to do in the other room with Sizzling Lips from Argentina, but I wasn't waiting around for a kiss-and-make-up session.

I was outta here.

Out.

Out.

Out.

I didn't come this far, which was only four houses away from home, to be treated like a nobody, stepkid, reject of a lady licker.

That was somebody else's job, not mine. I packed up all my belongings—four pair of jeans, four shirts, four pair of socks, and five pair of panties—and put them in a plastic bag, threw it over my shoulder, and headed toward the front door. By this time, Miss Felicity and her friend were in Miss Felicity's bedroom, low talking. You know what low talking is, right? That's what grown-ups do when they're bad-mouthing somebody; they talk real low so nobody can hear what they're saying. It didn't matter no how, 'cause I was leaving, going right outside the front door and over to the railroad tracks, where I would catch a ride on the back of a railcar and be carried over to a new life, far away from this one. My first stop would be Baton Rouge to pick up Aerial. Mama said Aerial was hurt real bad, but I knew that once she saw me, she wouldn't be hurt no more. I'd take *all* the hurt away. Twins have the power to heal each other. I made my way to the tracks with my plastic bag thrown over my shoulder like a real-life hobo. I sat and waited on those rusty, cold tracks like I was waiting on the last ticket to heaven's front door.

In a glance, I was staring at the black-shelled remains of the place I used to live. Home never looked so good, even though it was long gone, and soon the city was going to come and tear it down. It was an eyesore to the neighborhood. Really, *every* house on this block was an eyesore, but our house was a "heart sore," because somebody died inside, and even those who didn't die in the blast still lost their lives that night.

It had been close to a whole month, but in some ways it felt more like a whole lifetime. I never thought I'd miss looking at the ashy, black skin of Mr. Rufus James, but today I almost wished I could see him somewhere inside the charcoaled remains of that house, barely standing on shaky ground. I wished I could see his tall, skinny body stumbling around all liquored up on Wild Turkey and Captain Morgan. Never thought I'd miss looking at Mama in that faded, coffee-stained, waitress getup she used to wear, the one that her hips were outgrowing.

"Woman," Mr. Rufus used to say, "you gonna have to go up a couple sizes in that there uniform; your ass is as big as the whole state of Texas!" And mama didn't appreciate that at all. I never thought I'd be here on the street, looking at the city dump from this side of the railroad tracks, a stranger in my own neighborhood.

I sat and prayed to God that one of those raggedy railcars that used to ride my nerves so bad would come and deliver me from Ms. Lickety Split. It was the same railcar that I used to hate to see from my bedroom window. The same exact one that I used to curse and raise my fist up to in the early morning hours for shaking me awake without apology every single day. It's funny how the same thing can suddenly look very different if you need it bad enough. I used to call that railcar "ugly," but today it was the most beautiful piece of transportation on the road. Indeed, it was. I guess anything can become beautiful under the spell of desperation. I waited, waited, and waited some more, but there wasn't a train in sight for miles. I looked far to the east, so far that I could see forever. Seeing forever was easy, but spotting that train was another story. But just as I was about to give up, I heard a whistle blow from the west. My heart picked up speed, 'cause I knew that I was about to be free, but instead of freedom, I turned to see Miss Felicity whistling after me, like I was a cow or something.

Oh brother.

There she stood with one hand on her hip and the other wrapped around one of those nasty little cigarettes. She was wearing low-hanging booty shorts with high heels and a tight shirt that made her chest look even bustier. Her blond hair was buried beneath a loud red scarf, and she was wearing giant gold hoop earrings. Actually, they used to be gold, but now they were green, which meant they were never really gold at all. That's right, and there she stood, staring, no, *glaring* at me.

I sighed big, rolled my eyes, and turned my head the other direction. She had another think coming if she thought I was going back to that broke-down rat hole of a dive she called a *house*. Her place should have been condemned by the city, too, just like our burned up, raggedy old house four doors down. There wasn't much difference between the two houses, and if you asked my eleven-year-old opinion, both places were going straight to hell.

I could feel the ground shake as Miss Felicity's big awkward feet stomped across the street, over to the side of the railroad tracks where I was sitting in absolute peace, up until that very moment.

"Just what do you think you're doing?" she asked, huffing and puffing across the street.

"Leaving!" I said with determined arms resting against my chest.

"Where are you going?" she asked.

"Who's asking?" I asked, nose turned up.

"I am," she responded defiantly.

"Baton Rouge," I bellowed.

"What you gonna do there?"

"Pick up Aerial."

"Then what?"

"What do you mean, then what?" I snapped.

"Then what?" she asked.

"Then . . . *life*," I said.

She took another hit off that cigarette, and I looked at her with the most disapproving look that I could possibly muster.

"How you getting to Baton Rouge?" she asked.

"Train," I said, turning my eyes back to the tracks.

"How much money you got?" she asked.

"I got about fifty-three cents," I said.

"How far you think you can make it on fifty-three cents?" she asked.

"About six feet," I said.

She paused, looked at me. "Then what?" she asked.

I didn't answer Miss Felicity.

The conversation had started twirling in circles.

"You ever been hungry?" she asked.

I turned, looked at her a beat before responding with indifference, "Sure."

"You ever been really, *really* hungry?" she asked.

"Guess so . . ."

"How you plan on fixing that if you ain't got no money?"

"I'll make do," I said.

"Where you gonna sleep?" she asked.

"Somewhere," I said flatly. "There's always *somewhere*, even when there ain't nowhere else."

"You ever spend a whole night outside by yourself?" she asked.

I didn't answer. Obviously, she knew the answer to that one, so I just turned my back to her and rolled my eyes.

"I ran away when I was about your age," she said, plopping her big booty down beside me. "Maybe a year or two older than you are now."

I didn't say anything. Guess I didn't have to; my eyes said it all with their surprise.

"I got tired of my daddy coming in after me every night," she said in a low voice; then she took another hit on the cigarette, held the smoke for a long time, and blew it out real far. "So I packed up one of them little bags, just like you got, threw it over my shoulder, and climbed out the window, right in the middle of the night air."

There was silence for a long time. She didn't say nothing, and I didn't say nothing. But funny thing was, by this time, I had taken such an interest in the story she was telling me, I really did want to talk to her.

"Where did you go?" I asked.

"Somewhere," was all she said. "There's always somewhere, even when there ain't no place else to go, right?" she said, winking at me.

I half smiled. I didn't really want to, but it was kind of funny that she threw my own words back at me.

"I found a tree at the park about two blocks away from my house," she said, "and I climbed it and sat there for the night and most of the next day, while the whole town looked for me."

"Really?" I asked with a wide-eyed expression.

"Yep," she said. "They was calling after me, shouting my name, like I was going to come running home like Lassie, or something."

"Now, that's impressive," I said. "You had a whole town of people looking for you."

"Yep," she continued. "But, you see, I ran into a little problem up there in that tree."

"What kind of problem?" I asked.

"Well," she said with a slight pause, "eventually Mother Nature came calling, and I had to take a piss," she said.

"Oh," I responded. "Well . . . duh . . ."

"And I had to eat at some point, and take me a good shit, and that tree didn't come with all those kinds of accommodations."

"Oh," I said. "So what did you do?"

"I came down," she said.

"You gave up?" I asked.

"Nope," she said. "I just came down."

"You went back home?" I asked.

"Yep," she said.

"What did your parents say?"

"My daddy whipped me real good with a nice-sized switch," she said. "Then, after my mama went to bed, he crept into my bedroom and it was back to business as usual."

There was silence.

Silence.

Silence.

Till I broke it . . . "You think your mama knew about your daddy?" I asked.

"Yep," she said.

"Yeah?" I asked, surprised.

"How you know?" I asked her.

"'Cause she caught him once," she said. "Came in the room while he was on top of me."

"What?" I squealed.

"Yep," she said.

"What did she say?" I asked with bated breath.

"She said, 'Buck Hardaway, you make sure that thing is covered up with something. I don't need that girl coming up pregnant.'"

I frowned and was stunned into silence. "Is that why you like ladies?" I eventually asked, the words rolling off my tongue like cold steel hitting the ground, burying themselves deep. "Is it 'cause of what your daddy did to you?"

On the edge of my words, there was a rip in the silence. I had never seen Miss Felicity like I saw her that day. I could see in her eyes a deep, hollow sadness. It looked like the kind that never really leaves. In that instance, she and my mama looked like *they* could have been identical twins. Pain has only one face, and that's what makes it a universal expression. We might all wear it different, but it doesn't matter how you wear it; in the end, it all looks the same.

"I don't know why I like ladies," she said. "Maybe 'cause their skin is soft."

"I ain't never met nobody that liked ladies," I said. "How long you been liking ladies?" I asked.

"You sure ask a lot of questions for an eleven-year-old," she said, puffing away. "I been liking 'em for as long as I can remember liking anybody."

"How does that happen?" I asked.

"How does what happen?"

I turned, looked at her, but didn't say anything else for a minute. "You know . . . that thing you do?" I asked with my face scrunched all up, like I was in some kind of pain.

"You talking about being a lesbian?" she asked.

"Is *that* what you call it?" I asked, excited that I had learned a new word in my vocabulary.

Miss Felicity almost laughed out loud. "Yeah," she said, nodding.

"So, tell me about being a lesbian," I said.

She shot a look at me that spoke a voice all its own. It said something like, *You better back up off me with all these questions.* So, I took a liking to the more quiet side of my personality.

"Ain't nothing to tell," she said. "I am who I am. I'm Felicity Hardaway. Best barber in town. I drink too much. Cuss too much. Smoke too much . . . and sometimes, I am a barbarian."

"What's that?" I asked.

"Something like an animal," she said, "Just kind of rough on the edges. I don't do good with *please* and *thank you.* . . . "

"No kidding," I said.

"But my heart's always in the right place—it was in the right place the day I stood up in that big crowd of people and promised your mama that I'd look after you for a while."

I didn't say anything; I just looked down somewhere toward the dirt.

"I'm sorry, Blaze," said Miss Hardaway, "but I can't let you get on that train for two reasons—one is 'cause the train don't run on Sundays, and today *is* Sunday. The second reason is, I always keep my word."

Miss Felicity stood up and started walking back toward the direction of her house. She didn't dare turn around to see if I was following; she just asked me a simple question from where she stood, marching forward. "So, what you think, young Blaze?"

Slowly, I rose and began to follow behind her, in her footsteps, walking on exactly the same ground she stepped upon, only with smaller feet. We were two different people who had been in the same set of shoes once upon a time ago, and upon that ground we would build an understanding of each other.

"I think . . . I think . . . you shoulda stayed up in that tree," I said. "That's what I think."

After that day, we found our way, Miss Felicity Hardaway and I. And she became to me, by way of definition, one of the greatest loves of my life. Aerial James would always be my very best twin, but Miss Felicity Hardaway had a place in destiny as my very best friend.

Chapter 11

Twelve

If you count the days as they come and go, you can literally watch life speed by in person.

I woke up on the morning of my twelfth birthday feeling unusually smart. When I opened my eyes, Miss Felicity was standing over my bed. She was dressed up in what looked like church attire, which was strange for Miss Felicity, 'cause the last place on earth you'd find her was in somebody's church. She was wearing a long, tight blue skirt that almost covered her knees and a matching jacket with a hat. I thought for a second that somebody had died, till she leaned over and handed me a big white box wrapped with a pretty red bow.

"Happy birthday," she said with an extra-wide grin.

I shot straight up and grabbed the box, anxious to open it up and see what Miss Felicity had gotten me. "Thank you, Miss Felicity!" I said enthusiastically. So far, this was my only present. Mama had already told me not to be expecting *anything* this year, with Mr. Rufus's funeral bill and Aerial's hospital stay. She said she was "fresh out of supply." My grandmother, Ms. Dixie, had been helping Mama out a whole lot since the accident, and even though I kind of understood, I really didn't understand at all.

I opened my box and pulled out a beautiful pink dress with

fancy lace and a matching pink bow. Beneath the dress sat a pair of matching white tights and a pair of shiny, patent-leather shoes.

"Wow!" I yelled, pulling all the stuff out of the box. "This sure is pretty," I said, holding up the dress.

"Come on! Come on!" said Miss Felicity, slapping me on the knees. "I got something special planned for today!"

"What?" I asked anxiously.

"Never you mind; just get dressed," she said, walking out of the bedroom. "And don't forget to scrub the dirt off those ankles!"

I got dressed as fast as I could, even cheated a little bit on the bath. I splashed around in the water without doing a whole lot of washing with soap.

Scrub those ankles!

Scrub those ankles!

I got all gussied up in my new birthday outfit, and Miss Felicity put the pink bow in my hair, walked me over to the mirror, and showed me to myself. I couldn't help but notice that womanhood was knocking on my door, and I was starting to look more like a girl than a boy and more like a woman than anything else. A previously flat chest was sprouting the buds of breasts in the making, and there was hair starting to grow in unmentionable places on my body. But I was trying to stay looking more like a boy than a girl. It seemed like breasts and pubic hair would cause way more problems than I'd know what to do with.

"I am impressed," said Miss Felicity, coming up behind me, staring in the mirror. "Now, let's go! Can't stand in front of the mirror all day admiring yourself on your very first twelfth birthday."

"Well, seeing as how I'll be thirteen on my next birthday, this is also my very *last* twelfth birthday."

"Indeed," she said, nodding.

As we headed toward the front door, my smile faded and I stopped right where I stood. I looked out the window and stared at the empty space between *here* and *there*. Miss Felicity turned and saw the expression on my face. I must have been as white as the sheets I used to pee on. Notice I said *used to*; I'm not a bed wetter anymore.

"Blaze?" she asked, concern plastered on her face as she walked back toward me. "What is it?"

I just stared out the window.

Miss Felicity turned her eyes in the direction of my gaze, hoping to see what I saw. She would never see what I saw, 'cause what I was looking at wasn't outside; it was *inside*.

"Young Blaze?" asked Miss Felicity, staring out the window. "What is it?"

"Today is Aerial's birthday too," I said, numb and still.

Miss Felicity didn't say anything, just looked at me. Then, after a few seconds, I put one foot in front of the other and walked out of the house. Eventually, Miss Felicity followed.

The drive in the car was pretty quiet the first few minutes. Well, I guess it wasn't all that quiet with the noise the engine was making. Her car was old, raggedy, and loud. You could hear her coming from at least two, three miles away. You could see her, too, 'cause sometimes that raggedy car would smoke for no good reason. That's funny, 'cause Miss Felicity and her car had something in common—they both smoked like a chimney.

"Where we going?" I asked.

"You'll see soon enough," she said casually.

"Give me a hint," I said.

"Nope," she said.

We rode another twenty miles in silence; then all of a sudden, I saw a sign that read **BATON ROUGE, 200 MILES**, and I couldn't help but start screaming out of control.

"Aaaaaeeeerriiiaaaal!" I screamed. "You're taking me to see Aerial!"

Miss Felicity started smiling real big. I jumped across the seat and wrapped my arms around her and started kissing all up and down her cheek.

"Get off me kid!" she said. "It ain't *no* big deal; no big deal at all!"

"Yes, it is, Miss Felicity, and you know it is!"

"I don't know nothing!" she said, laughing.

"You know plenty," I said, rolling down the window so I could stick my head out of it and SCREAM.

Miss Felicity just looked at me, laughed, and shook her head. "Get back in here, you crazy kid."

I brought my head back inside and rolled the window up.

"You miss her, don't you?" she asked, looking at me as I sat in my seat, grinning ear to ear. "Reach over in that backseat and pull out that box, she said to me.

I did as she asked and leaned over in the backseat and pulled out another big white box with a red bow. "What is it?" I asked.

"It's for Aerial," she said. "We can't have you being the *only* cute one, now, can we?"

I smiled. "That's real decent of you, Miss Felicity," I said. "God's gonna save you a special place in heaven, you know."

"I doubt it," said Miss Felicity.

"Why?" I asked. "Don't you believe in God?"

"It ain't that I don't believe in God," she said. "I doubt God has a whole lot of faith in me these days."

"Why you say that, Miss Felicity?"

She didn't answer, but I could see by the look on her face that she was judging herself, and I knew why.

"What?" she asked, looking back at me. "What?"

"You think God won't let you in heaven because you like ladies, don't you?"

"I ain't never said no such a thing," she said, lighting up a cigarette.

As I watched Miss Felicity light that cigarette, I could tell I was starting to know her. I knew things about her that most people didn't. I knew that she always reached for a cigarette when she felt scared or threatened in some way. She also grabbed a cigarette if she didn't know the answer to something. She would also smoke if she was angry, confused, or frustrated.

"You don't have to," I said.

"Don't have to what?" she asked.

"Say sorry for being who you are."

She laughed nervously.

"Are you ashamed of being a lesbian?" I asked.

She didn't answer.

"I thought so," I said, nodding.

"You know where we are?" she asked. "We are in Louisiana—heart of the Bible Belt."

"So?"

"These are good, Christian, God-fearing folks," she said, smoking, smoking, puff, puff. "Homosexuals are going to hell."

My eyes widened, and my mouth dropped. I was surprised to hear her say it so raw like that. "You think you going to hell, Miss Hardaway?" I asked.

"I think I'm already in it," she said without skipping a beat.

"Well, I don't think you're going to hell," I said emphatically. "Who said you was going to hell?"

"The reverend . . ."

"The reverend don't know everything," I said. "If he knew *everything*, he'd know his own daughter climbs out the bedroom window every night and sneaks down to the swamp with a boy so they can kiss and do *other* things . . . if you know what I mean."

"Shut your mouth, young Blaze," said Miss Hardaway, laughing. "Not the holy, holy reverend's daughter."

"Yes, siree," I said.

"The reverend's daughter is a HO!" screamed Miss Hardaway, laughing.

I laughed, too, and once the laughter faded, there was only silence. And we both let it be, the silence. We had no reason to change it, inserting words where none belonged. Sometimes silence is necessary so you can hear what you may have forgotten to say. The rest of the drive went that way, till we arrived into the city of Baton Rouge, Louisiana, and Miss Felicity pulled out an envelope with a return address that Mama had sent me in a letter.

"We gotta find this address," said Miss Felicity.

"Do they know we're coming?" I asked.

"Nope," she said. "It's a surprise . . . as much of a surprise for them as it is for you."

"Really?" I asked, my eyes lit up with anticipation.

"Don't you know birthdays are magic?" she asked. "You should always expect the unexpected on a birthday."

We drove around for what seemed like FOREVER, looking for the address on that envelope. When we finally pulled up to the address, we saw it was an old, run-down, faded pink apartment building with about ten units. They were real old and rickety-looking. It looked like a good gust of wind could blow the whole doggone thing down to the ground. Maybe this was the place that my grandmother, Ms. Dixie, had rented for Mama while Aerial recovered. It had been three months since I had seen Aerial, and I could hardly wait till the car rolled to a stop before I was opening the door to jump out.

Miss Felicity grabbed my hand and pulled me back. "Blaze," she said.

I stopped and looked at her. I could tell she had something to say, 'cause her face came across with a real serious expression. "Don't tell your mother . . ."

"That you're a lesbian," I said, finishing the statement for her. She looked as though she almost felt ashamed for even mentioning it.

"She wouldn't understand," said Miss Felicity.

"Do *you* understand, Miss Felicity?" I asked, looking deep into her eyes. She just looked at me, kind of surprised by the question. She smiled, but no words were said. I took that smile to mean a yes, so I said, "Well, then, as long as you understand, that's all that really matters here, now, ain't it?"

I got out of the car, and that was the end of that conversation, at least for that day anyway. I turned all of my attention to the joy of seeing my Aerial. "I'm coming, Aerial," I whispered. "I'm coming." But little did I know that life was about to change again, never to be the same. Truth is, it had already changed, but I just didn't know it yet. But soon *I would*.

Chapter 12

French Toast

The apartment number we were looking for was 108. And from the looks of things, it appeared to be off to the side and around the back.

Miss Felicity fussed with her skirt, straightening, brushing, twitching and swishing it to the side. She fussed with me, too, fixing my hair, licking her fingers, and then flattening my eyebrows out with her spit.

"Okay, okay," I said, pulling back. "That's spit."

"Spit works for a lot of things," she said, smiling, as we walked around the side to 108.

We both took a deep, deep breath, and Miss Felicity gave me a once-over to make sure I was in good, presentable condition.

"Well?" I asked. "How do I look?"

"You look mighty fine to me, young Blaze. Mighty fine, indeed."

We both stood on the doorstep, and I could tell by the way her forehead had started to sweat that we were both a little nervous. I slowly knocked on the old, crusty, white, rod-iron door. I knocked again, again, and again, but there was no answer.

"You think they're home?" I asked Miss Felicity. She looked at me and shrugged her shoulders, as if to say, *How would I know?* Miss Felicity moved me off to the side and knocked a few more times on her own, but there still was no answer. And just as we were about to go back to the car, we heard the sound of a chain being undone and a dead bolt being released. I was so anxious that the door seemed to come undone and open in pitiful slow motion.

My heart was racing, pounding, and thundering inside my chest. Miss Felicity's forehead was almost dripping in sweat, and the makeup she had on her face had started to cake up and flake a bit. I had no idea why we were both so nervous. Maybe it was because we were unannounced. Maybe because in the time that I had been away, I had not only been away, but had also grown apart.

The door opened at a snail's pace. It was as if it was too heavy for the small hand that opened it. Once the door finally opened, I was able to see the frame of Aerial as she came into view. And what I saw in that moment will haunt me for the rest of my life. It was the most frightening and horrific encounter I had ever had. The little girl who opened the door wore the body of Aerial. I recognized the hair, because it was identical to mine. I recognized the simple green dress she wore, for I, too, had the same outfit. I recognized the shoes. I, too, had the same pair. My reasoning mind suggested that this was, in fact, Aerial James. But when I looked at the face behind the screen, my crazy mind grabbed hold of me. It was *not* the face of Aerial. No, Aerial's face had been exchanged in the most unfair of trades. This little girl's face was the picture of a monster. It was as if someone borrowed Aerial's body but forgot to bring along her beautiful face.

Where did you put your face? I wanted to ask. *Get that one off of there and bring your real face back.*

Who would play such a cruel, cruel joke? And where was mercy now? Who would crinkle your skin and burn it so? Who would disfigure your nose and separate your eyes, and make them lopsided like that?

In that moment, I shot a look to Miss Felicity, who looked as surprised and equally as horrified as I. Her eyes widened and she knew not what to say. Neither one of us did. And although we only stood for a fraction of a second on the porch, when Aerial James opened that front door, time stopped and stood still right where we were.

Aerial shot back from the door, screamed, and ran back into the apartment, slamming the door.

"Aerial!" I shouted, banging on the door. "Aerial!"

Within moments, Mama opened the door and nearly fainted when she saw me and Miss Felicity on the doorstep. She reached for her forehead and fell backward a beat.

Miss Felicity reached for me, but I yanked open the door and ran inside, almost knocking my mama straight over. "Blaze!" she screamed. But before she could finish the last and only syllable of my name, I was already out of her reach.

I quickly surveyed the interior of the apartment, for a hint of direction on where to go from here. It was a simple little place and not much to look at by way of decoration. The living room was beige, and had one couch, one chair. The dining room was plain with one table, four small chairs. Naturally, I found my way to a long hallway, and that is where I would go, seeking Aerial.

"What are you doing here????" screamed Mama to Miss Felicity. "Why did you come?"

"I'm sorry . . ." I could hear Miss Felicity saying, stumbling and stuttering over her words. "I didn't know . . . didn't know . . ."

"This is NOT how I wanted Blaze to find out . . ."

"I didn't know . . . I didn't know," she stumbled.

I ran to the back bedroom where the door was shut, and I started pounding on it. I tried to open it, but Aerial was pressed against it on the other side.

"Let me in, Aerial James!" I demanded. "Let me in! Let me in!"

"Get out!" she screamed. "Go back home! Go back home!" I could hear Mama cursing out Miss Felicity in the other room, and I could hear Miss Felicity trying to defend her reason for coming up today.

"It's their birthday . . ."

"Does this look like much of a BIRTHDAY to you?" screamed

Mama. "You had no right—you had no right!" screamed Mama as she made her way down the hall to where I was held up, just outside of Aerial's door. Mama tried to pull me away from the door. "Blaze . . . Blaze . . ."

"Get off of me!" I screamed. "Get off me!!!!"

"Blaze," begged Mama with tears filling her eyes.

"I HATE you for doing this!" I shouted.

"Blaze," Miss Felicity called out, trying to comfort me.

"I HATE you for keeping me away from Aerial!"

Mama looked like she always looked in moments like this, like she was about to have a meltdown. Like she couldn't handle it. Like life, as usual, was just too much for her. Too big. Too grand. Too devastating. Too raw. Too real.

"Aerial!" I just kept screaming, banging on the door. "Open the door. Let me in! Let me in!"

"Go home!" she screamed at the top of her lungs, crying and sobbing on the other side of the door. "Go home!"

"Nooooo!" I screamed. "No."

Mama picked me up off the ground, kicking, screaming, biting, and clawing at her all at the same time and tried to move me away from Aerial's bedroom door and back into the living room.

I remember Miss Felicity calling my name and trying to get me to calm down and be normal, or as close to normal as they thought they could get me.

"Blaze," begged Miss Felicity. "Blaze . . ."

"Don't touch her!" screamed Mama at Miss Felicity. "You've done enough. This wasn't supposed to happen! It wasn't supposed to be like this! I wasn't ready for this."

Miss Felicity lowered her head, unable to speak, unable to respond to Mama and unable to console me. She stood there in the middle of the end. She stood there stampeded by a simple act of kindness. She meant no harm bringing me here, but only harm had come from it. She stood there, undone, unraveled, and unrolled. She had tried to do something right, something really, really right; but in the end, all she got was something really, really wrong. She just kept her head lowered, unable to speak, unable to think, unable to respond, unable to breathe. She couldn't be right, so she just stood there being wrong.

In the midst of this, Ms. Dixie, Mama's mother, opened the door wearing pants that were too tight and a wig that was too big, with a god-awful shade of red lipstick on her lips.

She came in the front door carrying a bag of groceries, which she dropped to the ground the moment she saw my face. There was a carton of brown eggs in the bag. They rolled out of their resting place, cracked open, and spilled all over the carpet. As I watched, I never realized how much me and a sack full of brown eggs had in common.

Jumbled.

Broken.

And spilled.

"Sweet Mother of Jesus," said Ms. Dixie, making the sign of the Father, Son, and the Holy Ghost against her chest. Maybe we all should have been making that sign. I made that sign, too, and so did Miss Felicity; she didn't even believe in that sign, but that's just about how desperate we were in the moment.

Mama stood in the center of the floor, her eyes dripping with makeup from her tears. Mascara ran down her face without apology. It was a look that I had seen her wear most of her life. Raccoon eyes were her signature.

Ms. Dixie didn't move.

Mama didn't move.

Miss Felicity didn't move, and I didn't move. We all just stood at complete attention, terrified of one another, but more terrified of ourselves.

"Does anybody want breakfast?" asked Ms. Dixie. "I'm making eggs." Her eyes cut to the broken eggs on the floor, and then she reconsidered. "French toast."

"We might like some French toast," said Miss Felicity, numb and dazed.

"French toast would be nice," said Mama.

"French toast it is," said Ms. Dixie. "You like sugar?"

"Everybody likes sugar, Mama," said Mama.

"Sugar would be nice," said Miss Felicity.

"Then sugar it is," said Ms. Dixie.

Ms. Dixie bent down and started picking up the broken eggs, and Miss Felicity jumped right in to help. Mama turned away and started down the hall, where she went into the bathroom and started running cold water over her face. In the blink of an eye, everything went back to normal.

Ms. Dixie was on her way to make French toast and Mama was freshening up for breakfast. Miss Felicity was still pretending to be an in-house cleaning lady, scrubbing egg off Mama's floor like I had never even seen her scrub her own doggone floor. Aerial was locked away in the back bedroom sobbing, because she was burned to a crispy crisp and NOBODY in the hell had bothered to tell me that my twin didn't even look like me anymore! My identical, mirror twin wasn't just a new stranger; she was a mother-loving, real-life, salt-of-the-earth kind of monster.

"I DON'T WANT FRENCH TOAST!" I screamed so loud that my voice echoed, bouncing off all four walls and ricocheting around the room with a thunderous blast.

Ms. Dixie dropped the bread. Mama froze in front of the mirror, and Miss Felicity stopped picking up egg. "I DON'T WANT FRENCH TOAST!" I screamed again.

Mama slowly walked out of the bathroom and back up the hall like a zombie. She came and sat down on the couch, numb, with no words. Ms. Dixie reentered the living room and sat down on the chair opposite Mama. Miss Felicity stood up, frozen in the center of the floor. The bedroom door slowly opened, and the heavy footsteps of the wounded made their way up the long stretch of hall. Aerial appeared and walked over to me in the center of the floor where I was standing. She stood opposite me, and we just stared at each other, searching for twinhood.

No words were said.

None were needed.

I reached my trembling hand up to her disfigured face and rubbed it against her once soft skin, now leatherlike in texture. I caressed the burns, examining them against the palms of my hand. I closed my eyes tight, and one by one, tears began to stream down my cheeks. Through lopsided eyes, she peered into my soul and I into hers.

"God knows you by name," I whispered into her ear. "And you're gonna be just fine."

Aerial put her arms around me and didn't let go for a long time. We held on to each other for life, for breath, for air. Nobody would dare separate us again.

Mama just sat in the chair, head lowered, in silence, along with Ms. Dixie and Miss Felicity.

"Can somebody please make me some French toast?" asked Aerial. The room had felt like death till she asked for French toast; then all of a sudden, our birthday just got a little brighter.

Chapter 13

Strangers

We stayed at Mama's apartment most of the afternoon, Miss Felicity and I. We were noble guests, who even helped wash the breakfast dishes. I found it of great interest that even though I was with family, home felt like a place far, far away from here.

I presented Aerial with her birthday present, courtesy of Miss Felicity. She opened it, and we all stood around and watched. Her face beamed like a light, through a mangled reflection, as she held up a beautiful, pink-laced dress, identical to mine, resting it against her chest and rubbing it like shiny, new money. It was the same pink dress that I wore, but we all knew she wouldn't look like me in it. We all knew it, but no one dared say it.

"Go try it on!" suggested Mama, always trying to lighten the mood, to pretend it didn't exist at all. Mama was real good at pretending, and Aerial obeyed. I knew she was pretending, too, 'cause it made everybody feel better.

How does she really feel? A beauty turned beast before her time. When Aerial disappeared down the long hallway with the dress and shoes in hand, Mama leaned over to Miss Felicity and whispered, "Thank you" in her ear.

"My honor," said Miss Felicity, who up to this point had been as quiet as a deaf mute. I had never seen her so low-key. She had even temporarily given up cigarettes *and* swearing, something I thought I'd never see in this lifetime. She was stiff and unexpressive. I hardly recognized this Miss Felicity. You could tell she was a zillion miles away from her comfort zone. She didn't know whether to smile or throw up, piss on the floor or sit ladylike with her legs crossed. It was almost funny, as I watched her desperately search for the right expression for this particular unique set of circumstances.

When Aerial reentered the room, she was wearing her new birthday dress, and we looked like twins again from the neck down, but only from the neck down. Everyone in the room pretended for the rest of the day that we were still identical. But no matter how good the acting was, we all knew we weren't and never again would we be.

Always twins.

But never again identical.

So half of Aerial and I seemed to be missing, but none of us pretended to know that. And that's what made us all grand liars, in a strange sort of way. Aerial would be the first to admit it, and in fact, she did during a private moment I had with her later that day in her room.

"You finally got your own room," I said, looking at the simple little room that belonged only to her.

"Guess so," she said, sitting on the bed by herself till I decided to join her.

"What's it like?" I asked her, paused a beat, then continued. "Being *you?*"

"Burned?" she asked for clarification.

I nodded.

"It's like walking into a room kinda like this one," she said, looking around her tiny bedroom, "and once you get inside, the door disappears."

I glanced at the door and thought real hard for a second, maybe even two.

"You know there's a door," she went on to say, "because you had to get in some kind of way."

"So, it's like living in a world where there's no door to the outside?" I asked.

"Exactly," she said.

"Maybe you *are* the outside now, Aerial."

"Then I want to come back in," she said, squeezing my hand tight, "to the way I used to be."

"Make a new way now," I said, looking into her eyes. Most of the time, I tried to look around her outside reflection, kind of like everybody else did. I didn't want her to feel bad or myself to feel bad, but I guess we had gone way past feeling bad. I didn't mean to stare, but I *needed* to stare. It was so hard to look at her once-beautiful face, now gone, but I knew I had to get past it, because Aerial was inside of there.

Somewhere.

Behind the burned skin.

"Wouldn't you?" she asked. I had almost forgot what we were talking about, because I had gotten so lost in her reflection.

"What?" I asked.

"Wouldn't you want out?" she asked me.

I did not respond. How could I when the answer itself was so obvious?

At the end of our visit, Mama walked me and Miss Felicity outdoors. Aerial stayed behind with Ms. Dixie. There were no long, drawn-out good-byes and not even one of those I'll-see-you-real-soon kind of lies uttered by any of us. In a bizarre way, I felt like I was leaving an unfamiliar place, where the people seemed somewhat familiar but little more than that. Mama, Ms. Dixie, and even Aerial—I knew them once upon a time ago, but now they were all different. Or maybe it wasn't them at all; maybe it was *me* who was different now. Like I said before, only one person may have died that night, but everybody in that house lost a life, and that included me.

As we walked out to the street, Mama pulled me off to the side. Miss Felicity just kept walking, more out of respect than obligation.

"I'm sorry, Blaze," she said. "I'm sorry you had to find out like this. I'm sorry I didn't tell you the truth. I was just trying to protect you."

"From what?" I asked with a harsh ring in my voice.

"From life," she said.

"I don't need protecting," I declared with certainty. "I'm *not* weak."

That stung her.

I saw.

"Every day after the accident," said Mama with a tremble in her voice, "she just kept peeling—layers and layers of skin, till I didn't even recognize her no more. It was god-awful, Blaze, ripped my insides straight out of my body, and I didn't want you to have to see it. She's still not out of the woods; there's a lot more surgeries, recovery, doctors . . ."

She rambled on, but I didn't say anything in return. There were no words to fill in the anger. There was just anger to fill in the anger. "Sweet Jesus, don't hate me for it, Blaze," said Mama.

Again, I did not respond, which may have been an indication to her that I already did. Maybe I hated her for loving Mr. Rufus too much or maybe just for not loving herself like she should have.

"You come back again real soon," she said, "you hear?"

"Like a visitor?" I asked.

Silence.

"Like family," she said, leaning down and gripping my shoulder with her hands.

"Looks like you got a whole new life without me," I said, looking at the old, beat-down complex.

"It's temporary," she said, folding her arms against her chest uncomfortably. "Just till we get Aerial back on track. She's still under a lot of care at the hospital. They been real good to her."

"What about me, Mama?" I asked.

"You're in good hands with Miss Felicity, ain't you?" she asked, glancing over at Miss Felicity, who had eased her way into the car and was waiting inside for me. She couldn't hear my conversation with Mama. "She's doing right by you, ain't she?"

I half-smiled.

"What, Blaze?" she asked. "Don't you like her?"

"Some days," I said, "I feel like you're walking through life with a paper bag dumped on top of your head."

I turned around and tried to open the door, but Mama pushed it shut. "Don't you dare judge me, Blaze LeDoux James!" she insisted. "I am doing the BEST that I can for my family."

I looked at her, then straight through her. The words she said meant nothing to me. I opened the door, got in the car, and locked the door. She knocked on the window, commanding that I roll it down.

Reluctantly, I did so.

"You have no idea what it's like to be me," she said. "Don't judge me till you do." And with that, she kissed me on the forehead. I said nothing, just turned around to face the front and rolled up the window, as though she wasn't even there.

Miss Felicity waved to Mama, started the car, and drove off real slow. The ride back home was long and silent. It felt like we were leaving a funeral. When we got back to Shreveport and pulled up in Miss Felicity's driveway, I closed my eyes and just sat there. It was nice to be back on steady ground. The air in Baton Rouge didn't breathe so easy.

Miss Felicity turned off the engine, sat back in the seat, and took a deep, deep breath and blew it out. She had smoked about thirteen cigarettes on the drive back home, and I could tell she was a nervous wreck. She took another deep breath, blew it out, and declared, "I could have shit on myself today!"

"I thought at one point you did," I said without expression.

She laughed out loud. It sounded like a mighty roar, coming out from her belly and echoing throughout the car; then she took a breath and it was sucked back in. Then we fell in between the crack of silence again.

"What are you thinking about?" she asked, looking at me.

"I'm thinking that was the nastiest French toast I ever did eat," I said sincerely.

Miss Felicity laughed.

And laughed.

And laughed.

And eventually, so did I.

Chapter 14

Good-bye

One thing about life, it just keeps going.

We stop.

It moves on.

If we fall flat on our face, it will roll over the top of us without apology to keep its course.

It has to.

It's life.

If life paused for our sad songs, slow dances, pitiful moments, uncertainties, and failures, the whole universe would collapse in on itself. So, life cannot afford to be too concerned with our personal problems. In fact, I would put a wager on it that life knows nothing of our struggles.

How could it?

It's got to support everything in existence. If it hiccupped every time we stubbed our toe, everything breathing would stop. So, this is my very poetic way of simply saying life goes on. And it did.

It did for me and it did for Miss Felicity. After our surprise visit to Mama, Aerial, and Ms. Dixie in Baton Rouge, it was almost like me and Miss Felicity came back to New Orleans and pretended right along with everybody else. Miss Felicity went back to cutting boys' hair, and I went off to summer school to make up for all the days I had missed from the chaos of the year.

Miss Felicity went back to pretending that she liked boys, but when nobody was looking, she was in the back room licking girls every chance she got. Every now and again, the woman from Argentina would fly into town and spend the night. She would never stay with Felicity longer than one night, but I think that was on account of me. She'd pop up like a ghost in the late-night hours and then disappear before the sun came up. And even though I never saw her, I always knew when she was around, because the walls would giggle with their sweet pleasure in the midnight hours, and Miss Felicity would wake up ever so cheerful the next day.

Mama kept on pretending and playing her usual part of the caretaker/martyr. She gave up waitressing, and caretaker/martyr became her full-time job. Her obligatory call came every Sunday morning, 9:00 A.M. sharp.

"How you doing, Blaze?" she'd ask.

"Fine," I'd say, stalelike.

"Miss Felicity treating you nice?"

"Yes," I'd respond flatly.

"You eatin' good?" she'd ask.

"How's Aerial?" I'd ask, cutting her off and shrinking her twenty questions down to one.

"She's coming along," was her constant reply. "Coming along just fine."

"Good," I said. "Let me talk to her."

"She's sleeping," she'd always say. Aerial was always sleeping. *Sleeping.*
Sleeping.
Sleeping.

"Gotta go, Mama," I'd always say after that.

"I'll see you soon," she always said, "real soon."

"Sure," I said, hanging up, knowing that was a lie. Mama had gotten real good at that, and I just pretended not to notice. We had all become so good at pretending, one day I woke up to discover that pretending was what we did best.

I pretended that the house four doors down had never belonged to me. I also pretended that the people who lived there were more like historical figures and not actually part of my *real* life. It was just easier that way.

I pretended not to feel a thing when the city came out and leveled the house to the ground, bringing down the charred walls and ash-black frame. I was walking to school that morning when I looked over and caught eyes with a worker who stood on the same sacred ground that Mr. Rufus had died upon as he took saliva out of his own mouth and spit it on the ground. I just looked at him, shrugged my shoulders, and kept going. Out of the corner of my eye, I saw another worker turn to the side, unzip his pants, and drop his urine in the same space that Aerial and I had shared when we were babies. But I just kept going, kept walking, didn't stop, and didn't look back.

Now I was being like life—roll over the top of your sadness and just keep going, without apology. Just keep going. I pretended another three, four months maybe. Till one Sunday morning Mama didn't call. It was the first Sunday morning that her very prompt 9:00 A.M. did not come. Something else came instead—a knock on the door.

Miss Felicity was in her bedroom, and I was sitting at the kitchen table, eating a bowl of oatmeal.

"Blaze!" yelled Miss Felicity. "Get the door, doll!"

"Okay," I said, shuffling to the front door without thought or concern that my life was about to change forever *again*. When I opened the door, my expression went blank and my mouth dropped all the way to the wooden floor.

Mama stood on the doorstep wearing church clothes—a big hat, a skirt, and a nice shirt. She was wearing soft, pink lip gloss, and her face looked flawless, eyes bright and hopeful.

"Mama?" I asked, surprised. "What are you doing here?"

"Hi, baby," she said.

"Who is it, Blaze?" asked Miss Felicity, coming around the corner, holding just as much surprise to her face as I held to mine when she saw my mama.

"May I come in?" asked Mama.

"Sure," said Miss Felicity, pulling me away from the door. "What's going on?" she asked.

"Well," said Mama, standing in the center of the floor with her arms crossed. "I've come to pick up Blaze."

Huh?

"We're moving to Pasadena, California, with my mother," said Mama. "It'll be a new start for us."

Huh?

"What?" I screamed. "What are you talking about?"

"Okay," said Miss Felicity, who sounded about as surprised and confused as I.

"There are some really good doctors there who can help Aerial," said Mama.

"So go and come back!" I screamed.

"It's a chance for a new life," Mama said to me.

"What life?" I screamed. "We have no life in Pasadena!"

"We'll make one," said Mama.

"I don't wanna make one—I already have one!" I screamed.

"Blaze," said Miss Felicity.

"This is crazy!" I screamed. "Don't I have a say-so in my own life?"

"You're twelve years old now," said Mama. "Don't make a scene in Miss Hardaway's house and embarrass me," she warned. "She's been real good to you, but it's time to go now."

"I don't want to go!" I protested.

"Blaze," said Miss Hardaway. "Your mama's come for you, so it's best you go. I'll be moving out of here anyway by month's end, and I'll be on the road traveling most nights, so I won't be able to look after you no more."

"Go get your things," said Mama, growing impatient. "It's time to go."

"But . . ." I protested, head spinning with confusion about where Miss Felicity would be.

"I won't hear another word," said Mama. "Not another one. Go right now and get your things, young lady!"

I looked into Miss Felicity's eyes, and she looked about as awkward in this moment as she did the day we had gone to Baton Rouge to surprise Mama and Aerial.

There was a long pause and a pinch of deafening quiet, and

no one dared say anything. Who would speak for me when I could no longer speak for myself? I was twelve years old. Somebody had to speak up, but all tongues fell silent and all ears fell deaf. Deflated, I turned and walked back down the hall like a zombie, walking to the death chamber.

Pasadena?

Mama and Miss Felicity turned and looked at each other, and politely they made small talk. Both were equally uncomfortable, and neither knew what to say.

"Thank you for being so kind," Mama said to Miss Felicity.

"No problem," said Miss Felicity.

"I don't have much money, but I'd like to give you something for your troubles," she said, extending a hand with several bills in it to Miss Felicity.

"No trouble at all," said Miss Felicity, shaking her head, rejecting the monies.

Silence again.

I reentered the living room, feeling as if there were a brick inside of my chest as big and heavy as the whole state of California.

Pasadena?

"Come on," said Mama, extending a hand to me. Of course, I didn't accept and walked right past her to the door. This made Mama even more uncomfortable and almost apologetic-looking to Miss Felicity, who at this point couldn't have looked more confused and ill at ease. I turned and looked at Miss Felicity, whose eyes caught mine and locked.

Sorry, she said without words. *So sorry.*

I walked out without so much as a thank-you to Miss Felicity, who in total had taken care of me for about eight months and counting. "Blaze," said Mama, "what do you say to Miss Felicity?"

What do I say? To sum it all up in a word, I said, "Good-bye."

Miss Felicity nodded and accepted my farewell without words. Her eyes said enough.

"Blaze," scolded Mama. "*Thank* Miss Felicity for looking out for you, child."

"Thank you," I said without emotion or eye contact. I didn't want Miss Felicity to see my tears *or* my hurt. I didn't want her to see my regret about leaving, even though I really didn't live here at all and was only a visitor all these days and nights that I slept here. But somewhere along the way, I forgot I didn't live here, or maybe I didn't forget; maybe I was just "pretending" that I did live here.

I could feel the heaviness of Miss Felicity's stare as she watched me walk out her door. I could feel the gaps between the words she couldn't say, or *wouldn't* say.

Mama was close on my heels, and I could feel the air around me get tight, because she was in my space. I had the urgent impulse to stop on a dime and let her ram into the back of me and smear her pretty pink lip gloss all over the side of her cheeks.

"Blaze," called Miss Felicity, and with that I did stop on a dime, and Mama did in fact run smack dab into the back of me, but she didn't smear her lip gloss, not even a bit. I finally looked at Miss Felicity, and with tears in her eyes, she said, "I love you, Blaze James."

What?

Miss Felicity Hardaway had said the *L* word. In that moment, I could not hold it back, all the love I felt for Miss Felicity Hardaway, all the time and distance that had come and gone; all the fights and misunderstandings. We were two lost people, she and I, somewhere in the middle of nowhere and everywhere else in between. But somehow we found each other, and that in itself was a miracle of God, because when we found each other, by accident we found a little bit more of ourselves. How do you sum all of that up in a moment? How do you go from a tragic night of dead flesh and burned down dreams and the promise to "take care of this one" to "bye-bye"? Fasten a big pretty red bow around it and call it a wrap. My unspoken affection for Miss Hardaway poured out of me like a chocolate fountain that just didn't know any better. It poured out in the innocence of a child, because no matter how much of a genius I was, I was still a little girl. It came out in tears, in sobs, in gasps to take in more air than I could possibly breathe, in the terror of leaving the only other person in the world I had ever loved besides my twin,

Aerial. I shot past Mama and over to Miss Felicity, who wrapped her arms around me real, real tight, and she squeezed me till I couldn't breathe anymore. She held on to me till all the air in my lungs rose up and out of me.

"You matter," I said to her, "and don't you EVER forget it, Miss Felicity Hardaway. You matter a whole, whole lot."

I kissed her on the cheek and turned away, and I will never forget the look on my mama's face when I turned to catch eyes again with her.

She lost and she knew it.

If Mama lived a thousand years, and I, a thousand years and one day, I would never love her like this. She lost and she knew it, even though she was a long way from trying to win anything, least of all my affections. She knew that I loved Miss Felicity in a way that I would never love her, and perhaps that was the greatest loss of all.

Not ever.

Not ever.

Ever.

Not ever.

Chapter 15

Clarification

Life in California was no great shakes. Flip a coin and try again, Mama. How about we do something really outrageous and move someplace else? I don't know . . . let's say Shreveport, Louisiana, maybe? How about we do something really brave, like get the heck out of here and go home?

I sure did miss Felicity Hardaway. I missed her with all of my heart. Sunday mornings, 9:00 A.M., used to be Mama's time to call me. Now it was my time to call Miss Felicity. Our conversations were always brief, because I had to respect the three-minute rule: It's long distance. You got three minutes. And no more. Get off the line. Click.

I think Miss Hardaway missed me as much as I missed her. She never said it, but I could tell by the way she liked to linger on the line. I think she was downright lonely without me.

"How's California?" she asked during one of our recent telephone conversations.

"Big," I said.

"Big is good," she said.

"Not if you're little," I insisted. "You moved yet?"

"Soon," she said.

"Where you going?" I asked her.

"Anywhere but here," she said.

"Three minutes, three minutes," Mama cackled in the background.

Okay, I motioned to her. *Okay.*

"You doing all right?" asked Miss Hardaway.

"I'm doing," was all I could say.

"How's Aerial?" she asked.

"She's doing too . . ."

"Three minutes," said Mama. "Hang up."

"Gotta go, Miss Hardaway," I said.

"Thanks for calling me," she said. "Send California my regards."

"I always do," I told her. "And California sends it right back to you, wrapped up in a nice big gust of cancer-causing smog."

Miss Felicity would start laughing and that would be it. Mama would literally click the phone off while I was still on it. That's when I gave her the evil eye, because I knew it had nothing to do with the flipping phone bill. She cut me off 'cause she didn't want me talking to Miss Hardaway for too long, cause she knew I loved her more, and she was jealous.

"Stop complaining about California, you hear?" scolded Mama. "Stop all that complaining. This is a beautiful state."

Palm trees, sandy beaches, and movie stars are all fine on the back of a postcard, but that's not *real* life. We would drive past all the big mansions, fancy cars, and pretty people on the way to our real life—a cramped two-bedroom duplex in Pasadena.

Ms. Dixie had a room, and Mama, me, and Aerial shared the spare bedroom. There was clutter and chaos in every corner. Ms. Dixie collected stuff, and by "stuff" I do mean *everything.* Newspapers, magazines, antiques, fake fruit bowls, vintage clothing, odd fixtures, everything. We stepped over, around, on top of, and beneath clutter to get from one inch of the house to the other.

"Jesus Christ!" I screamed one morning, trying to find the bathroom at 3:00 A.M. but instead found a batch of prickly sewing needles Ms. Dixie had left out on the floor.

"What's going on?" Mama called out from the bedroom as I stood in the hallway with a bleeding foot.

"Ms. Dixie's sewing needle just got stuck in my foot."

Mama got out of bed and made her way zombielike to the middle of the hall where I stood, inspecting my foot. "Let me get a look," she said.

I showed her.

"It's not so bad," she said.

"Feels worse than it looks," I said.

"Wash it off, Blaze, and keep your voice down. We don't want to wake Ms. Dixie and Aerial."

Mama patted me on the head and went back into the bedroom. I found my way into the dark, cluttered bathroom and sat on the commode, where I thought about killing myself. I didn't want to be dead; I just didn't want to be here, so right about now, any death would do.

This was the absolute worst move Mama could have ever made. We had been in Pasadena almost a whole month, and Aerial hadn't been to see one doctor. Her face was still burned up, and Mama wasn't doing much of anything every day except talking a good game about all these so-called grand doctors who were going to "heal Aerial's face and make it brand, spanking new." But like I said before, Aerial hadn't been to see any of these dynamos, 'cause Mama didn't have any dough.

Zilch.

She was broke as a joke. We were living off Ms. Dixie's retirement wages, and I knew Ms. Dixie was good and sick of that. Ms. Dixie was also feeling cramped in this cracker box of a house she owned, because three extra people took up a whole lot of breathing space. Matter of fact, our whole life was about to take a big, fat turn for the worse, and the next day at the breakfast table sure did prove that to be the truth.

I sat on one end of the table and Aerial sat on the other. It was the end of summer vacation, so neither of us had a thing to do all day long except sit around and listen to Mama talk about Aerial's face healing.

"I'm going to take Aerial to see Dr. Burns next week," said Mama to Ms. Dixie. "He's one of the best plastic surgeons in the whole state of California."

Ms. Dixie's mouth twisted, almost like she didn't want anything to do with any part of Mama's delusions. But Mama kept right on talking, pretending she didn't see Ms. Dixie's *real* expression. "Dr. Burns is a very talented man," she said. "He's fixed up many a burn victim in his day."

"Well, is he fixing them up for *free?*" snickered Ms. Dixie as she laid out her typical spread of bacon, eggs, toast, and grits.

Mama pretended like she didn't hear Ms. Dixie's comment and just kept right on talking. "He's got an office here in Pasadena," she said enthusiastically. "I'm gonna call and make an appointment for you, Aerial."

Aerial smiled.

"Don't go getting her head all puffed up, Aliyah James."

"Just what are you trying to say, Mama?"

Ms. Dixie looked away.

"She's trying to say you ain't got no money," I said to Mama, since *somebody* needed to translate and stop pussyfooting around the truth.

Ms. Dixie, who by the way was stiff and down-right snooty, never did appreciate my display of honesty. "That's not so lady-like," she would scold me when I was truthful. And I would grin real, real big, and Mama would shoot an eye to me, which translated to *knock it off* and *shut it up*.

Ms. Dixie, who was always dressed up so properlike at the breakfast table, wearing a big old wig and blood red lipstick with a shiny red leather bag at her side, would often sigh, exasperated by it all.

Breakfast was tense every single morning, because truth is, Ms. Dixie was just plum tired of us. She wanted her little cluttered house back to herself, and most days she looked at us with this unspoken notation between her big, furry eyebrows that read, *Are we done yet? Now, can you please go home?*

But this particular morning, things were extra tense. Ms. Dixie was passing dishes, plates, and glasses and setting them down hard on the table.

"Pass the grits," Ms. Dixie asked Aerial. Aerial did, and she slammed it on the table. Mama jumped. "Pass the bacon," requested Ms. Dixie. I passed the bacon, and she slammed the dish down so hard on the table, I thought it might have broken. Mama and Aerial both jumped. "Pass the eggs," requested Ms. Dixie.

"Uh," interrupted Mama, "I'll do it for you."

Ms. Dixie didn't look too appreciative of Mama helping her, because she had something in her throat she was just itching to get out. I knew it, Aerial knew it, and Mama knew it, but the real question was this—who was going to scratch up that itch?

"Something on your mind, Mama?" asked Mama. *Looks like Mama is going to scratch it.*

Ms. Dixie shook her head at first, then put the fork down and took a big gulp of orange juice. Guess she was clearing room for it to come up. "Well," she said, hemming and hawing.

"Well . . . what is it, Mama?"

"Just seems a little cramped 'round here, don't you think?" Ms. Dixie asked Mama.

Silence.

And more silence.

"That's 'cause it's so junky," I spoke out of the silence. Mama smacked me on the hand, just as quick as she could, but it wasn't in time enough to shut me up. Aerial started to laugh, which was nice, because she didn't do that much anymore. In fact, she rarely spoke at all, spending most of her time somewhere inside of her own little world, of which she rarely let anyone in, including me.

"I need a little breathing room, Aliyah," said Ms. Dixie to Mama. "Stretch out my arms and take in a good breath, if I want to."

"Ain't you breathing good now?" I couldn't help but ask. Another smack on the opposite hand came from Mama.

"Not as good as I ought to," said Ms. Dixie, shooting me a rather unpleasant eye. "I want to be able to walk around naked if I want to."

"Why would you want to do that?" I blurted out in disgust. Mama shot me a look, and instantly I hid both of my hands.

"I just need my place back," said Ms. Dixie to Mama.

Mama looked real hurt and rejected. "We ain't got no place

to go, Mama. What are you saying? You gonna put your own grandchildren out in the street?"

"No," said Ms. Dixie, uncomfortable in her seat, shifting from side to side, hugging the edge of a steaming hot coffee mug. "Don't be silly. I ain't gonna put you out in the street."

"Good," said Mama, relieved. Surely she wasn't dumb enough to think this was the end of the conversation.

"I got you a job," said Ms. Dixie, "as a live-in housekeeper."

"What!" exclaimed Mama and Aerial at the same time. I didn't say shit 'cause I knew it was coming. Excuse my Portuguese, but like I said, I knew it was coming.

Ms. Dixie was sweating in her seat. She looked real nervous, sketchy is more like it, even shady. She knew she had done wrong, wrong, wrong by us.

"What kind of job?" asked Mama, her face frowned up all the way to Tennessee.

"Live-in housekeeper," repeated Ms. Dixie without apology. "It's a real nice estate up in Rancho Palos Verdes. You've never seen such a place. The grounds are majestic, green and plush. You and the girls will live in the back house; it's called the maid quarters, but it's real, real nice—every maid wishes she could live so well."

We were all stunned into silence, even I. Mama looked down at her plate, crushed. Me and Aerial swapped all kinds of uncertain glances at each other; as for Ms. Dixie, she just sat there looking outright guilty.

"Mr. Willow owns the house," continued Ms. Dixie. "He's *real* nice—an oil man from Houston. He'll treat you damn good. Earn your keep and he'll reward you . . ."

"Mama, how could you do this?" asked Mama. "How could you do this when I need you the most right now?"

"Darling, I'm gonna be right here," assured Ms. Dixie. "We'll just live in separate places. I can stretch out and so can you and the girls. It'll be good for us."

"Good for *you*," said Mama. "I came here because I thought you would help me."

"It's been one year, Aliyah James," said Ms. Dixie with a sigh. "How long am I supposed to put my own life on hold? Aerial's fine," she said, pointing to Aerial. "Look at her—she's just fine." Mama kept her head lowered.

"This is as good as it's gonna get, young lady," said Ms. Dixie. "Life ain't going backward. We'll never be the way we were . . . Barbra Streisand sang that song a long time ago. We gotta move on."

"How 'bout I move on?" I piped in. "Back to Miss Felicity Hardaway. I knew this was a big fat mistake moving to California in the first place."

"Blaze," warned Mama. "I don't need your lip . . ."

"But I'm right, Mama," I said.

"We came here to help Aerial get better," said Mama.

"Aerial *is* better," said Ms. Dixie.

"She still needs surgeries," insisted Mama.

"Not till she's older," said Ms. Dixie. "That's what the doctors say—all the doctors say the same thing. They can't do nothing else to help her right now."

"I can't accept what they say," said Mama, crying a gang of tears into a hot plate of grits. "This isn't it for her."

"What isn't?" asked Ms. Dixie with fire on the top of her tongue. "What isn't?"

"This!" screamed Mama, standing up from the breakfast table. "This! This! *This!*"

"She ain't NEVER gonna look the way she used to!" screamed Ms. Dixie. "If you think one more surgery is gonna restore her face, you're crazy! She ain't NEVER going to look like her twin sister ever again! When are you going to *accept* it? Accept it and get on with your lives?"

The words came out of nowhere and rang a truth that was so violent, it almost shattered the windows *and* the walls. Aerial jumped up from the table, ran into the bedroom, and slammed the door. Mama and Ms. Dixie had a Mexican standoff in the middle of the dining room, both eyeing each other down to the ground. I was glued to my seat, like a desperate spectator, waiting to see how all of this was going to shake loose. This was better than an old black-and-white Western with one of them big shoot-outs at the end of the movie.

Mama and Ms. Dixie looked like they hated each other. Mama hated Ms. Dixie for telling the truth, and Ms. Dixie hated *herself* for giving so much hope to a hopeless situation. Ms. Dixie was right, you know. Aerial wasn't going to look no better than she did right now, which was the closest thing you could get to looking like a monster but yet retaining just enough recognizable parts to be called human. But sometimes, if you just looked at the exterior walls—Aerial's skin, face, eyes, nose, lips—the line could get blurred. Most days she looked half human/ half monster. I couldn't blame Mama for wanting to fix her, but I also couldn't blame Ms. Dixie for saying, *Look, woman, the jig is up.*

"When does my new job start?" Mama asked Ms. Dixie with the coldest voice I had ever heard her use.

"A car is coming for you this afternoon at two o'clock," said Ms. Dixie.

"Fine," said Mama. "I will pack our things and be out of here *today.*"

Mama turned her back to Ms. Dixie and snatched me up in the process, grabbing me by the scruff of the neck, like one of the litter from a new batch of puppies.

"I didn't mean no harm!" yelled Ms. Dixie, but Mama didn't respond. She just went into the bedroom and slammed the door so hard the windows shook.

At 2:00 P.M. sharp, a black Lincoln Town Car pulled into Ms. Dixie's driveway. A white man wearing a black suit jacket and nice gray slacks emerged from the car and knocked on Ms. Dixie's door.

We were all packed and ready to go. Mama had made us sit in the bedroom till the driver knocked on the door, and then we all three made our way to the living room door. There was a strange feeling in that moment, like a scene out of another bad movie.

Ms. Dixie had made her way into the living room at the same time as the rest of us. "I've done everything for you that I could," she said with tears in her eyes, "and now you wanna make me wrong for wanting my life back?"

Mama didn't respond, just said to me and Aerial, "Go get in the car."

"Good-bye, Ms. Dixie," said Aerial, offering her an embrace before shuffling out the front door.

I followed suit. "Thanks for everything, Ms. Dixie," I said, which almost sounded funny, the words themselves, considering the way we were leaving. Mama looked like she was about ready to not just smack my hands, but also cut them off at this point. Unlike Aerial, I didn't offer Ms. Dixie an embrace, just a nice wave. Heck, it wasn't that deep, my relationship with Ms. Dixie. Through her tears, Ms. Dixie smiled. It was a simple, faint smile.

Mama just looked at her, then walked out, almost pushing me out the front door in the process. "Move it!" she snapped.

"Ouch," I said. "All right."

We had a giant suitcase, which housed everything we owned. It wasn't much, but it was enough to make it across town to Palos Verdes, California, which is where we were headed.

Ms. Dixie watched Mama plow down the walkway. No words were spoken, but a lot was said in the silence. Before we reached the black car, Ms. Dixie scurried out of the house and followed us down the walkway, grabbing Mama by the arm. Mama looked down, almost daring Ms. Dixie to not turn her loose, but Ms. Dixie kept holding on. It was desperate, and maybe the only way Ms. Dixie knew to reach Mama, but I could tell by the hollow stare of Mama's big, round, black lagoon-looking eyes that their relationship was as good as dead—and Ms. Dixie knew it too. That's why she was holding on so tight, 'cause when she let go of Mama's arm, she'd be gone forever. And with that, Ms. Dixie did let go of Mama, and Mama turned her body away from Ms. Dixie, and with a deliberate step headed full-steam ahead toward the big black car.

The ride to Palos Verdes was long and quiet. Aerial looked out one window, and Mama looked out the other one. I stared at the bald spot of the white man driving the car.

Heck of a view.

I could see him eyeing us in the rearview mirror, especially Aerial. He was probably trying to figure out what the heck happened to her. Most people did when they saw her, just stared. That's why she *hated* going outside. Matter of fact, she hated going anywhere. So we rarely did, go anywhere, that is.

"How much farther?" Mama asked the bald driver.

"Twenty minutes," he said, eyeing Mama through the mirror.

I see you, dirty white man, staring at Mama's breasts. She had huge breasts that looked like two big honeydew melons. "Mr. Willow's expecting you," said the slimy driver.

Mama nodded.

"You ever met Mr. Willow?" asked the driver.

"No," said Mama quietly, eyes focused on the window. "What's he like?"

"He's like God," said the man. "*Everything* belongs to him."

"Pardon, do you fit under the category of *everything*?" she asked the driver point-blank.

I reared forward in my seat, because I couldn't wait to see how baldy was going to answer this question. But Mama took that as a sign of me being nosy, and of course she pushed me backward and gave me another one of her threatening looks. The driver didn't answer; he just grinned. It was a stupid kind of grin. Aerial looked at me and I at her.

We both shrugged our shoulders, but of course, in true Blaze style, I had to ask. "Just for clarification," I said, clearing my throat, "was that a yes or a no?"

Mama smacked me a good one on the left side of my cheek that day. Needless to say, baldy didn't answer, but even though he didn't answer and my cheek was pink and stinging, it was so worth it to ask just for a little *clarification*.

Chapter 16

Slaves and the West

This place was by far the most fantastic thing I had ever seen with my own two eyes. If I had three eyes, it would have been the same story. This was a cozy little community that hung off the edge of a cliff, hovering just above a large body of water. One of Los Angeles's most affluent suburbs, the city answers to the name of Rancho Palos Verdes, California.

"Holy Mother of God," mumbled Aerial as the big black car turned up into the estate at the very end of the street. There are no words to describe or articulate the Willow estate. This place was so magical-looking, it felt like *Alice in Wonderland*, or maybe just Alice in *wonder*, in awe of it all. It was pure white, this castle at the edge of the ocean. The driveway was winding and spinning, twirling and singing. That's right, this house was so rich that even the driveway had its own song—and so did the trees, the vines, the fountains in the center, and the fish in the pond leading up to the front door. So did the big picture window at the entrance to this palace that was as tall as a New York City skyscraper. So did the tennis courts and swimming pool, the horse stables and fine stallion that inhabited their own piece of paradise. "Holy Mother of God," said Mama with dropped jaw.

The driver looked at our gawking reflections through his

narrow, little mirror and laughed. "Welcome to the kingdom of Heaven," he said.

Guess he wasn't kidding after all.

God really does live here.

The car rolled to a slow stop, and the three of us in the back looked scared to get out. We just sat there looking at each other, almost daring each other to get out. We were afraid of being sucked up through the concrete for standing on such wealthy grounds with so little money in our pockets. I didn't have any money and neither did Aerial. Mama had double our worth, which was all of about ZERO twice over.

What do you do in a place like this where everything is too pretty to touch? You look with your eyes and hold yourself absolutely still, like one of them marble statues in that there driveway, lest you breathe, sneeze, cough, burp, or fart and disrupt any of the beauty of this wonderland.

When the driver yanked open the back door, you would have thought he was ripping it open to rob us, and we all jumped in synch.

"Welcome to the Willow estate," he said, extending his hand toward a gigantic, stained-glass door. It looked like something from one of them fancy Baptist churches back home. The ones where the preacher steals all of the members' money and puts it toward pretty costumes and nice decorations.

"Thank you," said Mama, hands close to the side of her body, cradling herself almost. "Come on, girls," she said, summoning us out of the automobile. We slowly exited the driveway and stood in awe of this place. It was even more unreal on the outside of the car.

"This way," said baldy, leading us into the house.

I almost threw up once we entered the house, not out of disgust but because I was scared to death. I had never seen anything so magical in all of my life. There were giant chandeliers hanging in the two rooms I could see. The rest of the interior looked like it went on for days and days and days, like you'd have to buy a ticket to get from one side of this place to the other. It had the most formal-type living room I ever did see, with a grand piano and two sets of winding staircases that ran like a snake from one end of the house to the other. And the floor, Holy Mary Mother of God, it was the shiniest thing I ever did see.

Aerial came in shortly behind me and gasped when she saw the guts of the house, covering her mouth in a dramatic sweep. Mama was standing in the middle of this place they called a foyer, her eyes wide open in great shock.

"Don't touch nothing," she said to me and Aerial in a voice that was too low for anyone else to hear, "not one thing."

"You must be Ms. James," said an older white lady wearing a maid's uniform who suddenly appeared as if out of midair.

I took a good look at her and, figuring she weighed somewhere in the neighborhood of 200 pounds, knew she couldn't have fallen out of midair without the kind assistance of an extra-heavy crane.

She was a husky white lady for sure, with a head full of silver hair and harsh winter-type skin. She looked kind of gruff, like she had worked the Southern cotton fields her whole life or something.

"Yes," said Mama.

"Come with me," she said to Mama in one breath, and "Don't touch nothing," she said to me and Aerial in the other. She led us through the magnificent palace and out the back to a small plain-looking apartment. It was not much different than Ms. Dixie's place. We went from the rich and fabulous to the shabby and underrated in thirty seconds flat. That's what I would call *express poverty* for sure.

"This is the maid's quarters," she said without a whole lot of friendly in her voice. "You can get set up and report back to me in two hours in the kitchen."

"Where's the kitchen?" asked Mama.

The old lady didn't look like she had patience for dumb questions like that, and even though I didn't know where the kitchen was either, it seemed like it was something that all the help should have known just because . . .

"That way," said the white lady harshly. "Keep walking till

you run into something with a handle on it," she said sarcastically. "That would be called a door—open it and come inside, and I'll put you to work."

She walked away without so much as a friendly good-bye. Her big old thighs were rubbing together like two pieces of dried wood. I actually felt sorry for Mama, because she looked a little on the overwhelmed side. I bet she was cursing Ms. Dixie sixty-nine ways to Tuesday right about now. We went from beauty and grace to living quarters that could arguably be much less comfortable than the horses' quarters.

It was a two-bedroom, plain-as-the-day-is-long apartment. No color on the walls. No marble staircase. No crystal chandeliers. Just plain beige walls and a drab pine table and chairs. Little refrigerator and small stove, and two tiny bedrooms with beds that almost looked like cots. The apartment had the tiniest of bathrooms that were so small, you almost had to pee standing up. God forbid the owner sacrifice a square inch of his living space for the comfort of those who would take care of the space that he lived in. I guess Mr. Willow wanted to make sure the maids knew the difference between working and living. The workers lived on the grounds, but the owners dwelled there.

A big difference it was indeed.

The owners could take bigger breaths, because they paid for the air. We took quick spurts and hoped not to get caught for being greedy with the oxygen. Admire *their* beauty, but just don't dare touch it, and everybody told us so.

Don't touch.

Don't touch nothing.

Don't touch nothing.

At one point, I wanted to kindly post a sign on every nook and cranny of the yard, castle, and ocean—**PLEASE REMOVE HANDS BEFORE ENTERING!** Jesus Holy Mother of God, we used to drive past the California postcard, but now we lived *inside* of one, and trust me, that was worse.

Mama's first day on the job was nothing too pretty. I couldn't believe that they put her to work so soon after we got there. But what was even more disliking to my taste buds was that I had to go along with her, while Aerial got to stay behind. Aerial always got to stay home, because she was sensitive to strangers staring at her face, and Mama was even more sensitive to strangers than Aerial was.

I became the poster child for the James family, because nobody wanted people gawking, staring, whispering, or asking questions. That pretty much axed all communication with the outside world.

"Hurry up, Blaze," snapped Mama as we rushed down one long walkway and another. I, on the other hand, was in no big hurry to report to duty as one of Los Angeles County's youngest maids. "Hurry up!"

We came up on a beautiful glass door, which Mama knocked on lightly, turned the handle, and entered. She reached back and snatched me up with her.

The husky white lady was in this beautiful kitchen preparing a feast. My eyes widened when I saw such a spread of meats, cheese, fruits, and grains.

Wow!

Rich white people eat so good!

There were spices, oils, and bottles of wine on display. This was mind-boggling to me and something you'd never see in our kitchen back home. Step into our kitchen and all you'd be impressed with was how many jars of generic peanut butter Mama was able to squeeze into that itty-bitty cupboard.

"Put this on," said the husky white lady, tossing Mama a maid's uniform. "There's a restroom around the corner."

"Okay," said Mama quietly. She gave me one of them looks before stepping into the bathroom that said, *Don't even think about taking a good breath in these white people's kitchen till I get back out here.*

I tried to ignore it, seemed so extreme. When Mama disappeared, I just stood in the center of the floor looking at the white lady, who was chopping meat on a butcher's block and staring at me with eyes that revealed a certain dislike to people with my particular combination of color coding, but I couldn't be sure, so I just let it be.

"Y'all ain't from around these parts," she said.

"No," I said, shaking my head.

"I wasn't asking," she said sharply. "I was just stating a fact."

I felt a silent confrontation happening between me and her, but she didn't know who she was messing with. I was Blaze LeDoux James, and I mattered enough not to let some husky, big-butted, bitter wench talk to me in a disrespectful tone. "The way I see it," I said, glancing around this million-dollar kitchen with shiny gizmos and fancy stuff, "the only people from around here would be the ones who own this place, not those who work in it. So the way I see it, you ain't from 'round here neither, is you?"

The husky white lady almost fell on the floor, missing the chop block and almost cutting her own finger straight off. "But that wasn't a question," I said with fire. "It was a statement. My name is Blaze LeDoux James, and I come this way by one of the finest cities in the United States of America—Shreveport, Louisiana."

"Shreveport, Louisiana!" The white lady burst into laughter. "What's so great about Shreveport?"

"Me," I said with a definite stare-down into her eyes. "I matter . . . I matter a whole lot."

I heard Mama cough, or maybe she was choking on her own spit, because she had heard what I said to the white lady. She entered quickly from the restroom wearing a plain Jane white uniform, with a little white hat, a wide white skirt, and some white shoes. I looked at Mama's face, and there stood a beautiful queen, squeezed down to the size of a small fist or a worthless dime, small enough to fit the imaginings of a glorified slave.

"You look white!" I exclaimed before bursting into laughter. But neither Mama nor the husky white lady had any appreciation at all for my sense of humor. Next thing I knew, me and Mama was "on pots" washing and scrubbing, rinsing, cleaning, scouring, shining, and polishing. Scrubbing floors and wiping off doors *and* doorknobs. Dusting crystal and polishing chrome. Disinfecting, decontaminating, deodorizing, and with me as her sidekick, philosophizing on the newfound plight of the Negro, immigrant housekeeper.

"Mama," I said, as we stood outside scrubbing the windows and polishing the walkway. "Who polishes the outside of a house?"

"Blaze," she said, sweating under the sun and humiliation of it all, "when you got as much money as this man, you polish everywhere you walk, inside *and* outside."

"Mama, you wanna hear something funny?" I asked.

"Sure," she said, keeping her focus on the window washing.

"We came from a poor, raggedy neighborhood in the South, where we lived as free people, to a rich, white neighborhood in the West where we signed on to be slaves." Her eyes widened, and her expression went from zero to ten, toting a mixture of fear, hysteria, outrage, and panic. "What you think about that, Mama?"

"Well," she said with an attitude, "I damn sure don't think it's *funny*." She stomped off, and I think that was our last discussion on the uncomfortable subject of slavery in the West.

Later that night, back in the maid's quarters, I soaked my two sore feet in a bucket of hot water while Mama prepared leftovers from the royal kitchen. It was a humble feast we had managed to bring back, which consisted of dark-meat chicken, red potatoes, and salad. Aerial stood at the entrance of the tiny bathroom, staring at me. I felt like she was gawking or watching me as if I was some kind of circus attraction or something. In that moment, feeling the sweat of my twelve-year-old brow, I began to feel resentful of Aerial.

Why didn't she have to help? Why was Mama always trying to exclude her from everything breathing, just because her face didn't look so pretty anymore? It didn't seem like a good enough reason not to participate in the role of hired help to me.

"What?" I snapped, looking at Aerial's distant, vague eyes.

"Nothing," she said, shaking her head.

"What are you staring at?" I asked her again.

"You look funny," she said, humored by the fate of my feet.

"What's funny?" I asked, annoyed. "You think *this* is funny?"

"Blaze," warned Mama in that overly desperate tone that she always used when I was pushing the line, which, by the way, was always, because I was always pushing the line when it came to Aerial. Everybody pushed the line, in Mama's mind, when it came to Aerial. If it was up to Mama, even God would have to ask permission to blow the wind where Aerial stood. It was like Mama was trying to make the world perfect for her, because she was all burned up. Mama wanted her to think that the rest of her life would be as cozy as a plate of sweet cucumbers.

Oh, darling daughter, it was like she was saying, *you don't have to worry about a thing. You don't have to lift a finger to wash a plate or even wipe your own behind; me and Blaze will take care of that for you.*

What?

What?

Me and Blaze?

Blaze who? I wanted to ask.

Blaze *me?*

Yeah, said Mama without words. Blaze *you*. She committed me with every word she never spoke, in between pauses and in gaps in the conversation, quietly and out loud, with my consent, but mostly without it.

Blaze will do it.

Blaze will handle it.

Blaze has got it covered sixty-nine ways to Tuesday night. Blaze will wash it, spit-shine it, polish it up, and make it pretty before the sun rises on the edge of a new dawn. Blaze will pick it up, dust it off, and breathe life into it again. Blaze is the old night, the new day, and every other beat of time in between. Blaze is. That's her new job. She's taken on the role of being *everything*. And it was here that I began to resent my twin. It wasn't the same between me and Aerial anymore. Ever since Aerial's accident, Mama was so busy trying to make sure she was okay at all times and in every possible way. Mama wrote Aerial the biggest apology letter of all times and handed it to her on a silver plate, which, of course, was the plate I had scrubbed clean with my own bare hands, and it was called *life*. And in between the commands and demands, I had begun to resent the twin I had loved all of my life, Aerial, the beautiful girl who had come out on the wrong side in a meeting of destiny between her and a hot flame. The taste in my mouth had grown bitter in the month since my return back home. Mama overcatered to Aerial James for fear she may accidentally catch on fire again just by walking too fast or straining too hard to pass a log of poop.

Geez, Mama! A little work never hurt nobody.

"Blaze, set the table!" shouted Mama from the other room.

Now, let us reason this together. I was sitting my tired butt on the commode, with my two little feet in a bucket of hot water to ease up the ache of a long, long day, and Aerial was standing at the doorway, with her arms crossed, about to share in a feast that came as a result of all me and Mama's good hard work today. Could it be, the reasoning of a madman to expect that Mama might ask Aerial James to set the dead, blasted, dog-gone table?

"I am soaking my feet!" I shouted back. "Aerial can do it!" I cut eyes to Aerial, and she cut eyes right back to me, as if to say, *Bite your tongue* for even the thought.

"No, she cannot!" shouted Mama. "Your turn!"

"It's my turn *every* night!" I shouted.

I heard the dishes slam down on top of the table, and everything in the background stopped. Mama was in front of that bathroom door in two seconds flat, moving Aerial to the side and staring me down like I had robbed and killed a pair of old blind ladies when nobody was looking.

"When I ask you to do something, I do expect it to be done!" she yelled.

"Why can't Aerial do it?" I asked, glaring at her with untold amounts of disappointment.

"Because I asked you," was all she said.

"Why do you ask me to do *everything*?" I asked. "And you never ask Aerial to do *anything*?" She didn't answer, just kept steady eyes on me with one of those looks that said, *Shut your filthy little mouth, little girl*. But I've never been one to make a whole lot of investment in anybody's threatening looks, including Mama's, so I just kept right on talking. "She's not dead, you know. You act like if you ask her to do so much as wipe her own behind, she's gonna break into a million little itty-bitty pieces!"

Well, needless to say, those were the last words that came out of my mouth that particular night. Mama stepped into the restroom and shut the door behind her so Aerial wouldn't have to see her inability to handle the bloody, unwrapped truth.

The next morning, I woke up with my bottom lip busted, and Mama and I got ready at five o'clock in the morning to prepare Mr. Willow's breakfast. Aerial, of course, slept in. I do not believe I uttered another word to Aliyah or Aerial James the rest of the week. As far as I was concerned, they were both as good as dead as Mr. Rufus. And it would only be a matter of time before I was gone for good.

Chapter 17

Embarrassed

We had been slaving at the Willow estate for a good week before we even caught an eye of Mr. Willow himself. He traveled the world and worked long hours, and we were rarely assigned to anything more than kitchen duty, so it was unlikely that we would be in any place that Mr. Willow would. When you have cooks cooking, servants serving, and maids cleaning, why would you ever need to step a single foot in that unglamorous room called a kitchen?

But one day he did come in, and me and Mama was working, under the direction of the unpleasant husky white lady, who I would eventually come to know as Mary Agnes.

Mama was cutting meats and preparing food, and I was washing windows, floors, and shining doorknobs. This older white man wearing a fine three-piece suit came around the side of the kitchen and stopped dead in his tracks when he saw Mama.

"Well, good morning," he said, clearing his throat of a whole lot of rich people's mucus. "Who might you be?"

Mary Agnes spoke up immediately. "Oh, Mr. Willow," she said in the most suck-up tone of voice I had ever heard her use, "this is Ms. James."

"Oh," said Mr. Willow. The white hair on the back of his big hairy neck was standing up as he looked at Mama. I could also see a bulge in the middle of his pants that stood up, too, at the very same time.

Yuk!

He was a big white man with rosy-red cheeks and slicked-back silver hair. His stomach was round like a big glazed donut, and his arms were fat and hung down the sides of his rounded body. He smiled real big at Mama. He had one of those kind of smiles that looked rich. It was the kind that said, *I paid all of my bills this month, and I still have money left over to eat.* In fact, it looked like that's all he did was eat. Shame on me for thinking it, but I know it smells something awful when he goes in the bathroom for a poop. I hope we don't ever have to clean up that room. Let the other slaves do that.

"Oh yes," he said, "Dixie Mae's daughter."

"Who, sir?" asked Mary Agnes.

"Dixie Mae," he said, waddling over to take a closer look at Mama. "The nice lady I play tennis with at the club sometimes."

"Oh yes," said Mary Agnes.

Now, truth is, I don't know what she was "yesing" about. Mary Agnes didn't look like she had *ever* played a game of tennis in her life, and for that matter, neither did Mr. Willow. He probably didn't play for real. More than likely, he paid somebody to hit the ball on his behalf, 'cause I can't imagine him dragging around all that big behind on a tennis court, fast as those balls come and go.

"Ms. James," he said, licking his lips. For a second, I got scared and thought he had confused Mama with a big old turkey wing and was about to take a nice-sized bite into her pretty brown thigh. And even though Mary Agnes had made Mama wear that white uniform, which by the way, was a hideous sort of thing to ask a human being to wear, Aliyah James was still arguably one of the most beautiful women in the world. I was not a big fan of her these days, but even a blind man could see that nothing short of an explosion could take all of her pretty away. "Welcome to the Willow estate," he said, halfway to drooling.

Good Lord.

"Thank you, sir," said Mama, bowing like some type of

maidservant. Boy, throw a little uniform on a person, and it sure don't take long before they start acting the part. It's a pity to dress down for a role, ain't it? "This is my daughter Blaze," she said.

I half-smiled.

"Well, you sure are a pretty little girl," he said, waddling his way over to me.

When he got within a couple feet of me, he smelled so violently of cologne, I wasn't sure which way to go, the door or the floor, 'cause I was about to pass out at the strength of his scent. That was some kind of wild musk he was wearing. Boy, rich people overdo everything. *Ease up on musk, man!* That's what I wanted to say, but instead I opted for, "Nice to meet you, Mr. Willow." After all, I, too, had to play a part, since we were in Hollywood, and the whole family had taken up the role of acting the past year of our lives.

"What do you do for fun, young lady?" he asked.

Fun?

My eyes bugged a little on the edge of that question. *Slaves don't know fun by name.* I could feel Mama's body heat rise up with all kinds of nerves. She was frantic, hoping I wouldn't embarrass her with my smart mouth.

"Well," I said, "when I'm not traveling around the country, I pretty much like to sit poolside and work on a plan for world peace."

I do believe his big old rich eyes hit the polished floor before his jaw did. So did Mary Agnes's and Mama's.

Mama laughed out loud, real nervous and apologetic, because nobody knew what to say. "She . . . she . . . wants to go into politics someday," said Mama, stumbling over her words, trying to make sense out of what I had just said to Mr. Willow. I, on the other hand, had not an ounce of concern. The answer I provided him was as stupid as the question he asked. So, I will leave it at that.

He looked at me oddly, patted me on the head, cleared his throat, and got the heck away from me just as fast as he could. Mary Agnes shot a death look at me, and when she turned around, I stuck out my tongue at the back of her big old head. Mama raised one good fist at me and shook it. It looked like we might be going for a busted top lip by the end of the night.

"It was charming," said Mr. Willow to Mama as he made a swift exit from the kitchen.

"You know," said Mary Agnes to Mama with all kinds of unfriendly in her voice, "it would do well to get her under control."

"I got plenty of control," said Mama, not taking too kindly to Mary Agnes butting into her business.

"Your kind never can get their kids to mind, unless they beat them. Maybe you should . . ."

Mama stopped cutting the meat, but still grasped the knife in her hand. "Maybe I should what?" Mama asked Mary Agnes, swinging the knife.

Uh-oh.

Aliyah James was turning into the Big Bad Witch of the West. A white lady was about to get chopped up and served for dinner right alongside the pot roast tonight.

Now, from where I stood, this was an interesting kind of scene that was starting to unfold. Does the big white lady keep on speaking to the tired black woman who just lost everything in her life that remotely mattered, or does she fall back on good common sense and zip her lips?

"Maybe you should beat her," said Mary Agnes.

Mama slammed down the knife into the butcher's block and pushed up on Mary Agnes in the most ungraceful kind of way. It didn't look too ladylike from where I stood. My eyes got big just watching. "Now listen," said Mama to Mary Agnes. "Listen up real, real good. I have had just about *enough* of you."

"I don't mean no harm," Mary Agnes stumbled over her words. "There's no need for violence."

Mama looked at me, then at Ms. Mary Agnes, and I could tell she was in between a rock and a stone, trying to figure out what the right thing would be to do, whether to back away from Mary Agnes or beat her down to the concrete. Before Mama could turn back around and get another good word in, Mary

Agnes had run to the intercom in the kitchen and screamed, *"Security! Security!"*

Mama wound up in the private office of Mr. Willow himself, and I was told by Mama in no uncertain terms to "stand outside" and "wait till this boils over."

Of course, I never *fully* complied with any kind of instructions, 'cause after all, my name was Blaze LeDoux James, and I did have my own free mind, if I do say so myself. So I cracked the door, just a taste so I could peek into Mr. Willow's office and see what kind of chastising Mama was getting. But to my surprise, it didn't look like much chastising was going on; it looked more like fraternizing. Mama was seated across from Big Belly Willow in this leather chair, and he just sat on the opposite end, swiveling side to side. I think his belly was rocking more than the ocean outside, which by the way, you could see real good from his window. They were separated by a cherrywood desk, and everything in this room looked mighty official. It looked like the kind of place million-dollar deals went down just for the heck of it.

Mama was laughing, cozying up to Mr. Willow, because it probably did feel good to rub up against some money, even if it came with a deadly blast of wild musk. And I held on to my position right outside that door as I tried to figure out what all the big fuss was about in the first place. "Pay Mary Agnes no mind," said Willow to Mama. "She's a rather stuffy old broad." Mama laughed again, but I knew her well enough to recognize a fake laugh when I heard it. And, boy, was that a *fake* one. It wasn't a real belly laugh. Now Willow, his was a belly laugh, because he was one big, gigantic belly, so it couldn't help but to be one.

"Ms. James," said Willow, trying to push himself from his seat, which eventually he did, coughing and wheezing as he made his way to where Mama sat. He stood over the top of her like some grand structure, breathing heavy, wheezing and such. "I would like you to attend a function that I'm having tonight," he said with some real authority in his voice.

Oh boy, I thought. *We're working again tonight.* School was starting back in two weeks, and for the first time in recorded history, I was actually glad to be going to school instead of staying at home.

"Okay," said Mama with hesitation in her voice. He couldn't hear it because he didn't know her, but I knew her, and even though she said *okay* with a smile, she really said, *The hell I will* with a frown, but again, he didn't hear that, because you can only hear what people are willing to tell you when you don't know them. But if you do know them, and know them well, you are privy to all the stuff they *don't* say out loud. I shut the door, because it made no sense listening to anything else. We were working slaves, and tonight we'd be back on duty. What else did I need to know?

"Blaze," said Mama later that afternoon when we got off work and were walking back to the maid's quarters. "Now listen real good," she said. "We're going back to Mr. Willow's tonight for a dinner party."

"I'm done working for the day," I huffed as we walked back down the cobbled walkway.

"We're not going to be working," she said. "We're going as guests."

"Guests?" I asked, eyes wide and wild-looking.

"Guests," repeated Mama.

"Why?" I asked.

"'Cause Mr. Willow wanted to invite us," she said. "Actually, he invited me, but I'd just as soon take one of you girls."

"You mean *me*," I said. "I don't think you'd just as soon take Aerial."

Mama got that *look* on her face. It was the same look she always got when I brought up anything having to do with Aerial making a public appearance. "Are you ashamed of her?" I asked Mama.

She never bothered to answer the question. She didn't have to. I could tell by that run-through-by-a-sword look on her face that it was a hurtful, hurtful question—but only because the answer was painful, not the question itself.

Yes, she was ashamed, because Aliyah James had been the most beautiful girl in the neighborhood all of her life, and her daughters were equally as pretty, and everybody knew us by *pretty*, and one of us didn't fit anymore. And it wasn't just one of us; it was Aerial James, daughter of the most beautiful girl in the world.

So what do you do?

You can't throw out the baby with the bathwater, especially if the baby is your own flesh and blood. And I do believe that's the real reason Mama wanted Aerial to have those surgeries so bad. She was scared that if people saw her own fruit and blood looking like some kind of monster, it might make Aliyah James just a little bit smaller. And she had already been squeezed down by Rufus James to the size of somebody who was barely there anymore, so she couldn't afford any more minimization. Of course, Mama loved Aerial with all her heart, but I think there was a little space inside of her, maybe a twisted chamber or two, that was also a little bit, just a little bit, *embarrassed*.

Chapter 18

Nipple Rubber

Later that night, Mama and I both gussied up for Mr. Willow's big-time dinner party. I wore the pink lace dress Miss Felicity had bought me, and Mama dolled up in a red-ruby number with some matching ruby shoes. They were the tallest pair of shoes I ever did lay eyes on. I used to call them the "red towers," and she was as tall as the roof itself with them shoes on. Maybe she needed a little height every now and then to make up for all the days she lived so doggone small. It was the only fancy dress she owned, but when she put it on, you'd never know. You'd think she owned a million of them. Boy, if Big Belly Willow had any kind of heart condition, he was gonna bite the dust tonight, 'cause a million-dollar woman who glides around a room on ruby-red stilts is a showstopper for sure.

While Mama put the finishing touches to her face paint, I busied myself in the bathroom brushing my hair. In the mirror's reflection, I caught Aerial peeking several times, but when I fixed my eyes to look at her, she quickly turned away.

I'd look.

She'd turn.

She'd turn and I'd look again, but not before she turned away. It was a sick dance, because she wanted to stare at me just as much as I wanted her to turn away. And before long, she was in the bathroom with me, pulling the brush from my hands.

She began to brush my hair. "You don't have to feel guilty," she said in a soothing tone.

"What would I feel guilty about?" I asked. It seemed an odd statement, or maybe I just was being defensive because I *did* feel guilty.

"For not being me," she said, brushing my hair soft and gentle.

"And why would I do that?" I asked.

"Because you got away," she said casually, still brushing my hair. I looked at her tattered reflection in the mirror, and she seemed not even there. The Aerial I loved had died in the explosion, and this was her replacement. She was a stranger to me and someone who was greatly bitter at life. I know I shouldn't blame her, because if I stood in her shoes, I'd probably feel the same.

"You know how you got away?" she asked. I didn't answer, but it didn't matter none, 'cause she wasn't looking for an answer; she was looking to make her own statement. "By being a bed wetter," she said with finality. "Don't you find that strange?" she asked, brushing my hair now harder and harder, till it began to feel as though she was pulling it out by the roots.

"The only thing I find odd is the manner in which you are brushing my head," I said before sharply turning around and snatching the brush out of her hand.

She held an empty hand in the air, where the brush once sat, and stared at me as though I had stolen something of value from her. Maybe in her opinion I did—her face.

"Aerial," I said to her as I turned around and continued brushing my hair in the mirror, fixing the part she had messed up on purpose. "I didn't steal your face." The words hit hard, and her eyes reflected it, because in that moment we both locked eyes in the mirror. We were identical twins without an identity anymore, and we barely knew each other by name. "What do you want from me?" I asked.

Her lip began to quiver, and she looked a wretched kind of sad. "I want you to be not so pretty," she whispered, barely able to release the words. "I know that sounds cruel . . . sounds like something the devil himself would say," she whimpered, "but *that* is what I want from you."

I didn't know what to say. I set my brush down on the sink and just stared at her sad reflection as my eyes filled with tears. As awful as her thoughts were, mine were just as bad, 'cause I was thinking it was a pity that we hadn't had a funeral for Aerial James. And even if we didn't have a corpse to lay inside a coffin, we would have had a cup filled up with Aerial's spirit, because it was dead, and all that remained was a shell with an angry spirit keeping the flesh warm. And if that's all she was, she might as well lay the body down. It wasn't much good to her anymore, damaged inside *and* out.

"You wish I had died, don't you?" she asked, because twins can read each other's minds, so she knew what I was thinking.

"I find it very difficult to wish for something that has *already* happened," I said, pushing past her and back down the hall to the front door, where I would wait outside for Mama.

By the time Mama came outside, I had cooled down a bit. She offered a peculiar look, wondering what my exchange was with Aerial James. As we walked down the walkway, I turned back, only to catch eyes with Aerial as she stared out the window. And even though I was mad at her, I couldn't help but feel sorry. She looked like a prisoner behind those drapes and behind her skin. I can't imagine what it must feel like to be locked inside a corpse but still be very much alive. And I wouldn't get much opportunity to ponder it, because it was time to put on our party face as we walked around to the front of the house instead of using the side entrance.

"No fidgeting," said Mama.

"Okay," I said, fidgeting.

"Be polite and respectful, speak only when you're spoken to, and don't be nosy and butting in grown folks' business," she spewed. "Make sure you sit with your legs crossed, and be mindful of the way you are chewing your food at the dinner table. And by all means," she said with a sudden halt and a swift turn, "watch that devilish tongue of yours and no smart-mouthing these white people."

I smiled, but it wasn't really a smile; it was a smirk. I could pretend to acknowledge what Mama had said, which I did with a polite head nod, but it wouldn't really be the truth at all. I could make an attempt at being polite and respectful; after all, it wasn't completely out of my character to be any of those things. I could also entertain the possibility of minding my own business; sitting with my legs crossed, since I was wearing a dress; and chewing with my mouth closed, because we would more than likely be dining on the good stuff, by way of China. But as far as my "devilish tongue" and "smarting off to the white people," it was here that we had a breakdown of communication. There could be no guarantees in this department. After all, I was Blaze LeDoux James and as such had a moral obligation to be truthful to the truths that I told.

"Don't you embarrass me tonight," was Mama's final word. "And I mean it." It was here that I nodded again, politely, of course, because I was not about to commit to anything by way of verbal confirmation. "I mean it," she said as we rang the doorbell.

We had keys to the side entrance. I don't know why she insisted on us walking twice as far to go the front door, and then once there, ringing the bell and waiting in the cool night air for somebody to open it. She must have read the contents of my mind, because she took one look at me and snapped with a quick reply, "We're guests tonight. Not hired help."

Okay, Cinderella, I thought. *Call it what you want. Live out the fantasy any way you see it fit. But come tomorrow morning, you'll be out of those ruby-red slippers and back to wearing all white and rubber shoes, asking the same people you're dining with tonight whether they prefer tea or coffee.*

The door opened rather swiftly, and to our surprise, Mary Agnes was the one who let us in. And, oh boy, if you could have seen the look on her face when she saw me and Mama all dolled up. At first, she didn't recognize us, so she smiled, but the moment she did recognize us, she did a double take, and that fake smile curled upside down and twisted itself around and into the most unattractive frown you ever did lay eyes on.

"Ms. James," said Mary Agnes, surprised, almost choking on her own spit. "What are you doing here?" Without words, Mama pushed past Mary Agnes and carried herself inside the Willow estate like some type of royalty. And, of course, I saw this as an open invitation for me to do the same.

Mr. Willow's home was dressed up for the occasion, if that was even possible. *How do you dress up what is already a castle?* There were candelabras lit up all over the place, with about twenty-five or so snobby-looking people in this entertainment room, drinking cocktails and eating bite-sized pieces of food. Most of them were well-to-do-looking couples, the "who's who" of the neighborhood. There were butlers and serving ladies walking around with silver trays, offering drinks and cheese. Soft music was playing in the background by a real live piano player, who played a white baby grand in the corner of the room.

"I see my dinner date has arrived," said Mr. Willow, entering the room from a distance with a big old cheesy grin on his face. Low and behold, he was wearing a tuxedo, and I just knew he had doubled up on the musk. *Yep.* The moment he crossed my path, he almost blew me over. "Well, Ms. James," he said, bumbling and fumbling. "Aren't you just a feast for my beloved eyes to look upon," he said.

Oh boy, I thought. *Mama may lose a thigh yet.*

"I could suck you up in one giant scoop!" he bellowed, pulling Mama in close to him. When he scooted in for a hug, there was still a good distance between the two of them, 'cause his stomach was as big as the whole state of Missouri. Mama looked like she was scooting in, but in reality, she was just digging her red-ruby heels deep enough into the carpet so that she wouldn't tip over from his tugging and hugging. When he kissed her neck, I thought that this is where I might just throw up.

Yuk!

Then he turned and winked at me. "Hey there, little lady!" he said. "You're just as pretty as your mama!"

The hell I am, I was fixing to say. Especially if he had one good thought on making his way over here and squeezing me. *Don't you even think about it*, my body language suggested, which he understood, and with that, he turned his attention back to Mama, who really was dazzling under these lights.

I could tell by the way that all the rich people who were standing in Mr. Willow's entertainment room were staring at Mama, especially all the white men, that they thought she was pretty too—and so did their jealous wives. Aliyah James was a sight to behold for any man and a force to be dealt with by any woman who was with *any* man, looking at Mama. Mary Agnes was still stuck on the fact that we were inside the Willow estate as *invited* guests and not hired help.

"Come, darling," said Mr. Willow to Mama. "I want to introduce you to some of my friends." He whisked Mama away, and she shot me a look on the way to the other room that said, *Hope you can make do for yourself, kid. I got somewhere else to be.* It didn't surprise me none. It was easy for Mama to get swept up in her environment. She was fickle like that and just became a part of whatever picture was being drawn.

I stood in the center of the room, alone, not knowing who to talk to or what to do. I was a pretty sophisticated twelve-year-old, but this particular moment left me awkward. No one looked pleasing to my eye, at all. Most of the people here were grown-ups wearing expensive clothes and plastic faces. Fragmented bits of conversation spread throughout the room, hitting on everything from religion to politics to business dealings to boob jobs.

"What's your name?" somebody asked, tapping me on the shoulder. I turned quickly in the direction of the disturbance, and it was a young girl, not much older than me, but for a young person, she sure had an *old look* about her. She was rather unique, by way of her facial features, wearing bronze skin and long silky black hair. Her body sparkled with some kind of glitter stuff, and she looked like some kind of exotic animal. She wore big earrings, loud lip gloss, a gaudy ring, clinging bracelets, and high heels with a wide base at the bottom, and she looked to be a cross between a runway masterpiece and a sidewalk-sale disaster. She was right in the middle, and it could have gone either way, depending upon who was judging the situation. She wore a bright red party dress with the whole back cut out. The dress was so tiny, I could only hope she caught it on sale for 50 percent off, 'cause half of it was surely missing.

"The name's Blaze," I replied with a bit of attitude as I turned back around to my own world. A few beats passed, and then she tapped me again. "Yes?" I asked, turning back around, this time with a little more attitude.

"I'm Carmen," she said.

"That's nice," I said, not really interested in making conversation. For whatever reason, after we got to Mr. Willow's party, I found myself not wanting to be bothered.

"You live in the neighborhood?" she asked.

"Yeah," I said with a hint of sarcasm.

"Where about?" she asked.

"Around the corner," was all I said. "Literally."

"Really?" she asked, excited. "Cool. How old are you?"

"Thirteen next year," I said. *God forbid I just say twelve and someone think me young for my age.* Maybe that's retarded thinking, because twelve *is* young for an age.

"Sweet," she replied with her arms crossed. "I'm sixteen."

"That's nice," I said casually. "I *feel* like I'm sixteen." I was sounding more and more retarded by the minute. I don't know why I was letting all of that crazy talk come out of my mouth.

"It's pretty boring here," she said, looking around the party, staring at all the people, her arms crossed. Finally, she and I had something in common, so I turned around to talk with her. I figured she couldn't be *all* stupid if she was able to figure out by herself that this was probably the most boring event happening right now on planet Earth. "Let's roll," she said, leading the way. I followed, because she seemed to know where she was going. And even though I didn't know where we were going, it seemed like a whole heap of a lot better than where we were right now.

We went out the front door and over to this fancy convertible white Mustang, which was parked a few doors down from the Willow estate. She pulled out a set of keys and opened the door. "Hop in," she commanded.

My eyes widened. "Huh?"

"Get in," she said, shutting her door and opening the door of the passenger's side.

"Oh no," I said, shaking my head. "I'm not going to jail tonight for stealing nobody's car."

"It's *my* car, silly," she said with a laugh. "Get in."

I slowly got in, and I do mean real slow. I had never seen a sixteen-year-old with such a nice automobile. Back home, sixteen meant you could ride the bus by yourself, but to hell with having your *own* ride. You were lucky if your parents had a car, much less you get one too.

I could hardly believe this beautiful car was hers. Once inside, she turned on the radio and started dancing around, bopping her head. She was listening to something that was so foreign to me, I had no words for it but asked, "What's this?"

"It's a group called Styx," she said. "They're hot, right?"

"Okay," I said, hardly in agreement, "whatever you say."

"You never heard of Styx?" she asked with the most shocked look on her face, like I had just said I'd never heard of Martin Luther King Jr. or something.

"Only sticks I heard of is, sticks and stones can break your bones."

Carmen started laughing again, then rubbed on my cheek like a little old lady rubs the face of a French poodle. "You're real cute, Blaze."

"I'm just me," I said without a lot of thought behind it.

"This car was a birthday present," she said, smiling real big.

"Wow!" I said. "I'd hate to see what you got for Christmas if this was a birthday present."

"Oh," she said, staring at me real hard, "I got a really nice Christmas present last year."

"Yeah?" I asked.

"Yeah," she said real fast. "You want to see it?"

"You got it with you?" I asked, looking around her ride, thinking maybe it was under the seat or something.

"I carry them with me everywhere I go," she said, lifting up her dress. "Hold on!" I shouted. *What is going on here?* But before a good word could come out, her dress was up and her naked breasts were exposed.

"My Christmas present," she said, cupping her two breasts with both hands. My eyes widened even more. "My daddy bought these for me for Christmas."

"Really?" I said with either no emotion at all or so much, it couldn't even register as emotion it was so far off the chart. "You got your breasts enhanced?"

"Aren't they beautiful?" she asked, rubbing on them like they were her lucky charms or something.

"They're big," I said, trying not to gawk. They really were big, and the nipples were hard and pointy too.

"I'm a D now," she said with a certain pride.

"Your daddy let you wear a D breast?" I asked in absolute shock. "Boy," I said, exasperated, "white people are some kind of different."

And with that she laughed again. "We aren't so different," she said. "And besides, I'm only half white; my mother's Cuban."

It didn't make a bit of difference to me. She was on something altogether different than Blaze LeDoux James was accustomed to. Fancy cars, fancy clothes, and fake boobs. Shreveport, Louisiana, didn't know no kind of foolishness like this. Folks back in my neighborhood wouldn't even believe a story like this. A teenager with a new car, a convertible nonetheless, and D breasts that her daddy bought off the rack like shoes at Payless.

What in the Sam hell was going on? California was on something altogether different.

"You wanna feel them?" she asked, her dress still hiked up in the air.

"I . . . I . . . don't think so," I stuttered.

"Come on, they feel great," she said, insisting. "It's the most natural thing on the planet, a woman's breasts."

Not when they're filled up with a bag of silicone. There's something about that that just sucks the natural juice right out of them, I wanted to say but didn't.

"Come on," she said, "Give me your hand." I hesitated greatly, to say the least. "Come on, Blaze," she said, insisting. "They won't bite you." She laughed.

I couldn't bear to put my hand on her breasts, and she knew it, so she took my hand and wrapped it up inside her hands and laid them against her breasts. Once I touched them, the nipples turned hard and real pointy as she cupped my hands around her breasts and slid them from top to bottom and back again.

"Don't they feel soft?" she asked.

They did feel soft, and they *did* feel good.

She brought my hand to her hard nipples and began to circle the nipple with my finger, and the nipple even got harder. She looked at me and smiled, and began playing with her nipples, using my fingers as a puppet. "Don't they feel good?"

Sweet Jesus from the Holy Motherland itself, if my mama walked out here right now and saw me sitting in this white girl's convertible Mustang, with her dress hiked up in the air and my hands rubbing on her breasts, that would probably be the end of God's holy kingdom of creation as we know it today.

The whole good state of Louisiana would collapse into itself, roll over, and die with its tongue sticking out. The papers would fire off headline after headline, at the top of the news: BLAZE LEDOUX JAMES PLAYS WITH A WHITE WOMAN'S NIPPLE IN THE FRONT SEAT OF A MUSTANG, LISTENING TO SOME STYX. *Good Lord, up in heaven.* This was all a bit much. I snatched my hand back and jumped out of that car so doggone quick, you'd think my britches was filled with the vengeance of a whole sea of red fire ants.

I hightailed it straight back to Mr. Willow's estate just as fast as my two legs—in white tights, covered by a pink laced dress and wearing patent-leather shoes—could carry me. I burned a hole straight through the concrete with a newfound sense of urgency. I could hear it now, Mama asking, *What did you do tonight, Blaze? You disappeared for a spell of time.*

Oh, Mama, I'd say. *Nothing out of the usual—ate some cheese, drank some soda, and rubbed up on a white woman's fake breast, till the nipple turned hard as a rock.*

Sweet Jesus up in heaven. I hadn't lived in California but a good minute, maybe two, and now I was just as crazy as all the rest of these white folks out here.

Oh Sweet Jesus, I thought to myself, burdened by my own opinion. *God bless the great state of Louisiana. This would be some kind of unacceptable to the good people back home.*

On the walk back to the maid's quarters that night, Mama sensed that something was surely wrong. "You feeling all right?" she asked me.

"Feel fine," I responded quickly, hoping she would drop it.

"You didn't eat much," she said.

"Wasn't hungry," I spilled out of my mouth even quicker.

"You didn't talk much either," she noticed. "Which is unusual for you . . . you sure you feeling all right?" she asked, pressing the back of her hand to my forehead, checking my temperature.

"I'm fine," I said, pulling away. "Stop making a fuss over me, Mama!"

She stopped midstep, and cast her big brown eyes at me, looking up and down, real suspicious-like. I was scared she was going to smell the scent of white woman's nipple on one of my hands, so I pulled them close to my side, lest they give off Carmen's scent and give me dead away.

She didn't say nothing else that night, just kept eyeing me, looking for it. Like a bloodhound, she knew it was there. This made me real edgy and jumpy, and impatient as all get-out. She just kept looking, like she could see it. In the back of her mind, she was shouting, *Nipple rubber! Nipple rubber! You're a dirty, filthy nipple rubber,* but she just couldn't prove it.

Yet.

But still that didn't stop her from looking for it. As far as I was concerned, this was the end of innocence. It started going downhill from here, and before long, it picked up speed and went straight, straight, straight to hell.

Chapter 19

The Nitty-Gritty

What happened over the course of the next few weeks was incalculable by any man's estimation—Mama and Mr. Willow started sleeping with each other. Yes, it should have made world headlines. I can hardly believe it myself, and I cannot fix my face to write any more detail than that, but I know it to be a fact. Two weeks after that infamous dinner party, Mama stopped working downstairs and starting working upstairs, sleeping in the big house every night. She would be gone missing for what seemed like days at a time, tending to the affairs of Mr. Willow. Oh, she would pop her head in every now and again and check on us, but that was about it. She had made some kind of arrangement where Aerial and I would be tutored at home. Mr. Willow had agreed to pay for home schooling, because Mama wasn't too comfortable sending Aerial outside by herself, on account of her face and all.

The only good thing to come out of it was I stopped working in the house, though we had a set of "light chores" that Mama arranged for us to do every day. Simple stuff like pick up any trash on the grounds and keep the maid's quarters clean.

Me and Aerial remained in the maid's quarters for about a month, till one morning over breakfast Mama made a shocking announcement. "Girls," she said, gazing at us with a look that screamed, *I have sold my soul down the Nile River, and this is all that remains of me.* "Mr. Willow and I have been spending a lot of time together as of late . . ."

"Yeah," said Aerial, with distaste on her taste buds.

"Well," said Mama slowly before pulling back her left hand, turning it over, and displaying a rock the size of Gibraltar. "I'm getting married."

I choked on the eggs I was eating, and Aerial spit out her water midswallow. Mama didn't know which one of us to try and save first; but there was no need to save either one of us, because she should have focused all of her attention on trying to save herself. She seemed more desperate than we ever were, in this moment.

"What!" screamed Aerial. "You're marrying Mr. Willow?"

"Yes," she said, "in about six months."

"Six months!" I blurted.

"It'll be a quiet ceremony at the house," she said.

"I can't believe it!" said Aerial.

"Well believe it, 'cause it's true," she said, clearing off our plates from the breakfast table, right in the middle of our meal.

"I wasn't done yet," I said, trying to snatch a piece of bacon off one of the plates.

"Oh, you're done," she said with a twist in her voice, setting the dishes in the sink. "Now get ready for the tutor."

"That's it?" I asked, stunned.

"What else is there?" Mama asked.

"Where we gonna live?" Aerial asked.

"You girls are gonna get your own room in the house after the wedding," she said, "and Mr. Willow has agreed to be your new stepdaddy, so you girls mind him real good. He's a good man."

Both me and Aerial looked at each other with frowns. We didn't speak to each other much these days, except for light conversation, but today, we probably had a whole lot to say about this craziness.

"He doesn't even know me, Mama," said Aerial quietly. "He's never even seen me. Does he know about the accident?"

"Of course he does, darling," said Mama. "And he knows *me*, which is just about the same thing as knowing both of you."

"I wouldn't try to sell that crock of crap to anybody with half a mind of good sense," I said.

And with that, Mama smacked me right across the cheek. "I'll have NONE of that backtalk today!" she shouted. "You girls ought to be grateful."

"For what, Mama?" asked Aerial.

"For a nice life," she said. "We'll have a real nice life here with Mr. Willow. He's a good man. You'll get the best of everything—education, vacations, family trips, tutors, a beautiful home—and, Aerial," she said slowly, "you finally get to have all those surgeries to straighten up your face real pretty."

I was one good gulp away from a whole gallon of vomit coming out of my mouth and spewing all over the floor. "And what about you, Mama?" I asked, holding my stinging cheek. "What do you get out of this?"

She looked at both of us but didn't say a word. Me and Aerial just kept hard eyes on her, because we were both dying to know what the prize was for her.

"Yeah, Mama," Aerial asked her, "what makes it worth it for you?"

"Do you love him?" I asked, my nose and lips twisted up, because I couldn't imagine that she loved him at all. He was a good thirty years older than her and about 200 pounds fatter. He smelled of wild musk under the arms and cottage cheese about the breath. He was loud, big, and greasy. What could she possibly love about Mr. Willow except his cold hard cash? As far as I was concerned, he hardly had enough of that to make all of those exceptions seem worth it.

"I . . . I . . . wouldn't say I love him," she said, nervous and fidgety.

"Well, do you *like* him?" asked Aerial.

"Well," she said, shrugging her shoulders, "don't really know him well enough to say I like him either."

Aerial and I both frowned on that, because it made not a drip of sense.

"I can tolerate him," she said, trying to clarify her own mad reasoning.

"What does that mean?" I asked her.

"I can do it," she said, turning away, 'cause by now it sounded doggone crazy to her too.

"Why?" Aerial asked.

"The money's good," she said. "And we can live *easy* now." She paused. "And he's not *horrible* or anything."

Aerial and I just looked at each other, and Mama could feel the craziness of it all in our reflection, because we showed it to each other and then turned around and projected it back to her. Like I said from the get-go, she might as well have gotten a California tattoo stamped to the high point of her biggest butt cheek that said, *I have sold my soul down the Nile River and this is all that remains of me.*

The next night, we went out to dinner as an official family of four. It was the first time that Aerial would venture into the public facilities of Rancho Palos Verdes. It was a small but fancy place on the edge of town, overlooking the water. I guess that wasn't hard to do—*everything* in this whole city overlooked the water. The entire thing was sliced up sixty-nine ways to crazy, in my opinion. We had been brought by Mr. Willow's driver to the restaurant, and Mr. Willow would meet us there. Mama was dolled up in a short gold dress, with matching gold hoops. She was looking somewhere between a millionaire and a movie star every day of the week right about now. Being the chameleon that she was, she had taken on yet another roll, that of the glamorous, California housewife to the rich Texas tycoon. You didn't need to be too bright, too educated, too independent, or even too sophisticated. You just had to be pretty, and not just any kind of pretty, not your run-of-the-mill kind of pretty, but the kind of pretty that folks don't see too often, if ever. The kind of pretty that drops jaws, mouths, wallets, and future investments. That kind of pretty makes a white multimillionaire from Texas, living in one of the richest places on earth, propose to a Southern know-nothing, nobody from the good state of Louisiana. That was some kind of pretty *and* pretty extraordinary.

Mama had bought me and Aerial matching dresses for the occasion. She was a nervous wreck, because this was the first time Mr. Willow would actually meet Aerial face-to-face; up till now, he had only heard about her, 'cause she mostly lived as a shut-in, locked away behind shutters, windows, curtains, and doors. He knew she was burned, but I reckon he had no real idea of what she truly looked like, beyond Mama's weak description of the facts. And fact of the matter is fairly simple. She was just plain, downright, outright grotesque at first glance—*and* she was plain, downright grotesque at second glance too.

"Make certain to chew your food like ladies," said Mama to me and Aerial, giving us one last reminder on etiquette before Willow arrived.

"Versus what, Mama?" I asked. "Chewing our food like cows?" Normally, that kind of comment would have drawn a backhanded slap, but we were in a fancy place, and Mama was pretending to be fancy, and we all know fancy people don't slap their kids in public, or private for that matter.

But she did give me one of them famous Aliyah James looks and shook her head. "For the life of me, I don't know why you insist on being a donkey's ass all the time."

A donkey's ass?

Mama was learning new words for sure, living here in the free state of California.

Willow arrived wearing an all white suit, and, of course, you guessed it, too much doggone musk, again. He gave Mama a big old sloppy kiss on the mouth, which gagged both me and Aerial, and from the looks of it afterward, it gagged Mama too. I could tell that she couldn't stand him touching her. She would almost quiver in her skin every time he reached for her, which was constantly. Pulling, squeezing, rubbing on, feeling against, and sliding into her. Fat Willow didn't even allow *air* to get in the way of his contact with Mama's skin, hips, legs, thighs, breasts, lips, mouth, chin, cheek, hair, hands, and fingers. I had even seen him squeeze her baby toe one good time or two. He never let her be when he was in her presence. He never let her breathe, a good, clean gulp of California smog-filled air. Not a single solitary drop. If he had his way, Willow would breathe the air *for* Mama, recycle it through his lungs, and then give her mouth-to-mouth for sustenance. That's all it was anyway, recycled air. He gave her everything she needed, and every breath she would take following their bizarre romance would be at his sole discretion. And if he was in a not-so-giving mood, she had better economize and make due on a little, itty-bitty bit of air.

I had seen the way Mr. Rufus had touched Mama when I was coming up, and I knew she liked it, because she was always touching him back, but not Mr. Willow. Mama *never* touched him back; she just tried to hold on to her crawling skin while he touched, fondled, caressed, and breathed hot air and bad breath all over Mama's beautiful, satin-like skin.

"You must be Aerial," he said, extending a hand to Aerial.

She smiled and graciously accepted. I watched Willow's expression with great interest, and he was for certain a good actor. He stayed in character and did not flinch an inch by the appearance of Aerial's face, though I could tell most of the people in the restaurant, including our waiter, was very uncomfortable in her presence. Well, who am I to say for sure that it was Aerial's presence alone that was causing their discomfort? It could have been the big white man with the Grand Canyon–sized gut, cuddled up with the pretty little black woman and her two identical twins who looked not a single drop alike. We were an odd bunch for sure, and everybody knew it. We were Southern idiots who had taken up residence at the edge of the deep blue sea.

Dinner was long and uneventful. I mentally checked out before appetizers even arrived at the table. Actually, I had seen something in the restaurant early on that had caught my undivided attention—*a woman*. Yes, you did read my words, as precisely as I had written them, a woman. Like I said in the beginning, what had happened over the course of the next few weeks was incalculable by any man's estimation. Blaze LeDoux James was starting to like girls, and not in a friendly manner, but in a *friendly* manner. To make it more clear, I was starting to like girls in the way that boys liked girls, which was making me fast on the track to becoming one of them *L* people, kind of like Miss Hardaway. Maybe we had more in common than I ever knew when I was living with her; me and all my opinions of her *un-ladylike* behavior.

Lesbian.

The word itself sounds harsh, almost like some sort of permanent condemnation, as long as you stand on the side of the fence where women get down to the nitty-gritty of the licky, licky.

Lesbian, and almost thirteen years old, I was fast on the road to becoming something that would break every beating heart who ever loved me. My daddy, Mr. Rufus, would surely turn over in that cheap pine box and shallow grave if he had any inkling at all as to what was filling my head these days. And for lack of a better word, Mama would shit a brick the size of the entire Willow compound if she had the slightest clue. Aerial would spontaneously combust. My grandmother, Ms. Dixie, would disown me on the spot, and every good and decent citizen of Shreveport, Louisiana, would revoke my citizenship rights as a decent Southern girl for life.

It would be a cold, black day in a hot hell before anyone would allow me to breathe in lesbian air. In order to do that, I would have to extract both lungs up through my throat and out the opening of my mouth, without dying from suffocation. And that, by any stretch of a man's imagination, was just damn impossible, but I was growing more and more lesbian each day. My breasts and my private region below my belly button were growing in the direction of lesbian. I was starting to notice women and their breasts everywhere. Ever since that night in Carmen's Mustang, rubbing up on her breasts, I found a whole new feeling in the ground I stood upon. My body started doing crazy stuff, dripping and leaking a whitish liquid between my legs at the thought of Miss Carmen's nipples against the back of my hand. Shortly after rubbing on Miss Carmen, it was the first time ever, in the shower two days later, that I squeezed out, with my own two hands, all the tension that had built up between my legs, until it exploded out of me, making my body shake, rattle, and rumble.

I had *never* known a sensation like that, and there was nothing to do but do it *again* for good measure. Within days, it was all I wanted to do—get in the shower and squeeze out the pressure between my legs and explode my body into one gigantic explosion.

Pop goes the weasel.

It was a forbidden ecstasy nobody had ever told me about, but I discovered it on my own. The only thing was, I felt like a dirty birdie, because a woman isn't supposed to look at another woman like *that* and then have the good nerve to fantasize about her. What in the hell of all Sam creation was that nonsense about? What was the most natural thing in the world to me was the most unnatural thing to every other person on the planet, maybe except to Miss Carmen and Miss Felicity. Therefore, in this type of situation, who's wrong? And who's right? And do you die being wrong, or do you live being right? 'Cause either way it goes, death is a certain end, because you can't live how they want you to live without dying, and you can't live how you want to live without them killing you dead.

Chapter 20

The Happiest Day of My Life

The end of childhood came early. It was on the eve of my thirteenth birthday and the day of Mama and Mr. Willow's wedding ceremony. The wedding of the year was to be held at the Willow estate, which had been transformed into a charming fairy tale built of concrete and steel. There were heart-shaped flowers flown in from exotic locations all over the world to decorate the grounds for the occasion. Three hundred people would feast eyes on one of the most talked-about couples of the year. I didn't say *celebrated;* I just said "talked about," because though people would surely arrive in tuxedos and ball gowns, carting expensive gifts and wearing big fake smiles over the top of expensively capped teeth, in between the beat of every applause, I couldn't help but imagine they were really thinking, *How did this ghetto bitch luck up on this rich bastard here?*

There were wedding planners, photographers, florists, catering vans, pastry chefs, bartenders, a seating coordinator, and a live band featuring a whole choir of gospel singers. There were fireworks and bubbling fountains, a cleaning crew, a serving crew, and every other imaginable *and* unimaginable thing money could buy. It was everything you ever dreamed a fairy tale could produce, and after that, it still was so much more.

There was a giant ice sculpture of Mr. Willow down on one knee proposing to Mama. They did a "live sitting" the day before, literally hours, to have this life-sized sculpture created, and Mr. Willow flew in a special deep freeze to hold it all night. The sculpture was to be unveiled fifteen minutes prior to the ceremony, which was held outdoors in the fanciest tent you ever laid eyes on. It was decorated like the Taj Mahal, and they did it on purpose. The sculpture was to be left outside and allowed to melt down throughout the opening. According to Mama, it was supposed to be symbolic of their love, "melting in to each other," which was a crock of shit, because love had fallen off somewhere in the cracks of the zeroes that made up Mr. Willow's total net worth.

In his own words, Willow was "going all out and sparing no expense." At almost sixty years of age, he had never married because he had "thoroughly enjoyed the days of being a bachelor." But he was ready to give it all up for Aliyah James, a woman he refers to as "the pride and glory of the accumulation of all my days." He called Mama his "most precious and honest investment." But Willow wasn't no fool, and before Mama could so much as hire a window washer to wipe the streaks off the window on the day of the wedding, she had to sign a prenuptial agreement that in no uncertain terms made it very clear that should she and Mr. Willow depart, she would be entitled to the "exactness of what she owned" prior to their meeting. So, in the event of a divorce, all Mama would get is a white uniform and those white rubber shoes she wore on the day of their meeting. That's what she was wearing when she met Willow, and that's what she'd been wearing if she left him. But Mama wasn't leaving, ever. She had grown accustomed to telling people what to do and how to do it. She had also grown accustomed to being envied and hated by all her white peers, who under their breath cursed that "lucky black bitch for landing on top of a gold mine." She had found her own sense of what she called "a woman's power," but she had no idea it was rooted in the "weakness" of needing him for everything she *thought* she owned; she only owned it because he gave it to her, and the moment he changed his mind, it was snatched back, just like that. She didn't own a damn thing, not even herself, because that, too, had al-

ways been negotiable. Humbling, isn't it? Knowing that you really
do live under the condition of another man's say-so. But that
was the way Mama had lived all her life. She had done it with
Mr. Rufus, and now she was doing it with Mr. Willow. The way I
saw it, it was the same difference, only thing is, this go around the
sheets were nicer and the cup holders were prettier to look at.

Mr. Willow treated Mama all right enough, when he was in a
good mood, but sometimes, the devil himself would come and
visit Willow and walk around for a spell in his body. And when
that did happen . . . Lord, Jesus, Father, Mother Mary, and then
some, 'cause when Mr. Willow got the notion to catch a tree
stump up his big, white behind, it was nothing pretty to look at.
He would yell, curse, swear, treat the three hundred people who
worked for him like bitter slaves off a trading ship. He would
snort, fuss, muss, and double, triple cuss. He would tell you off,
fire you, curse you out, threaten to break your dog's legs, and
roll your wheelchair-bound grandmother into the nearest brick
wall, and all things breathing steered clear of him. Even plants
would dry up and wilt when he walked by in that frame of mind.
You know the saying by now—all that glitters sure ain't gold; for
all that it appeared that Mama had caught a catch like Willow,
she also inherited the great burden of all that came with it, all
the conditions, restrictions, obligations, appearances, and every
other word that you can possibly put in your mind to translate
into the ultimate loss of everything free, namely Mama's life,
because it now belonged to Mr. Willow. And just like his company, his estate, investments, and affairs, it was all paid for in
cash.

So, needless to say, Blaze LeDoux was never for sale, so perhaps that alone will alert you as to how Mr. D. H. Willow and I
got along behind the scenes. He didn't like me much, nor I him.
In fact, I think he may have hated me because I challenged all
that he was; he could not buy my peace. That was just not for
mother-loving sale to anyone, any place, any time, and at any
cost. Now, of course, Mama tried to tie a noose around my neck
to get me to behave lest "you mess up my good thing," she used
to say. I tried, tried, and tried, but obviously, *behaving* was not

my best asset, so why would the day of their *blessed union*, be exempt of me authentically showing up as my true self in true Blaze style.

Just hours before the wedding, we were in the costume room getting our faces painted and our hair swept into an updo, which I was looking to "undo" just as soon as I possibly could. Mama wore a figure-fitting, long white gown and was her most stunning to date. A giant strand of pearls lay delicately across her long slender neck. She was so drop-dead gorgeous that I could hardly believe she could possibly be any prettier than we had already seen her in the months leading up to the wedding.

Aerial and I wore beautiful bridesmaid dresses and layers of makeup, because we, too, right along with Mama, would be putting our best face forward. I was ready for my debut so I could hurry up and get it over with. It would be a long walk down the aisle, tossing rose petals on the ground before me, but Aerial was less than enthusiastic. I guess she would just have to make do with what the Good Lord had given her to work with.

In the makeup chair, I posed a question to Mama that shook her to her core. I didn't do it on purpose, but it didn't matter in the end, because she saw it loaded with bad intention.

"What do you think Mr. Rufus would say if he could see you today?" I asked Mama. Her glowing bridal smile curled to a sudden frown, and she shot me a look. The woman working on her makeup stopped for a second, as she was thrown by Mama's sudden burst of hostility. "You think he'd be happy for you?" I asked.

"Blaze," she warned, "are you *trying* to ruin my day?"

"Not at all," I said. "I was just wondering."

"Do me a kind favor," she insisted, "and take the rest of the day off from thinking."

"You happy, Mama?" asked Aerial, interrupting what was certain to be an unpleasant confrontation if it continued on in the same spirit. There was a pause, silence, and then a smile. "This is the *happiest* day of my life," responded Mama affirmatively.

"Then that's all that matters," said Aerial. Mama reached over and squeezed Aerial's hand. *Suck up*, I thought to myself with a single shot to Aerial's eyes. From the corner of my eye, I saw a woman whose big hair was immediately recognizable, even though it would take some doing to bring it fully into focus. Ms. Dixie had entered the private chambers, and we were all shocked to shit to see her, especially Mama.

"What are you doing here?" she immediately asked her.

"Mr. Willow invited me," she said softly, "After all, I am the mother of the bride."

Mama's eyes shot to the ground, but Ms. Dixie didn't back down as she examined Mama head to toe. "You can resent me for the rest of your days," she said, "or at least for the rest of mine, but it looks like you've done rather well for yourself here, miss lady."

"Curtain time," someone shouted from the other side of the door.

Mama jumped up and said, "Girls, take your places. We're starting." And then she turned and looked at me. "Blaze, *behave*." Those were her final words to me before turning to Ms. Dixie and saying, "You best take a seat up toward the front if you're planning on staying for the ceremony."

"Indeed I will," said Ms. Dixie with a half-smile. "Indeed I will."

The ceremony was short and sweet. He said, "I do," and she said, "I do too." Mama would carry the last name of Willow, but we would remain James girls. We wouldn't have it any other way. Ms. Dixie and Mama made up at some point during the course of the evening and even exchanged a real-life hug in between all the fake stuff.

The wedding was probably the most uneventful part of the whole night, because what would soon follow would single-handedly change the fate of everything breathing.

Later that night, during the reception, I found myself, as usual, bored silly in the company of Mr. Willow and all his friends. As I stood by the melting sculpture of Willow proposing to Mama, I heard the familiar sound of a past I had not forgotten.

"Bored, aren't you?" she asked, sounding smooth as an old jazz tune. I quickly turned because I recognized the voice.

Carmen.

This time she was even more wildly and exotically decorated than before, wearing a lime-green satin dress with matching shoes and a shiny lime purse. Her skin was still a beautiful bronze, and her breasts were as big as ever. She had done something new to her black hair—a set of blond streaks ran through it. She started to laugh as she looked at me, and I don't know why, but it annoyed me, so I turned away.

"You got a bad habit of sneaking up on folks," I said.

"I don't sneak," she said, easing up into my space and whispering in my ear as she pressed her breasts against my back. "I *never* sneak."

I turned around and looked at her, and I could feel my body tense up and swell up at the same time. My eyes landed on her breasts, and there I would let them stay a while. She saw me looking and could tell I was entertaining an idea or two.

"I knew it," she said.

"Knew what?" I asked.

"You like me," she said, running her finger across my jaw line, real sexylike.

"I don't even know you," I said, turning back around.

"Yeah," she said, leaning into me, pressing her parts against me, "but you want to."

"Don't believe everything you think out loud," I spat. "I ain't so easily impressed."

"I bet my new boobs that you *are* that easily impressed," she said with a laugh. I turned around and looked at her again. She held my eyes for a long time with a dare to her glare. "Dare you to follow me," she said.

And what could I do? I was fixing to turn thirteen tomorrow, and best thing I could do was rise to the occasion. She turned around and walked away, and I followed.

I followed her right inside Mr. Willow's house, which was now my house, and off down the hall to the far end of the walkway, to the death of something old and the birth of something new. She turned the crystal doorknob and entered a beautiful marble bathroom, which was decorated in red, black, and gold. There were nine bathrooms in the house, but this one was kindly situated at the end of the bitter earth. Carmen walked into the bathroom and turned on the light, and I followed behind her and shut the door. A critical error occurred in this moment, because I shut the door but did not *lock it* behind me.

Upon entering, Carmen turned around to face me with the kind of look in her eyes that wild animals get when they're ready to devour the young. I was young, and she was hungry to show me life me on the other side. And had I not hungered for it every night in my sleep and taken up squeezing explosions from my own private region in recent weeks with such devotion, I would have *never* followed her down this long hallway and into this bathroom.

Slowly, she sat on the vanity and hiked up her dress over her head, taking it completely off and allowing it to drop from her arms to the marble floor below. I looked at the dress but found myself much more interested in looking at her breasts. They were beautiful and ripe for touching, feeling, rubbing, sucking, and licking. I moved into her and grabbed them with my hands and started to suck the nipples, as if she were the mother lion and I the cub. Her body began to writhe against me as she became filled with the pleasure of my suckling. She took her hands and lifted up my dress and placed her fingers inside my panties and began to rub on my private area as soft and gentle as she could. Now, this had a certain kind of effect on my young woman's body, and I found that my hips began to rock to the rhythm of her movement, and I wanted to moan. In fact, I could not stop the animallike sounds that came from my mouth. I thought of Miss Hardaway and her friend from Argentina, and in this moment, I understood.

I wanted to moan out loud as I felt my underwear filling up with such wetness that it began to drip down my leg. And this is where Carmen would push me back and lay me down on hard ground, remove my panties, and spread my legs. She liked the wetness that was dripping and began to scoop it up with her fingers and lick them with pleasure.

"Virgin pussy," she said, licking, "is so good."

Virgin pussy? Is that what I had? If so, maybe virgin pussy was valuable. And as she buried her face into my privates, she began to dig deep in my interior with her tongue.

I felt like I had come undone and outside of my own body. It wasn't real. How did I get from Shreveport, Louisiana, to Rancho Palos Verdes in the first place? How did I go from being a little girl to a grown woman in a single night? How did I go from not even liking boys ever all the way to liking girls a *lot?* None of it made sense to me anymore. My head was spinning so fast I thought it would come clean off. I didn't know if I wanted Carmen to keep going, but I knew I didn't want her to stop. I thought it might be best to let her keep going; after all, she was taking me somewhere. It was somewhere that I wanted to go all of my life—the absolute edge of freedom and the foul, earth-crushing place that says *kiss my ass* or *lick my pussy*, whichever you kindly prefer.

I could feel it building up, an implosion that started at the bottom of my feet and was making its way up to the top of my brain. I tried to make words, but instead of words, I could only spill sounds, and they were foreign even to me. Just as I was about to release some sort of unidentifiable animal noise, I was startled by the sound of a gut-wrenching scream that ricocheted off all the walls, hit the skylight, and burst through the ceiling, almost breaking the glass dome in the roof.

It was not my call of the wild, nor was it Carmen's.

It was Aerial's scream, who for whatever the reason had taken it upon herself to find this bathroom at the very edge of the world and enter *without* knocking first.

In that moment, I was sure I had given myself a concussion, because my head slammed so hard against the marble floor that the whole room turned black and dizzy for a minute. Carmen jumped up and grabbed her green dress to cover her breasts. She picked a fine time indeed to be modest. Once I gathered myself, I closed my legs and picked myself off the floor, reaching for my panties and dress.

Aerial stood at the door, hand over her mouth, shaking like she had seen a ghost, or maybe two lesbians in action, and that was more horrifying than any corpse she could ever lay eyes on. Aerial's eyes were big and scary-looking, and she looked more like a monster than she ever had before. Carmen quickly put her dress on, and I just stood there, staring at Aerial, and she at me. No words were spoken, just the uneven exchange of twins who had loved each other deeply more than a single lifetime ago. But that love was as beyond repair as Aerial's burnt skin.

"*Mama!*" screamed Aerial as she pushed back from the door, seemingly in slow motion. It may have doggone well been slow motion, because everybody's life stopped right then and right there.

"Holy fucking shit!" said Carmen, trying to quickly dress herself in an all-out panic. "My father's going to fucking kill me if he finds out."

I didn't say a word, just slowly started putting my panties and dress on. "What are we gonna fucking do?" she asked, pacing the bathroom like a hunted possum.

"Don't sneak," I said sarcastically. Carmen had become a disappointment. She seemed so much bigger than life, till life grew teeth with fangs on the end; then she wasn't so big anymore.

"You're fucking crazy," she said. "We're gonna be in big trouble if that . . . that . . . tells."

"If what tells?" I asked.

"That . . ."

"*That* is my twin," I said in defense of Aerial, no matter how tragic I thought her own personal behavior was in this moment of time. "Identical twin," I continued, "caught on the wrong side of a fire more than one year ago."

"Well," said Carmen, crossing her arms, "your twin may have just cost both of us our ass . . ." And before she could finish the words, Mama, Ms. Dixie, Mr. Willow, and Carmen's father were all standing at the door, and this was beginning to look a lot like one of those wedding nights that was hardly going to have a happy ending, no matter how much money the groom had paid for the bride and spent on good food and wine. That giant ice sculpture was a big old waste of time and dollars, because it couldn't hold the cost of spit, in comparison to what was really going to be remembered on this wedding day.

Willow, you rented that deep freeze for nothing, 'cause in the morning, no one will give a damn about a big block of ice that probably took way too long to melt to the ground and roll back into the ocean.

Mama looked absolutely horrified. I had never seen her so pale and drained of color in all my days. She was so white, in fact, that Mr. Willow looked more like a Negro than she did in this moment.

"Blaze," she called out to me. "What . . . what . . . what," she said, trembling, unable to get the words out. Mr. Willow and Carmen's father stood behind her; *aghast* would be a good word to describe them all. Aerial was standing at Mama's side, stripped of all honor amongst twins.

Big mouth.

Blabber mouth.

Tattletale.

Traitor.

"What have you done?" asked Mama, devastated, as she looked into my eyes knowing what had happened. I knew that she knew, but that wasn't the hard part. She knew that she *knew*, and that was the part that was simply unbearable.

I lowered my head. What else could I do?

I didn't have an explanation or a word of comfort to make them all feel better about what had just happened. I didn't have some magic hocus-pocus, rhetoric bullshit that would convince them that it was all just a big misunderstanding. No matter how much they wanted to hear a lie, or I didn't want to tell the truth, we couldn't wish it all away or unring the very loud bell that was chiming in everybody's ears, including my own. How does one unspill the spilled flood, steadily rising in the middle of the bathroom floor? It was there, the devastation, along with my wet panties and overly active private area.

It's natural to run away from what we cannot bear to look at, but what happens when you *are* what you cannot bear to look at? And every single person in that room that night had become the unbearable moment, no matter how vile or disgusting they had judged it to be. We were all it, and in that hour, everyone tried to figure out how to walk around in *new* skin.

If I had been on the bathroom floor, smooching with a boy, Mama would have been devastated; but the fact that I was on the floor with a girl took it way past devastation into a place in a woman's heart where the incident in question is classified under a new category—*unrecoverable*. And that's about where Mama was, in the unrecoverable zone.

She began to weep out loud, in tragic sobs that echoed from ear to ear, wall to wall, room to room, world to world, from whence we came to where we had become. Mr. Willow tried to comfort Mama, but he could not, because she refused his comfort, his attention, his sympathy, his empathy, his passion, his trust, his loyalty, his virtue, his *everything*. And when she could no longer stand the touch of his skin against hers, she ripped his arms from her side, returning them to his own as she slowly lowered herself to the ground in the most beautiful dress she had ever placed on her delicate body. And it is there she would lay, wilting like a dying rose in spring, thorns and all, protruding, ripping to shreds the skin of every guest in attendance who heard her cries and made their way to the edge of a marble bathroom on the other side of the world to witness her fall completely apart on the happiest day of her life.

I never saw Carmen again after that night. Her father revoked the car, and on their way out the door, he was threatening to call the plastic surgeon in the morning and have her "breasts deflated." He said she did not deserve them if she was going to "abuse them with wild, reckless behavior."

The next day, my thirteenth birthday, I woke up in the mood for breakfast. At the table, Mama spoke not a word of the night before. She looked, in fact, rather close to a zombie. Mr. Willow uttered not a word, not even a "good morning."

Aerial did not come down for breakfast. I was hoping she had died in her sleep. Cruel, but true. And what of me? Well, I was just hoping my eggs turned out good. Like I said, I was really in the mood for breakfast.

Two days later, and under the direction of Mr. Willow and Mama, the staff packed up my things and I was shipped to a private boarding school in Hartford, Connecticut, where I would remain for the rest of my childhood.

It was the end of everything.

Life.

Everything.

Life.

Everything.

Chapter 21

Contradiction

Five Years Later

On my eighteenth birthday, I boarded a plane from Hartford, Connecticut, to Shreveport, Louisiana. After five years of boarding school, never again would I step foot in any institution of learning.

I had outgrown them all.

I was a woman now, all grown up in the spitting image of the beauty of Aliyah James. Even I could not have predicted the kind way in which Mother Nature would facilitate my exterior walls and bloom me into the most beautiful flower of spring.

With a height of almost five feet, ten inches and a voluptuous, desirable body, flawless skin, perfect hair almost to my waist, and deep, hollow eyes that told the tale of one thousand journeys, I was always the prettiest one in whatever room I stood in. But it didn't matter, because I was life's greatest contradiction. From young men to old men and all whom make up the male species in between, I was pursued for courtship. But neither did this matter, because not an ounce of my beating heart turned itself in the direction of *any* man. I was an official lesbian by all accounts. A loner by trade, I did not date men or women, nor did I entertain conversation surrounding my sexual preference. My sexual exploration was limited to long, hot showers and provocative mental stimulation in the imagery of breasts and vaginas.

I had gone from an outspoken know-it-all to a more reserved know-it-all. In the wisdom of my later years (i.e., life after the age of twelve), I found there was no great reward in speaking your mind about every little thing under the sun that it seemed fit to offer an opinion on.

Mr. Willow paid dearly for my tuition, room, and board in Connecticut. Mama also paid dearly, but her cost would not be in the form of money. No, it would come under a different set of demands. Hers would be the cost of our relationship, whatever remained of it after that fateful wedding night, when all crumbled to the ground and turned to ash. I would remain full-time on the East Coast for five years, even holidays and summer vacations, without returning to Rancho Palos Verdes, California. It was the most natural thing in the world *not* to see them and to work through holiday season on campus and do odd jobs in the summertime, under the guidance of supervising adults.

I accumulated a great passion for designing clothes while at boarding school and had become quite good at it. Mama used to send me new clothes every month, and in my rage against her, I would cut them up, put holes in them, and wear them around campus for display. I would then have pictures taken of myself wearing cut-up new clothes and mail them to the Willow estate in Rancho Palos Verdes. The clothes were an instant hit on campus, and though we would wear uniforms during the week, after hours, the kids wanted to display their own version of originality, which they did brilliantly through my designs.

Interestingly, the more clothes I cut up, the more replacements I was sent from California. At some point, I think Mama had set me up on auto-ship from a clothing manufacturer on the West Coast. And just like clockwork, new clothes would arrive the fifteenth of each month like a government-issued check or food stamps. And so it was in the heavily tainted world of passive-aggressive relationships between Aliyah James and Blaze LeDoux. Throughout the course of my five years at boarding school, I designed all kinds of wild outfits for the misfits on campus who kindly paid me a small fortune for the witty genius of ripped clothing. It was a lucrative business for a teenager, and by the time I graduated, I had managed to save close to $7,000, and with this money I would build a whole new life.

One week before my graduation, Mama had purchased tickets for Mr. Willow, herself, and Aerial to come to the commencement services. The day before the ceremony, Aliyah James and I would have what would be our last conversation, at least for a while.

"We are coming in tomorrow early afternoon," she said. "We're staying at a lovely hotel in the downtown area."

"Mama," I said interrupting her. "I'm not walking tomorrow." There was a long, heavy pause and a deep sigh on the other end of the line. "Well," she huffed, "whatever do you mean you're not walking tomorrow?"

"I'm *not* walking."

"Whatever foolishness you are plotting and planning, I want it to stop right now," she insisted. "Mr. Willow paid a good deal of money for you to attend this school, and I do expect that you will walk across that stage and receive your diploma."

While she was blabbing on the phone, I was counting hundred-dollar bills—$7,000 worth, to be exact—and it would be enough for me to establish independence and start doing things my way. No more of Mr. Willow's money or insistent direction from Aliyah James. She had done enough of that to last me a couple of good lifetimes.

"Don't bother coming," I said with finality. "I won't be here when you arrive. I already bought my ticket and I'll be flying home tomorrow."

"Well . . . well . . ." She gasped, huffed, and puffed. "This is a real big inconvenience—these tickets are nonrefundable."

I did not respond, but she knew me well enough to know my mind was not changing on account of her and Mr. Willow's plans. "What time do you expect to be here so that I can have the driver come pick you up?" she asked with a huge, dramatic sigh.

"I'm not going to California," I said. "I'm going *home*—to Shreveport."

"Have you lost your good mind?" snapped Mama. "Just what do you imagine you might do there?"

I didn't answer her.

"Blaze LeDoux James!" she screamed on the other end of the line. "Give me one reason why you're doing this.

As I continued to count my money, I knew that I had *seven thousand* good reasons to do it and not one good reason not to.

"I gotta go, Mama," I said.

"Blaze!" she screamed as the phone headed in a downward plunge, cutting her off. "Good night, Mama," I said *after* the fact, and then proceeded to disconnect my phone from the wall just in case she had a hankering to call back.

7:10 A.M. the next morning, I thanked Hartford, Connecticut, for the five years of hospitality and boarded a flight for Shreveport, Louisiana. I could not wait to return to the place from whence I came.

I had not been to Shreveport, not even for a visit, since that day Mama came for me. And though I kept in touch with Miss Felicity Hardaway for the first couple months after I left, I stopped calling and she stopped answering. Guess she did move on, just like she promised she would. So it wasn't like I had any connections in Shreveport. Most of Mama and Mr. Rufus's family was stone crazy, so it was unlikely that I would be looking *any* of them up.

I was glad that I had saved up this little money, because I could get a place, maybe rent a little shop, and start tailoring folks' clothes and designing some fashions. Shreveport probably wasn't ready for the cut-up look, but I could do some nice church outfits or something.

I flew into Dallas and took a small connecting flight into Shreveport. As I flew over the city, it looked as I remembered it, but it felt a whole lot different. This was home and life before it changed. This was life before it got complicated. This was life when it was easy. This was life, pre-lesbian. This was life pre-everything.

When we landed, I collected my bags and made my way to the curbside. I took a good breath of air as I stood on the curb. It was sure nice breathing in some down-home, Southern hospitality—fried chicken, collard greens, gold-toothed smiling, wide-grinned teeth missing air.

It was so damn good to be back home that I wanted to laugh out loud, shout, send both arms straight up toward the sky, hug the concrete, kiss the dirty sidewalk, and make love to the gravel on the side of the road.

I just stood there smiling till a dusty man from around the way approached, making a big to-do about nothing. "Oh wee," he said, wearing a superfly red pimp-daddy outfit with some pin-stripes, a big hat, and loud Sunday shoes that reflected the sun back on itself. "You sure is some kind of fine," he said, twirling all the way around me like a tornado.

I rolled my eyes and thought, *Here we go again.*

"What's your name, girl?"

"Who's asking?"

"Keith, the love doctor," he said with a gold-toothed grin. "What did you say your name was?"

"Blaze," I said, turning the other way, praying on a taxi right about now.

"Can I take you out for a crawfish dinner?" he asked, swarming around me like a fly on shit.

"I can't," I said.

"Why not?" he asked.

I didn't respond, just kept an eye out for any form of transportation right about now.

Bus.

Bicycle.

It didn't matter. I just knew I wanted to get the hell away from here. "You ain't from Shreveport, is you?" he asked, staring at me as if he could see right through my skin and into the part of me that was invisible. His words cut deep.

I ain't from Shreveport?

In no uncertain terms, I turned to face this funny-looking man and looked him dead in the eye and said, *"I am Shreveport."*

He understood the words beneath the words, so he backed off a bit, but not entirely. "You a Shreveport, girl, huh?" he asked, eyeballing me up and down.

"Yes, I am," I said.

"You is the prettiest girl I ever seen in this city," he said. "Can't blame a man for wanting to get close."

I rolled my eyes one more good time, wondering what a girl had to do to catch a ride from the airport.

"You gonna let me take you out?" he asked, hovering over me like a pack of mosquitoes.

"No," I quickly responded.

"You gonna let me take you out?" he asked again.

"No," I said harshly.

"I wanna take you out," he pressed. "You gotta let me take you out."

"No," I said again, but this time there was relief in sight. A taxi was approaching my way. I began to wave my hands wildly in the air as I ran toward the edge of the curb.

"Why?" screamed pimp daddy, baring his gold teeth and loud red shoes. "Why won't you let me take you out?"

The taxi pulled up and stopped, and just before I opened the door to get in, I turned around and said, *"Because I am a lesbian!"* And with that, he froze, his expression wide-eyed and shock-filled. Had I blown a simple breath in his direction, he would have shattered into a thousand pieces.

"Where to?" asked the cabdriver.

"I don't know," I said. "Just keep driving. I'll know it when I see it."

"Your dime," he said with a shrug.

As we drove through the city streets, I noticed a lot of people walking around outside, with no particular sense of direction. They all seemed to be in a big hurry to go nowhere, and then there was a whole handful that did not seem to care that they were nowhere, just that they were *now here.*

Through the corner of my eye, I kept noticing the driver staring at me.

"You not from around these parts, are you?" he asked.

"Born and raised," I said.

"Really?" he asked with that infamous look of surprise. "You the prettiest girl I ever seen around these parts who ain't just passing through."

Well, maybe I should have been passing through. Home didn't know me no more. Everybody thought I belonged to someplace else, and the only problem with that was, so did *someplace else.*

"Two-sixteen Turnpike!" I shouted from the rear. "that's where I want to go." And with that, the cabbie swung an illegal U-turn in the street and headed west. Guess I wasn't kidding when I said I was going home. May as well go all the way out and back to the place where the whole thing started from.

We drove for what seemed like days before turning on to my old street. I got a tingling in my spine just being here. As we proceeded up the road a bit, I was surprised to see how run-down the houses were, not that they were mansions back in the day, but now they looked like certified shit, and this could categorically be classified as a real-life ghetto. Almost couldn't blame Mama for not coming back for a visit. Rancho Palos Verdes was a million miles away from this heap of a dive, but there's something endearing about the place that you fell out of the womb into.

The cabbie pulled up right in front of 216 Turnpike, and I nearly dropped my jaw. The whole block looked like holy hell, with the exception of our old house. Something new and different had been erected here in the place of something old and corrupted. Something beautiful had replaced something torn down and grotesque. Something *healed* had replaced whatever it was that stood in time as wounded. It was a standout in the community, and this little place was its own version of Rancho Palos Verdes in the middle of a heap of trash.

The little house was white with yellow trim, a cute little white-picket fence, and a shiny new wooden door with the cutest little doorbell you ever did see.

I was so caught up in the viewing, I didn't hear what the cabbie asked for by way of his fare, so I handed him $50 bucks and said, "Keep the change." He jumped out of the car and handed me one large suitcase and peeled off with urgency. Guess he had more suckers to hustle and more fares to close in on. After all, this was Shreveport, and trying to make a living was a full-time job all by itself.

I was so mesmerized by the beauty of this newly constructed house that when I closed my eyes, I could see life in it again, in the form of me and Aerial playing freeze tag out front.

You're it!

No, you're it!

You're cheating!

I quit!

I remembered collecting june bugs and crickets, storing them up for experiments, which I usually conducted in our bedroom after hours in the dark, in the hopes that Mama and Mr. Rufus would never find out, lest they beat my natural black ass. Behind closed eyes, I could also see Mama pulling up in that raggedy truck she used to drive, wearing that stained uniform from the diner. I could see what Mr. Rufus was talking about with her hips spreading and all. I could also see Mr. Rufus peeking through the front living room, always keeping tabs on who's keeping tabs on him. *Paranoid bastard*, I wanted to shout. *Get out of the window for Christ's sakes.*

I slowly walked up the pleasant little walkway and stood on the welcome mat with my one large suitcase. I just stared at the words: **WELCOME.**

"Welcome," I whispered.

Suddenly the door swung open, scaring the living breath out of me. I jumped back a beat.

"I'm sorry," said the voice of a man through the screen door. "I didn't mean to scare you."

"I'm fine," I said, part defensive, the other part startled. He opened the door and stepped outside as I backed away.

"Can I help you?" he asked, coming into view. Once he was outside, I could see that he was a beautiful man, very fair skinned with blue eyes. I was certain he was African American, but I had never seen a black man with blue eyes. He was one of the prettiest people I think I had ever seen, with two big old dimples and the friendliest smile this side of the Mississippi. He was a little taller than me, which probably put him at about six feet. He was wearing a white T-shirt and some suspender pants with a funny-looking pair of house shoes. They were yellow and fuzzy and had a bird's beak at the crown of the toe. As my eyes scanned his length and rested there, on the bird's beak, he started to laugh and wiggle his toes. "Birthday present from my mother."

I smiled and he smiled back. We looked at each other for a long time, and I knew for a certain fact that he was very attracted to me, and had I any liking to men at all, I, too, would have been attracted to him. I saw that he was pretty, but no more than that. It didn't rev up my engine, resting my eyes on him, for this simple fact: *He was missing a vagina.*

"Are you lost?" he asked, looking at my one big suitcase. I laughed out loud when I imagined how this must have looked to him.

"No," I said. "Not really."

"Are you sort of lost?" he asked again, fixed on my bag.

"Sort of," I said, looking down at his WELCOME mat, "but not really."

He just kept looking at me like he was expecting me to explain my presence on his doorstep, but that might take a little bit of time, so instead I said, "I see your mat here says WEL-COME."

"Yes," he said, his eyes dropping to the mat as well.

"Is that welcome good for a stranger?" And with that, he smiled and let me in.

Once inside, I nearly burst into tears, as he had ironically designed his house with the same layout that we had growing up as children. I stood in the center of his living room floor, in awe, just staring at the walls. He stood behind me, watching, wondering, and pondering who was this strange woman in his house wearing such a familiarity to his surroundings?

"I used to live here," I quickly blurted, turning in his direction.

"You must have this house confused with another," he said. "I had this house built from the ground up a couple years ago. It was a vacant lot when I bought it."

"Six years ago, there stood a house on this very ground, exactly like this one, except it was an eyesore, old and raggedy, and not much to look at . . ." I paused.

"The James property?" he asked.

I nodded.

"That house burned to the ground in a gas explosion," he said, referencing his memory bank.

"Yes," I said quietly.

"Everybody died in the house, didn't they?" he asked.

"Only one person died, but everybody who lived in that house lost their lives that night," I stated like a robot who had not had the experience but had only read about it. In the silence, he could hear what I did not say as he focused hard on my eyes, with profound understanding from his own.

"You lived in the house?" he asked, finally adding up all the missing pieces. My lip began to quiver, just a bit, and he tried to move close to me, but I held up a steady hand to halt his intentions. He could not hug it away, and an embrace would not change the course of the James Family Destiny.

"I am Blaze LeDoux James," I whispered. "In that back room to the left, which is probably your bedroom, is where I grew up."

"I'm sorry," was all he could say, before a long period of unsettled silence crept in. "And what about you? Did you get hurt?" he asked with great compassion.

"I was not a candidate that evening for a tragedy," I said, walking toward the window, staring out into the backyard. "You see, I was a bed wetter, and on that particular night, I was over there," I said, pointing out the window, "trying to dry my sheets before my daddy could see what I had done *again*."

He lowered his head with no more words to offer. "And," I continued, "Mama worked for an all-night diner, so she didn't make it home till after the house blew up."

"I'm real sorry," he said.

"My father died and my sister was maimed for life," I said.

He lowered his head but had no words. What does one say to

change the beat of another's heart? Perhaps silence is best on those rare occasions.

"May I sit on your lovely sofa?" I asked, looking at his beautiful brown leather couch that rested in the middle of the floor.

"Sure," he said, extending a hand to help me over to it, not that I needed it.

I sat down and took a deep breath. "Maybe it was too much coming back," I said, "but I just wanted to go home."

"Do you live around here?" he asked.

"Yes and no," I said. And with that he looked confused. "I just moved back," I clarified, "from Connecticut."

"Connecticut?" he asked.

"I went to boarding school there," I said.

"What about your family . . . your mother and sister?" he asked.

I just looked through him, like a ghost with no face. *What family?* I wanted to say, but I couldn't say that to a complete stranger, so I opted instead to say, "My mother and twin sister live in California. My mother is remarried, and at this time, they have no immediate desire to return to Shreveport."

"Can't say I blame them much," he said, walking into the kitchen, fixing us a drink. "It's not the kind of place to live out big dreams," he said reentering with a glass of lemonade, which he surrendered to me.

"Thank you," I said. "For your hospitality," I added after a quick pause.

He nodded and continued right on with his story. "I bought this property two years ago, saved up all my money from working two jobs for the longest time," he said with a sigh. "I'm going to sell it one day and make a nice profit, which I'm gonna use to buy my tire business."

"Tire business?"

"Michelin, Goodyear, Firestone," he said, "tires."

I nodded and smiled slightly.

"I *love* tires," he said with a lit-up expression, "and I'm gonna buy a tire shop in Providence, Rhode Island."

"Providence, Rhode Island!" I shouted. "Why?"

"'Cause," he said with a shy little grin, "that's the only place in the country that would finance me for my own shop."

I laughed at the absurdity of it all, as well as the simple beauty and brilliance of it too.

"It's gonna be called Nate's Tires," he said, grinning.

"So, I take it your name is Nate," I said.

"How did you know?" he gasped, then burst out with a mighty laugh. He really was cute when he laughed out loud, and he was cute when he was quiet too. I guess any way you chopped it up, he was just dang cute.

"Nathaniel Wheaton," he said, extending his hand to shake mine. "I am most pleased to make your acquaintance, Blaze—"

"Yes," I replied before he could finish his sentence. It was like we knew each other, even though we were strangers; we had already met and become either the best of friends or the worst of enemies.

I couldn't prove it, but I was certain we had done this already before today, and it was as if he were posted up in this house just waiting for me.

Blaze LeDoux James, the great contradiction.

Chapter 22

Not with Him

I stayed with Nathaniel Wheaton that night. It was the most natural place to end up, back at home, so it did not seem an odd arrangement, nor did it seem particularly unusual for me to be there, as crazy as that may sound. I blended like the borders around the floor or the trim around the paint. It just made sense, the yellow over the white, and Blaze LeDoux, a resident of 216 Turnpike.

The same day of my arrival, Nathaniel Wheaton had off from his job at the local tire shop, and so we spent the balance of the afternoon talking. At the end of the day, Nate cooked me a plate of mile-high spaghetti with garlic toast and a root beer float.

"I guess you stayed true to your word," I said, sopping up the last bit of food on my plate.

"And what word is that, Blaze?" he asked.

"Welcome," I said, referring to his doormat at the front door. "That was a mighty tasty dinner. I am thoroughly impressed."

He seemed most pleased to have impressed me so, and this began almost what I could call his obsession to please me.

"May I bring you more lemonade?"

"No, thank you, Nate."

"May I bring you a soda pop?"

"No, thank you, Nate."

"May I run you a nice bath?"

"No, thank you, Nate."

"May I rub oil on your feet?"

"Really, no thank you, Nate."

"What may I do for you?" he finally asked in great frustration.

I thought about it a second and wondered if I could say it without it sounding mean. "Well," I said, taking a deep breath, "you could leave me alone for a minute." And by the sunken look on his face and lowering of his eyes, I received instantaneous feedback that, no, I could not say it without sounding mean or breaking his beating heart in half.

"I wouldn't mind a glass of lemonade," I said moments later, because he did seem crushed that he could not service me in some capacity. And with my request came his grand smile as he jumped from his seat to retrieve me some lemonade.

I spent the night in his guest bedroom, and the next morning, I awoke to a full table of fresh-squeezed orange juice, flapjacks, bacon, and all. There was also a vase of fresh flowers sitting at my bedside, which was not there the night before. Nathaniel had also run me a bath in his antique tub filled with bubbles, lavender, and rose petals; it was only 7:00 A.M., so I can only imagine what time he had to awaken to accomplish all of this.

I slowly made my way to the breakfast table, wearing a heavy robe, tangled hair, and, quite possibly, leftover drool from the night before, which had dried upon my chin. And interestingly, he thought I was still the most beautiful woman in the world as he sat at the table, reading his morning paper and drinking a cup of hot coffee.

"Morning," he said upon seeing me, jumping up to pull out my breakfast chair.

"Thank you," I said quietly, barely knowing what in the world to do with all of his good intentions.

"Did you sleep well?" he asked, pouring me a glass of juice and a cup of coffee, and fixing me a nice plate of flapjacks, bacon, and eggs.

"Yes," I said, staring at the breakfast in awe.

"I ran you a bath," he said meekly. "Hope you don't mind."

"No," I said a little dazed, still trying to take it all in. "Lavender?"

"Vanilla lavender," he said. "Hope you like it. It calms the nerves."

"Oh," I said, "I think I'm pretty calm."

He smiled at me with those big blue eyes and daringly handsome face and proud stature, and for the life of me, I could not figure out *why* he was being so damned nice to a complete stranger. His welcome had gone way past "welcome" and was now something else, teetering somewhere between being overly helpful and borderline psychotic. I did not know how to take it, for I had never seen such innocence and beauty, grace and peace, and the sheer outpouring of goodness in all of my life. I felt like pinching myself to see if indeed I was dreaming, or better yet, pinching him to see if he was real.

"How's your breakfast?" he asked with a glow of pride on his face.

"Very nice," I said, taking bites real slow, wondering if he was trying to kill me with kindness.

"I have to go in to the shop today," he said, "but I'll be done about six o'clock, and if you're up for it . . . I'd like to take you to dinner."

My eyes shifted toward my plate, and I did not bring them back up again for a bit of time, which led him to believe that there was a problem. And there very well might have been, because I was getting the feeling that Nathaniel was smitten with me. He had *crush* written all over his face. Now, had I been a heterosexual woman, this might have been a winning combination, but I was a lesbian, and no matter how beautiful he was, he did not move me in that way at all. It would only spell disaster to walk him down a dead-end road. And to make matters worse, he was staring at my hair with such keen interest, I thought that at any given moment he was going to whip out a hairbrush and start brushing.

"You have really beautiful hair," he said.

"Thanks," I said, shoving eggs in my mouth really fast, hoping that we would not have to stay stuck on the topic.

"Is there something wrong with your breakfast?" he asked, of course, gravely panicked about it, lest anything be less than perfect in the world of Nathaniel Wheaton.

"No," I said, but was obviously bothered.

"You look," he said, afraid to utter the words, "unhappy."

"I . . . I . . . ," I said, trying to find the words to go someplace with them.

"Oh no," he said, practically grief-stricken, "there *is* a problem. What," he asked, snatching my plate, "are your eggs cold? Flapjacks too dry?"

"Nathaniel," I said, "please . . ."

"What did I do wrong?" he asked. "Bathwater's too cold?"

"Nathaniel," I said, pulling back from the table. "This feels a little creepy."

He stopped dead and stood excruciatingly still, and by the look on his face, I could tell he was scared to make another move *without* my say-so. I didn't want to hurt him, because surely he had the purest heart I think I had ever known, but I was more afraid to mislead him by way of my intentions. And the truth of the matter was this—I was not intending to be in any type of romantic way with him, because from where I stood, it was a chemical impossibility. The best that he and I could ever be was great friends, *or* bitter rivals in a competition for the prettiest girl in the room. But how do you tell someone that when they are looking at you as though you are the woman of *their* dreams, and you are looking over their shoulder to find the woman of *yours*?

"I'm sorry," he said apologetically, pushing back from the table. "I didn't mean to make you feel creepy; I just wanted you to feel *welcome*."

I looked into his pretty blue eyes and could see very well how a "regular" girl could get lost behind his eyes. He was the whole of perfect, and there was nothing missing. He was sincere, charming, hard-working, some kind of handsome, *and* decent.

Who wouldn't want to keep his company?

"Nathaniel," I said, "I can't be more than your friend," I said.

He got on his knees and scooted his way to me, and taking both of my hands as he sat at my feet. "A friend is the best thing to be," he said casually. "Don't you think so?"

The moment seemed overly romantic for my taste, so I pulled my hands from his and nodded silently in agreement. "Well," I said, breaking the mood. "Thank you for breakfast and for your hospitality. I should be going."

"What about your bath?" he asked.

"Right," I said, turning around remembering, "thank you."

I quickly bathed, got dressed, and packed up my one big suitcase and headed toward the front door. Nathaniel was getting ready to head off for work. I stopped at the front door and turned with a big smile. "Thank you, Nate," I said.

He nodded and opened his arms for an embrace, in which we exchanged a quick hug. I could feel him wanting to linger in my arms, but I could not allow him the privilege to do so, for it may confuse him against the truth, and I *never* wanted to do that.

"Don't be a stranger," he whispered into my ear.

I almost wanted to laugh out loud and ask, *What else could I be, man? I'm gay.* But perhaps he would not see the humor in that exchange, so I opted instead for, "Of course not."

I hit the sidewalk and headed east, but I had no idea where in the hell I was going. I could feel Nate's eyes following me from the front step, so I was trying like hell to get away from his sight as quickly as I could. I felt about as free or as lost as a big gust of wind, depending on how you looked at it. I must have looked some kind of retarded lugging a big, giant suitcase on wheels down the road. It was the strangest thing. I *was* home, all the way down to the ground I slept on last night, but still, I wasn't home. It was then that I knew home was not outside the body, but *inside*. Being comfortable in one's own skin was home.

Just then, I heard a BEEP BEEP alongside me. I turned slightly to the right and looked over my shoulder, and there was Nate, driving in an old pickup.

"Where's your ride?" he asked.

"I don't have one, Einstein," I said with a hint of irritation, lugging the suitcase behind me.

"You need a lift?" he asked.

It only took about two seconds to realize that a lift was probably a really good idea. "Sure," I said, stopping. He jumped out of his truck and grabbed my suitcase with a big smile. As usual, he was thrilled to boast what was probably a common sentence in his rather ordinary vocabulary: *Good morning, folks. I saved the day again.*

I took a deep breath and walked around the front of his car, and just as I turned the corner on the other side of his truck, I saw a woman four doors down open the door of her house and come outside. She was beautiful, with sassy brown hair and wearing short shorts with a great set of legs in high heels. Her breasts were large and inviting. They offered a silent invitation that said something like, *Squeeze me, squeeze me,* and she walked with the kind of strut that I wanted and wanted to know. When she turned and looked at me, all I saw were two piercing green eyes, and I felt a sudden hiccup in my chest.

She never left Shreveport, I thought. *She's been right here the whole time, staying four doors down and across the street in that raggedy little house of hers.*

"Oh my God," I said, expressionless and white as a ghost, "Felicity Hardaway."

Nathaniel saw my expression and looked up the way to see what I was looking at. I forgot about him, and was so taken back by seeing Miss Felicity, I screamed out her name as loud as I could and started making my way down the street, running toward her.

"Miss Felicity!!!!!!!!!!!!!!!!!!"

My hysteria frightened her a bit, because, after all, I didn't look a thing like I did the last time she saw me. I had been a simple preteen, but now, for all intents and purposes, I was a grown woman. "Miss Felicity!" I said again, running straight up into her driveway and onto her front lawn. She backed up, and I stopped. "You don't remember me, do you?" I screamed, laughing and shouting with joy.

"Remember you?" she asked, smoking a cigarette, carrying

that same expression from six years ago. "I never even met you before," she said.

"Blaze," I said. "And I think you have met me before."

Her mouth dropped as her eyes scanned the length of my woman's body, head to toe, and she was utterly speechless. "Holy fucking shit," she said, dropping her cigarette. "You grew the hell up!"

"Yes," I said, spinning around for her to take a better look at me, like a horse at the auction. She was laughing, and I was laughing, and then she laughed some more before coming over and giving me the biggest hug in the free world.

"Blaze James," she squealed, pulling me back from her so she could get a good look at me. "How the hell you been?"

"Good," I said, nodding, "real good."

She grabbed me again and hugged me tight, and I noticed somewhere between her releasing me and bringing me back, my panties got wet. Just being pressed against her body felt like some kind of relief, and when I looked into her flawless green eyes, I wanted to stay there. This was different, very different, because I had not ever looked at Miss Felicity in *this* way before. I quickly looked away, lest she see something in my eyes that would give me away.

I was a strange bird indeed. I lived my life as though being a lesbian was my sole privilege and not to be shared with anyone, male or female. Not sure how realistic that would be long-term, but I liked to keep it to myself and did not like talking about it with anybody. I never told a soul at boarding school, and after that night with Carmen on the floor in Mr. Willow's bathroom with an audience of 200 people viewing the most private moment in recorded history, I was shy about expressing that I was a lesbian. Just as I turned away, I locked eyes with Nathaniel sitting in the truck, grinning up a storm. Yes, I was almost annoyed. I felt uncomfortable for fear that Nate would see it in my eyes that I had just looked at Miss Hardaway in a way that I could never in a million years look at him.

Miss Felicity looked upon Nate with a question in her mind, and I could see it, but she dare not ask it in the moment.

"You ready?" he asked.

Ready? I thought. *No.* In fact, hell no! I wanted to stay with Miss Felicity and catch up, talk, stare into her eyes, or something. I didn't want to go, and Nate sensed it. He could tell. It must have been that panicked look behind my eye.

"You want me to take your bag back to my place?" he asked, hoping like hell I would say yes. Actually, I wanted him to give me my bag so that I could bring them inside Miss Felicity's house and stay there, but it was an awkward moment to put her on the spot and ask outright.

"Yes," I said quickly to Nate, hoping that I could stay with him until I could find my way back here. And no sooner had I uttered the word yes did Nate do a 180-degree turn in the middle of the street and hightail it back to his house, where he unloaded my bag with obvious joy.

Even Miss Felicity laughed in observation. "I think he's real happy about the news—you staying and all."

"It's just for a couple nights," I said, trying to downplay it lest she think Nate and I had something going on or, worse yet, that I liked boys.

Yikes!

"I just met him yesterday," I tossed in the conversation real quick.

"Really?" she asked with a raised brow. "Interesting."

"Well," I said, on my way to stuttering, which also meant lying a bit, "I was just in the neighborhood . . . and . . . stopped by the old place to see who bought the land."

"Is that right?" asked Miss Felicity, looking at me like I was twelve shades of crazy.

"Well," I said, shuffling my foot back and forth, "it's been a while since I been back home."

"You'll have to tell me all about it," she said before kissing me on the cheek and turning toward her car, "but right now ain't that time. I'm late for work."

"You still working at the barbershop?" I asked.

"Yeah," she said. "Where else am I gonna go?"

I nodded, just as Nate drove up again, beeping the horn. "I

left the door unlocked for you, darling!" he hollered. "See you at six!"

Miss Felicity looked back one more time and started to laugh as she jumped in her car and backed out of the driveway. Nate was grinning, waving and carrying on, driving down the street giddy out of his gourd.

"Great," I said, walking back to his house. "This is just great."

Six o'clock came sooner than I wanted, and Nate came busting home with a smile and a pack of handpicked roses.

"For you," he said.

"Thanks." I half smiled.

"You ready for dinner?" he asked.

"Yes," I said, not so enthused but borderline faking it.

"Let me catch a quick shower," he said, "and I'll be right with you."

I nodded in agreement, and he quickly disappeared into the bathroom. I could hear him singing to the top of his lungs when he got in the shower; he did seem to be some kind of doggone happy.

It was annoying. He was oblivious. Maybe I should tell him over dinner that I was a lesbian and then have him kindly drive me to a hotel for the night.

I found myself being lured to the curtain, looking outside and into the street, watching the empty road, and my eyes landed on Miss Felicity's driveway. She still hadn't made it back home yet, and as I stood in the center of Nate's floor, I could feel my heart pick up in beats. I wanted to see her, just a glimpse, a glance, a peek, a moment, a beat, a pause in or out of time. I wanted to lay eyes on her once more. I wanted to see her breasts and imagine what they might feel like in the palms of my hands or in the deep end of my throat.

My breath got heavy just thinking about it, and my panties began to leak with the familiarity of excitement. I had not felt a rush like this since I can't remember when, if ever. Not even with Carmen and our experimentation did I feel such a push between my legs that wanted to find its own way out. I had not been able to stop thinking about Miss Felicity since I had seen her this morning. She had been occupying all the free space in my head, but it was not like I had any free space to give for no good reason. I had a lot of other things that should have been in my head, like What was I going to do? And where was I going to live? And what would life look like in the very small town of Shreveport, Louisiana, that somehow seemed to have shrunk down to the size a shoebox since my last visit? No, this was not the time to corral with idle fantasy and excretions and expulsion between my legs, but I could not seem to halt the raging river of hormones that had now begun to consume me. And as I stood in the window looking out, I ran my hand down the front of my breasts, then inside the front of my pants, where I began to twirl my clitoris for pleasure. I kept one steady eye fixated out the window, thinking about Miss Felicity and dreaming about her, calling her up in between my legs as I began to writhe to the rhythm of a slow snake, grinding air and fantasy to create so much friction that I came all over my hands with an implosion that left me barely able to move.

But I did move in the next moment, and rather quickly, because Nathaniel cleared his throat directly behind me. I jumped and turned. He looked white as a sheet, for I do believe that he had stood in the center of his own living room and watched the whole damn thing without interruption. But, of course, he was too much of a gentleman to utter a word about it.

"You ready?" he asked with a hint of hesitation and embarrassment.

"Yeah," I said, trying to act like it was no big deal, even though I was mortified that he may have seen what had just happened in front of his own living room window. "I'll grab my purse."

"Okay," he said before stumbling over a friendly suggestion. "You may also want to wash your hands . . ."

I looked at him, but his eyes shot away from me and down to the floor.

"Okay," I agreed, expressionless, and as I eased into the bathroom, I saw Nate walk curiously to the front curtain and peer out. And it was here that I wanted to laugh, because he could stand there in that same spot for a thousand years and *never* see what I saw. He'd have to invite himself inside of my head for that kind of view, and that sure in the hell wasn't about to happen in this lifetime or any other.

Minutes later, we landed on the black top of Nate's driveway, where I stood outside his truck, waiting for him to lock up and secure the premises. It was just then that Miss Felicity drove up. She got out of her truck, looking tired from the long day, caught eyes with me, and smiled. She then looked up and saw Nate, and shook her head with a chuckle. A wave of heat flashed through me like a lightning bolt. "Damnit," I whispered to myself. *She thinks I'm with him. She thinks I like boys.*

"Shit," I said out loud.

"You say something?" asked Nate, approaching the truck.

"No . . . just talking to myself." I looked back over at Miss Felicity, who had opened the door and gone inside by now. And there I stood on the opposite end of Nate's truck, in a heap of frustration, desperate to take both a good shit and a nice deep breath.

Chapter 23

Quiet Lesbian . . .

I woke up the next morning, desperate to get out of Nate's house and over to Miss Felicity's. I had dreamt about her all night long and had awakened twice in the middle of it to masturbate. I had to get out of here and over there somehow. She had awakened something inside of me that was akin to nothing I had ever been introduced to before.

I had to see her today.

I just had to.

I leapt out of bed almost in a panic and started packing my bag. Again, there was another lavender bath waiting on me, along with a four-course breakfast, and Nate with that big goofy smile on his face, sitting at the table reading the morning newspaper.

"Good morning!" he said when he saw me, pleased as spiked punch and just as oblivious today as he was yesterday.

"Good morning," I said hastily. "I won't be staying for breakfast."

"Why?" he asked, jumping up from the table.

"'Cause I have to go Nate," I said, running over to the window to see if Miss Felicity's truck was in the driveway. *Yes*, it was still there. *Good!*

"You can't leave without putting a little something in your stomach," he said.

"No," I said, "that's okay."

"I won't hear of it," he insisted. "Sit down and at least have a glass of juice while I get your things, and I'll drive you anywhere you wanna go on my way to work."

"Okay," I said anxiously. "I'll have a glass of juice, but don't worry about giving me a ride. I can ask Miss Hardaway next door."

"Who?" he asked.

"Miss Hardaway," I said, pointing that-a-way. "She's your neighbor, a few houses down and directly across the street."

"Oh," he said. "Yes."

"I'll just hop a ride with her," I said.

"I don't think so," he said.

"What?" I asked, jumping up.

"Ain't that her truck right there?" he asked, looking out the window.

"Shit!" I screamed, running over to the window, where I saw her truck backing out of the driveway and pulling off down the road.

"No worries," he said. "I can take you."

"But I . . . I . . . ," I mumbled, "need to see her."

"She'll be back tonight," he said with a grin, "if you want to wait."

I sat down at the table. "Yeah," I said with a great big sigh, putting my head down. "I'll wait."

Later that day, I felt like I was going to come out of my skin waiting on Miss Hardaway to come back home. I was pacing back and forth, to and from the window, nervous and anxious. It all seemed a bit much, but just as I began to feel overwhelmed, I remembered the name of her shop, near downtown—Cutting Up. "That's it!" I said, quickly calling a taxi for a ride.

Within the hour, I was at the front doorstep, looking cute in a pair of my own latest fashions. Once inside, I could see the place held true to rumor. It was as crowded as all get-out, especially for a Thursday afternoon. Miss Felicity was the center of attention, wearing her typical shorts and high heels, low-cut blouse, and big earrings. She was doing that voodoo that she was known for doing on heads and laying down some fresh hair-cuts. When she caught eye of me, she paused a beat. It was ever so slight, but nonetheless, I could see the interruption of her flow and every other male species in the room. All eyes sat either on my front side or my backside.

"What you doing down here, girl?" she asked, staring me down, head to toe.

I didn't have a real answer, so I had to make one up in a hurry, and to my surprise, it was something unexpected. "Hair-cut," I said.

"What kind of haircut?" asked Miss Felicity. "Trim the ends?"

I ran my hands over my long beautiful hair and decided that maybe it was time for a real-life change.

"A little more than the ends," I said.

"Well," she directed with a smile, "have a seat, and I'll be with you shortly." She took another good look at me and shook her head. "I can't believe you that little James girl from up the street."

I smiled on the outside but felt a blow to the chest on the inside. *I wasn't just the little James girl up the street. I was the girl who lived with you for almost a year. You taught me the definition of lesbian in action. You and Miss Lolita, or whatever her name was, were my original teachers. I didn't know it back then, but I was a lesbian, too, and now that I'm here, I just want you to recognize me. Not just as the kid up the street . . .*

"Come on," she repeated a second time with a bite.

"Huh?" I asked, coming back from my own interior conversation.

"Come on," she said again.

"Okay," I said, jumping up and into her barber's seat. She grabbed a cape and put it around my neck snuggly, before running her hands down the length of my hair.

"Nice head of hair," she said. "What do you want to do with it?"

"Cut it off," I said before I had a chance to stop myself.

"Off?" she asked, wide-eyed in disbelief.

"Yes," I said with confirmation. "I want something sassy."

"Sassy?" she asked.

"Yeah," I said defensively, "why not?" I felt as if she was looking at me like some kind of child, and though I had not been an adult for a long time, I was a long way from being a kid. I don't know why, but I desperately wanted Miss Felicity to take me seriously and not just as someone worthy only of dismissal. I could be sassy; after all, my name was Blaze LeDoux James. As she pulled her long fingers through my hair, caressing, lifting, twisting, twirling, and ultimately cutting, I could feel the energy between us. It was thick enough to stand a popsicle stick in the middle of.

"You don't remember me, do you?" I asked her as she leaned in close to cut my bangs.

"Sure I do," she said.

"You act like I'm a stranger," I said.

"You *are* a stranger," she said, spinning my chair around to face the mirror, where she and I would speak through our reflections, both real and imagined.

"I lived with you for a year," I reminded her.

"You were just a kid," she spat, cutting me off at the knees.

"But I remember you," I said.

"That's nice," she said in an almost sarcastic, piss-ass tone before spinning me around and leaning in real close, with her breasts pressing up against me while she continued to cut and style my hair. I could feel the rise of body temperature between us. It felt like a wave of heat rolling back and forth, from me to her, to me and back to her. But it was confusing, because she was *pretending* she didn't feel it, too, which made me question whether or not I was just damn crazy and fabricating the whole thing within the interior of my own heart.

"You don't act like you remember me at all," I said adamantly.

"What do you want from me, Blaze?" she snapped. "College tuition . . . what?"

In that instant, she hurt my feelings beyond repair of the moment. I felt flustered, because in all the days of me being a quiet lesbian, I had finally looked into the eyes of a real-life person who I wanted to be out loud with. I wanted her. I wanted her really bad. My childhood fascination with Miss Felicity had grown to a new level. The biggest difference was this—when I was a kid, I wanted to be around Miss Felicity, but as an adult, I wanted to be *with* her. And that wasn't so easy to explain, especially to someone who held you so close to the image of being a kid with no plausible concept that you were a full-grown lesbian.

I was so drawn to her, and I felt like she just didn't get, see it, or want it. So I didn't say another word and let her finish my haircut without further incident. The way she had behaved toward me had already leveled me, preventing me from making further progress by way of conversation.

By the time she finished, she had been reduced to small talk to cover up the uncomfortable gaps in the dialogue between us, or better yet, the gigantic crack that her distance had created. But when she spun me around in her barber's chair for the last time, she delivered to me the image of true beauty, looking back at me. I was brand-new with a gorgeous short bob, a little longer on the right than the left, and layered elegantly in the back. It was sweeping, breezy, and fun. I swung my head wildly and laughed. Miss Felicity nodded with approval, pleased with the job she had done.

"I love it!" I screamed.

She pulled the cape off and smiled on the edge of her final words. "It's on the house."

And though it was a kind gesture in honor of our "friendship," I wanted to pay her, because I was not in need of charity or a kid discount. Hell, I had $7,000 in my suitcase back at Nate's. I didn't need a *free* haircut. So I stood up, standing a good inch taller than her in my heels and standing before her, we stared each other down. Her green eyes against my brown eyes made an interesting backdrop. I stood a little more than six feet with my heels, and so did Miss Felicity. Neither of us would back off from our stare, and with that, I slipped a tip in her bra and stepped off.

"Bold move, Blaze," she said to my back as I strutted in the sexiest runway-model walk I could muster toward the door.

"Thanks for the haircut, lady," I said with a whole lot of sass.

Later that evening, back at Nate's, I sat across from him at the dinner table, eating a gourmet meal he had prepared for us. He was smiling at me, and I was looking at him with polite observation. It was my observation that he was mad about me, and it was probably going to be a huge problem in the very near future, if it had not already become one.

He took a bite of food.

I took a bite of food.

He chewed.

I chewed.

He stared.

I looked back.

He took a sip.

I took a sip and then he sipped again.

I was beginning to feel like an old married couple, and I had only been at his house for two nights.

"I love your hair like that," he said, gawking and eyeing me like an ice cream sundae.

"Thank you," I said, trying to put more food in my mouth than conversation.

"You're so beautiful," he said.

I almost choked.

"Nate," I said, "can I ask you something?"

"Anything," he said, eager to respond.

"Do you have any friends?" I asked.

His expression dropped.

"Not that I . . . I . . . ," I said, trying to make it sound a little more gentle. "How do you invite a stranger into your home and never ask them to leave?" I asked. "It just seems a little . . ."

"I just like you being here, I guess," he said, deflated as he moved away from the table and into the kitchen, where he began washing the dishes.

"Shit," I said beneath my breath. I had hurt his feelings, but it was true. It didn't seem like Nate had much of a life if he was willing to let me in at first knock. Needless to say, the rest of the night was quiet as he sat silently on the sofa watching reruns of some show from the '70s.

"Good night," I said quietly.

"Good night," he said without making eye contact.

"I think it's best if I get a hotel tomorrow," I said.

"You might be right," he said, glancing at me and then through me before turning his attention back to his show.

The next morning, I awoke to the empty sound of nothingness. There was no breakfast, no fresh flowers at my bedside, no lavender-vanilla bathwater or clean bath towel. There was no display of affection or fondness of me anywhere present. In fact, Nathaniel had already left for work, and the only evidence of our actual meeting was in the form of a note he left by the door. It was a simple scribble that read *Please lock the door behind you.* I had hurt him, but it was not intentional. I wanted to apologize but just didn't know what to say. Perhaps he and I would meet again, and in that meeting, we would make amends. But not before another brush with Miss Felicity, who was standing at Nathaniel's door just as I opened it, waiting on me with the hundred-dollar bill I had slipped into her bra yesterday as a tip.

"Nice try," she said, shoving the money into my chest and walking away.

"Hey!" I said, finding my way off the front porch and following on her heels back down the street.

"I don't want your money, Blaze," she said.

"What?" I yelled after her. "My cash don't spend?"

"Not in my world it don't," she said.

"What's your problem?" I yelled.

"You insulted me by giving me that money!" she said, steadily walking but not ever looking back to face me.

"Your ego shouldn't be so big and your common sense so little!" I shouted in the middle of the street. "By the looks of this house, seems like you could stand to use the money!"

She walked inside her house and slammed the door.

"You have anger-management issues!" I screamed from the street. "Seek help!" I kicked the empty air I was so doggone mad, because, not only had she shut the door on me, but she had *shut the door* on me. And all I wanted to do was be with her and around her like a puppy dog. I wanted to lap her up like a warm bowl of milk, like a hot cup of tea.

I stood in the middle of the street between here and there, everywhere and nowhere at all, eyes darting back and forth from Nate's house to Felicity's, Nate and Felicity.

I wanted to cry. Reach out. Scream out. Fall out. "Why are you being such a bitch?" I screamed from the middle of the street. And when I turned around to walk away and back down to Nate's, where I would catch a taxi to my next adventure, Miss Felicity opened her front door and reappeared with hands on her hips, in the place where only empty space had stood before. As I turned my face and body back toward her, she seemed to make peace with a simple gesture of kindness somewhere between a wave and a head nod, encouraging me to come inside. Then she moved away from the front door, leaving her invitation at its opening, should I choose to accept. I did as she requested and moved very slow toward the front door, but I was cautious just in case the invitation was a setup for an ambush.

Once inside her home, I gently shut the door, where memories of childhood met me. I could feel my heart pick up speed and could hear Miss Felicity in the kitchen boiling a pot of tea.

"Come on," she said, setting two cups down on the kitchen table. The second I stepped foot in the room she occupied, I wanted to melt, especially when she looked at me, then through me with the most intense green eyes that I had ever seen. It sent a great spark immediately through my spinal column and up through the base of my neck. She was wearing shorts and a little tank top, accentuating her breasts, but this time she was not wearing heels, just bare feet and real pretty toes.

"Sit down," she said. I did as she asked, quietly and obediently. "So," she said. "What's your deal, Blaze?"

"Don't know that I have one," I said, fondling the outer edges of my cup.

"What do you want from me?" she asked straight out as we stared into each other's eyes, iris to iris. She was going straight for the soul, and I could tell she wanted to bypass all the bullshit.

"What makes you think I want anything from you?" I asked, beating around the bush so to speak, but no pun intended.

"Cut the shit," she said, lighting a cigarette. "How old are you?"

"Eighteen," I said boldly. I had already told her that before, but she must have forgotten.

"You don't know shit," she said, blowing smoke in my face. "I'm thirty-two years old—past all my twenties and on my way to a good midlife crisis, and you . . . you're just a teenager."

"So," I said in my defense. "I am what I am. What of it?"

"You walking around here like you got the whole Southern tip of the United States of America in your back left pocket," she said with another couple puffs on the cigarette. "And you don't know shit . . . you're fucking that boy down the street—"

"I'm not fucking him," I said quietly in my defense. "We're just friends."

"Right," she said sarcastically.

"No," I said frantically, "it's true." I could not bear to allow her, even for a moment, to think that I was not what she was.

"Okay, kid," she said, dismissing me.

"No, I'm not," I said again, frantic.

"Okay, Blaze," she said with a bite, "drop it."

"I'm not sleeping with him," I said.

"It's your business," she said.

"I'm gay!" I blurted. And with that, the room went silent, and her eyes locked into mine, and she slammed her teacup down on the table.

"I knew it!" she bellowed, and got up from her seat and walked back into the living room. I followed with urgency on her heels as she stood in the center of the floor with her arms folded across her big, beautiful breasts.

"How did you know?" I asked, coming up beside her.

"How could I not?" she asked, putting it back on me. "You think I don't know when somebody's checking me out?" she asked, all up in my face. I was embarrassed and ashamed. Perhaps I had been gawking without realizing. "Wake up, Blaze. This is the South. Lesbians communicate in code down here."

"I don't even know the code," I protested.

"You *are* the code," she said with a flat expression.

"I didn't know that," I said, impressed.

"Like I said," she repeated, "you don't know shit."

She moved from the living room to the bedroom, and I followed right alongside her like a puppy dog, thirsting for worldly ways and deeper insight.

"Get out!" she snapped. "I gotta change for work."

But I didn't go, just stood right there.

"I want to stay," I said, growing excited between my legs with the thought of her wearing nothing.

"Back off, Blaze," she warned. "I can read your mind. I've always been able to."

"What do you mean?" I asked.

"It's not going to happen," she said flat out. "No way in hell."

"What?" I asked, maybe because I just wanted to hear her say it.

"I'm not fucking you, Blaze," she said. "Is that clear enough for you?"

I do believe it was, but I was not about to tell her that.

"Don't come sniffing around here for an experience," she said. "I don't play with toys."

"I am *not* a toy," I said.

She removed her tank top, and her heavy breasts fell out and onto her chest, and my eyes immediately dropped to them. And she liked it; I could tell, but I opted not to push any further.

She grabbed a nice tight shirt and threw it on without bothering to search for a bra. She slowly removed her shorts and turned in the opposite direction, wearing only a thong, a tight shirt, and a beautiful set of legs.

I began to feel the hair rise on my arms. I wanted her so badly that I could taste her scent in the air through the distance that separated us.

"I'm not a kid," I said in my defense.

"So, what do you want?" she asked, still facing the opposite direction, her back turned to me. "A certificate of achievement?"

Instinctively, I moved toward her, but very slow. I felt very

much like an animal on the prowl. I wasn't trying to be preda-
tory, but the magnetism between us could not be denied. I was
drawn. It was as if she called, lured me, implored me and pulled
me to her, though she said nothing. She didn't have to because
this was beyond words, and it was here that I knew beyond all
knowing that I could not stop.

Would not stop.

Refused to turn around.

And go back.

She kept her attention focused on the interior of her closet,
or so it seemed, but I knew she was doing much more than se-
lecting a suitable outfit for the day.

I approached her from beind where I stood an inch from her
skin and a lifetime away from the longing for her touch. I ad-
mired the way God had made her. He made her similar to me
but different.

Different was good.

I liked different.

I liked her.

"I don't want no complications, Blaze," she said directly.

"It ain't complicated," I said.

"This ain't a game for the faint of heart," she said in a low,
direct voice.

"Who said I had a heart?" I asked aggressively.

"Somebody could get hurt," she warned.

I did not respond, nor did I allow her to engage in any more
critical self-talk. I simply allowed myself the pleasure of rubbing
her backside with my hand, softly sweeping it from side to side
and stopping in the middle.

She did not move or protest, but neither did she engage. She
stood naked on neutral ground, but there was no such thing as
neutral ground in a bedroom where two beautiful women were
pressed against each other pumping one million volts of live
wattage to both beating hearts. And in that moment I knew it,
and what had already been created in the spirit world would
have to be played out in human form. The drama where the
human heart would open wide, exposing itself in heights of

glory that only a god would know and speak of without remorse. Only celestial beings could be so free, to be more than
human in expression. As it was in heaven, so it would be on
Earth. As it was within, so it would pour without apology to the
outside world. As our interior thoughts revealed our most exterior revelations, this was the birth of a lesbian. And I had no
more fear, to be afraid of what I felt I could never express, except in silence to dead people, who had no tongues to talk and
share secrets to those who were living.

I wanted to melt my flesh down into brown liquid and pour
it all around Miss Felicity Hardaway and fuse our bodies together, and when we stood erect, we would stand as one body.
This was my true twin now, and Aerial, the masquerading one.

How do you get that close to a stranger who you've loved
since before the dawn of time and have no earthly explanation
to justify its origin or merit?

This would serve as the baseboard of insanity, which in some
ways would always bleed through the undercurrent of her and I.
And with that, I scrolled my hands around her waist to the front
of her body, where I snagged the front of her panties and pulled
them down, only to feel the moisture slide down the middle of
her legs from my interrogation. And once they arrived to the
ground, her panties, remained there, wrapped around her ankles, resting for some time while I explored her dripping interior walls with my fingers. She was soft and smooth, with little
hair to serve as interference. I massaged, fondled, rubbed, and
caressed her swollen and protruding vagina. And she did nothing but allow me access without restriction, to the point of
opening her legs even wider, as far as the panties around her ankles would allow, so that I could go deeper into her lesbian
world. In between my touch she would moan, and that was her
not-so-subtle way of saying, *Do continue.*

And with that, I spun her around and turned my focus to her
large breasts, where I lay my head, massaging her nipples with
an urgency to release the pressure that had been building up
since the great dam of puberty. With heavy breath, I began to
suck her nipples raw like a newborn at the tit for the first time

who was surprised to discover sustenance there. I found my own sustenance between her breasts, and there I clung for life, for breath, forever it would seem. Till she pushed me backward hard upon her bed and slowly but precisely and almost artistically released me from my clothing, where she began her own very personal exploration of my body like a voyager to the sea, on a new ocean of tumultuous waves. Once aboard ship, she parted my legs and drank of the Black Sea, till I came three times without pause, interruption, or the ability to recuperate to allow for another explosion, which came on the heels of another, then another, and back-to-back with such a violent force that the whole goddamned sea dried up and turned into a parched desert, a wasteland whose only longing was for Miss Felicity to come and pour her wetness into me.

Chapter 24

The Regrettable Lesbian

Felicity Hardaway never made it to work that day, and I never made it back down to Nate's to get my suitcase or catch a taxi to somewhere else. In truth, I did not wish to go anywhere else.

Felicity Hardaway *was* my somewhere else.

By six o'clock that evening, I began to get nervous. Nate would be coming home soon, and I knew that once he saw my suitcase, he would come down here looking for me. Felicity was also growing agitated, which was easy to tell by the fact that her cigarette smoking picked up speed.

Out of nowhere, she sat upright in the bed, her naked breasts taking up much of the spare room in front of her. "Blaze," she said with pending doom and gloom hovering around her voice.

Oh damn, I thought. *Here it comes.*

"We can't ever do this again," she said flatly.

When she pulled the word *ever* from her throat, I felt as though I had been stampeded by a herd of something wild. It could have been elephants, deer, rhinos, or even a herd of un-identifiable lesbians who had not yet made peace with their per-suasion.

"What?" I asked, sitting up beside her in a panic, hoping that I had misunderstood her words.

"You heard me—we can't do this again," she repeated, just as flat as she had spoken it the first time.

"Why?" I asked.

"Because," she said, getting out of bed in a huff, scanning her closet more earnestly this time for clothes.

"You can't just . . . ," I blurted, jumping out of the bed as well.

"Can't what?" she snapped.

"Can't stop," I said.

"Why?" she asked.

"'Cause this is special," I said.

She turned back around and shook her head. "Please don't tell me this was your *first* time."

"Of course not," I sharply replied. "It was my *second*."

"Fuck!" said Felicity. "I knew I shouldn't have—"

"What's wrong with you?" I screamed. She was just shaking her head wildly, pacing around the floor, mumbling to herself.

"What is wrong with you?!" I screamed again.

She approached me with a look of angst on her face. "This ain't love, Blaze," she said with finality. "It was just sex . . . and you're just too damn young to know difference."

"I ain't so young, you know," I said.

"Doesn't matter," she snapped. "It's over."

And with that, she threw on a pair of clothes and walked into the living room. I quickly dressed and followed behind her, where we squared off in the living room. She looked at me with hard eyes, and I at her. "I want you out of my house," she said in no uncertain terms.

My eyes filled with tears, and I stared at her, but she could not hold my stare, because her guilt got in the way.

"What do you want from me, for God's sakes?" she asked, depleted.

Silence.

Silence.

I did not answer. Instead, I simply turned and walked toward the front door and opened it, only to meet the face of Nathaniel, standing in the front door holding my suitcase in his hand.

Great.

The day just keeps getting better.

"You forgot something," he said, handing me the suitcase. We looked at each other with a long, hard stare. No words were exchanged, but plenty was said in the gaps of silence. Once I accepted the bag, he turned and walked away without further reply. I shut the front door and turned around to see Miss Felicity looking at me with an even greater interest in my bag.

"Where do you live, Blaze?" she asked.

"Out of this suitcase for now," I said, pointing to my bag.

"Damn, damn, damn," she said, walking back into her bedroom.

"This is temporary." She showed me the room I had stayed in as a youngster. "I'm sure you remember where everything is," she said with an attitude as she walked out of the room and back into her bedroom, shutting the door.

I closed the door to my room and sat down on the bed with a smile. Maybe it was only temporary, and in a few nights I'd be at a hotel somewhere downtown, but it didn't matter.

I was here . . . *for now*.

The next morning, I woke to the smell of fresh-ground coffee. Miss Feliciy was in the kitchen cooking breakfast, which reminded me of the good old days, which in retrospect weren't so good at all. Wearing a pair of silk pajamas, I eased out of bed and made my way into the kitchen, where Miss Felicity sat drinking coffee and reading the newspaper. I stood at the entryway of her kitchen and watched her with subtle eyes. She really was a beautiful woman in her natural state, without defenses. But it was rare indeed to find her in a natural condition.

"You going to come in?" she asked without making eye contact. "Or you just gonna stand there and stare at me?"

I smiled, entering the room with caution. One never knew how to predict the unpredictable moods of Felicity Hardaway. I took a seat at the table in silence, while Miss Felicity poured me a cup of coffee. She made heavy eye contact while pouring, which made me look away. "Thank you," I responded quickly, taking my cup and shoving it into my mouth to have something to do with my lips, tongue, mouth, hands, arms, and all the rest of my body parts that were not being used at that time.

"So, what's your plan?" she asked me.

"Don't really have one," I said.

"Don't you think you should get one?"

"I want to make clothes," I said.

"Interesting," she said. "You make clothes?"

"All the stuff you see me wearing, I made it," I declared with pride.

She nodded. "You got skills, girl."

"Thank you," I responded with a bit of a blush.

"Maybe I can hook you up down at my shop," she offered.

"Really?" I asked. "What kind of hookup you talking about?"

"How about you bring some of your fashions down to the shop and make some sales to the customers?"

"Serious?" I asked, perking up with great enthusiasm.

"Serious," she said with a nod.

"Great!" I said.

Later, Miss Felicity left, I called a taxi and got a ride to the garment store, where I would spend $2,000 of my $7,000 in material to create my unique form of fashions for the good people of Shreveport.

Over the next two weeks, I worked nonstop to create skirts, blouses, slacks, scarves, and all kinds of fashion accessories. Miss Felicity had started spreading the word to the townsfolk, and we scheduled an official fashion debut of my exclusive line, A Taste of Blaze.

It would seem that, for the time, Miss Felicity had found a peace with our new relationship, and when we were not working on my new line, we would find our way into her bedroom to engage in other activities.

It started out slow, with once, maybe twice a week, where she would surrender to the passion that clearly existed between us. On those occasions when we did make it to her bedroom, all that had been building up from the prior week would unleash itself, and like two wild animals we would consummate our love and devour each other without regret or apology.

In the midnight hour, we seemed to be inseparable, but by

dawn, the illusion would wear off, and I would awake in Miss Felicity's bed alone *again*, only to find her in the kitchen brooding over a cup of coffee and a Bob Marley song.

"You okay?" I would ask each time, the day after our lovemaking, which would seem like the birth of a new Holocaust, all over again.

"Why wouldn't I be okay?" she'd ask with a bite.

"You seem distant," I'd always say.

"I told you," she'd say, "we can't keep carrying on like this."

"You say that every time," I'd remind her.

"Well," she'd hiss, "I mean it *this* time."

On this particular morning, I was good and sick of Miss Felicity's wishy-washy, back-and-forth dance of the regrettable lesbian that she had been doing now for weeks.

"Why do you hate yourself so much?" I asked her.

"What?" she asked with shock plastered on her face.

"Why can't you just let yourself be happy?" I challenged.

"Well," she said, "I was just fine till you pushed your way up in here!"

"Is that what you think I did?" I asked. "*Pushed* my way up in here?"

"Seems so," she said.

That was it for me. I was good and done with Miss Felicity, and though I loved her so, I could not deal with her inability to deal with herself.

"You're all talk, aren't you?" I asked her.

"What are you saying?" she asked, getting up from the table and moving into her bedroom, where she would always retreat when she couldn't cope with the truth.

"You talk a good game, seem real confident, snappy, sassy," I said, following behind her, "but it's just for show . . . that's not who you are."

"You don't know a thing about me," she retorted.

"I know the most important thing about you," I said. "You've never been comfortable in your skin, and that's why you spent your whole life pretending."

"You don't know what you're talking about!" she yelled.

"The lesbian who never could," I said. "That's what you are. You lived your whole life on the edge of what other people would say about you. Pathetic," I said.

"I can do plenty," she insisted, "without you."

"Don't you love it when I touch you?" I asked, reaching her, but she grabbed my hand and threw it back to me.

"You're too young for me, Blaze," she said, reciting the words like a faithful mantra that she said each day.

"It's a funny thing," I said with a laugh, "but you never say that when I'm down there between your legs working it out."

"After your show," she said with a raised brow, "I want you out of my house."

I looked hard into her beautiful green eyes. They were the eyes that held a thousand secrets behind them, harboring the soul of a chained woman who never allowed herself to be free. She would never give herself what she would almost demand from every other person she knew.

"I want you out," she repeated, as though I did not hear her the first time.

"Gladly," I said without emotion. We had long since passed the days of sniveling and whining over our bipolar relationship that seemed as imbalanced as anything I had ever known in the days before it.

Combustible.

Passionate.

Exhaustive.

And violently changing. I should have labeled this relationship by its true name—*toxic*. But there was a part of me that could not write it off as such. It was the part of me that saw the real Felicity Hardaway and knew she was gentler than even the lightest feather; and all of her ranting and raving meant nothing of substance, because she had not a cruel bone in her body to follow it through.

Within one week of her asking me to move out, I previewed my new design line to the good people of Shreveport, Louisiana. And by the grace of Felicity's recommendation, because she was well known in the community, people turned out by the dozens And many of them remembered Aliyah James and Mr. Rufus, as well as Aerial.

This did much to boost sales.

There were a lot of inquiries on the whereabouts of Mama and Aerial, and I had little by way of information, other than the fact that they lived in Rancho Palos Verdes in a mansion, because Mama had married a fat white man about half the size of Manhattan. And though I had not laid eyes on any of them in more than five years, I dared not tell them that, because people may wonder how five years pass, and you grow up by accident without a mother and a sister.

None of us had good reasons for the absence, neither myself, Mama nor Aerial, but it was easier not to talk about it than bring it to light in casual conversation and go through a whole psychotic episode in desperate efforts to explain the unexplainable.

At the end of the evening, I had made almost $2,000, which offset the cost of my production line rather nicely. And as the last person was ushered out of Miss Felicity's shop, I felt I had at long last accomplished something.

"Well, how about that, girl?" asked Miss Felicity.

"How about that?" I repeated. It appears that both of us were rather proud of ourselves, and I split the earnings with her straight down the middle. But, of course, being who she was, she fought me in the taking of it.

"I don't need this," she said.

"Take it," I insisted.

"It's your money; you earned it," she said.

"Couldn't have done it without you," I said, setting the thousand dollars on her counter.

"Why don't you use this to get yourself someplace nice to stay?" she asked, placing the money back in my hand.

I don't know why, but whenever she talked like that, I felt such pain in my chest. "I don't want someplace nice to stay," I said. "I want to stay with you."

"Is that your way of saying my place is a dump?" she asked with a laugh.

And it did sound that way, and, yes, perhaps her place was a dive in comparison to the places I had seen since Mama married into Willow's money, but none of that mattered to me right now. All that mattered was that she and I could be together.

"Why do you hide?" I asked her, looking straight into those beautiful green eyes, trying to persuade her to look back at me. She turned away, uncomfortable, as usual. "What is it?" I asked her, following closely upon her heels.

She quietly turned and looked at me, and with tears in her eyes, she mumbled, "No complications."

I leaned into her, and we began to kiss, gently at first, then ferociously, because we never knew how far not to push it. And when we started, it just kept going, because we never knew how to stop it. With us, it always went from zero to ten, and that is why it always scared her so, because she wanted to control it, but you can't control what's too big for you to see, to hold, to touch, to embrace, to smother, and to try and chain.

In less than a minute, we were rubbing on each other's breasts, grinding on top of each other and making our way into the little room in the back, where we removed each other's tops and viciously go at it, like two hungry wolves, hungry for the other's touch. Almost insisting that the other give it here, give it here. And this is where we stayed for a while, feeding on each scent, skin, hair, flesh, bones, and soul, sucking out all that made us human and that which brought us closer to being gods. However, in the heat of the moment, there was a draft that blew through the room that felt like heavy eyes and stares of condemnation.

I sat perched on top of a little counter in the back room, with my legs wrapped around Miss Felicity as she devoured my breasts in her mouth, till I opened my eyes and focused my attention in the direction of the draft, and there stood three of the good people of Shreveport, wearing Sunday dresses and big hats, clutching colorful bags beneath their arms and sporting matching shoes on their feet. The horror-stricken expression on their faces told it all. They looked as though they had seen the dead reincarnate before their very eyes, or worse, two lesbians in active expression of great love.

"Lord Jesus," said the bigger of the three women, who wore a bright green dress sprinkled with hideous yellow flowers. "Have mercy on the souls of these women who have just damned themselves to hell!"

Upon hearing the voice of another, Miss Felicity must have jumped a mile straight up into the ceiling and beyond. Her skin turned clammy cold and she was off me, backed up nearly halfway across the room. In an instant, the women all turned and headed quickly toward the front door.

Call on Jesus!
Save yourself!
Satan is wreaking havoc through the streets of Shreveport.
Call on Jesus!
Save yourself!

We could hear them singing religious hymns of despair all the way out the shop. The door swung open and closed so damn fast, I thought it would nearly break off its hinges. And a glance, I saw Felicity, standing in the corner, looking down toward the ground as if she did believe that her very soul was on its way to a place no less painful than hell. The fact that her whole damn life had been confined to Shreveport was hell enough, wouldn't one think?

I did not know what to say. It had become very clear to me in this moment that this was her town, and these were her people, and somewhere along the way between losing everything and finding it all again, I had outgrown this town and these people. And I felt bigger than their small opinion of me and cared not that they had cursed my soul to damnation under the auspices of their own ignorance.

But Miss Felicity obviously did not feel the same way, and I came to know her desperate plight in the moment she reached up to a shelf and pulled to the ground all of its contents as she let out a mighty roar that sounded like hell had been unleashed from within and would cast a fury upon the streets of Shreveport, which would strike back with an iron that had been hand-molded straight from hell itself.

Chapter 25

"Piss-Ass Scaredy Cat . . ."

The days following what I would ultimately venture to call "the great reveal" would be excruciating. And Miss Felicity Hardaway would become the talk of the town by way of conversation and vicious rumor. I would remain at her home, at least for a time, while figuring out how to look as though I was leaving but really spending more time trying to figure out how to stay.

Miss Felicity was not well, in spirit and in health; she had contracted a nasty flu, sending her to bed for days, a most suitable place to find withdrawal of life. And I would take care of her, feeding her soup and wiping her forehead while she lay splattered out like one of the lost.

"I pulled the phone out of the wall last night," she said, pointing to the disconnected unit sitting at her bedside.

"Really?" I asked, noticing for the first time. "Why?"

"Because they kept calling," she said, staring into space.

"Who kept calling?" I inquired.

"Everyone," she said.

"And what did they say?" I asked, sitting beside her, holding her hand.

"'Pussy lover,' mostly," she said.

I shook my head and stood up indignantly and stomped away. "Why do you listen?" I asked.

"You see that disconnected phone, right?" she asked. "But tell me this," she continued, "how long do you think *you* can play deaf to the sound of their calls?"

"I don't give a shit," I retorted. "You're the one who cares about these people in this town."

"These people in this town are my livelihood!" she said forcefully, before succumbing to a violent coughing fit. I handed her a glass of water, which she eagerly accepted and began to drink. "They pay my bills," she concluded weakly.

"*You* pay your bills," I insisted.

"With *their* money," she shot back.

"That they give you for *your* skills," I concluded. "You're the best barber in this whole goddamned town."

"Not bad for a pussy licker," she said, staring off into space again.

"Maybe you should have left here a long time ago," I said, "and then you could have been free to be who you *are*."

She didn't respond.

"There is no freedom in this lifestyle," she finally said. "If you know what's best for you, you'll fall in love with some dick and get over your small fascination with the world of the underground lesbian hiding out in the South."

I started to laugh as I looked into her hard eyes and harder heart. "I don't fall in love with dicks or pussies; I fell in love with a person."

And with that, there was a loud knock upon the door. Miss Felicity sat upright in bed, almost with a look of panic on her face. "Don't answer it," she said, "could be trouble."

"What kind of trouble?" I asked.

"Shreveport kind of trouble." She got out of bed and threw on a robe just as fast as she could get it off the foot of the bed. The knock came again, louder this time. I walked toward the front door.

"Don't," she repeated, alarmed. "Don't answer it." She pushed past me and made her way to the front door, where the silhouette of a woman wearing a big hat was waiting on her doorstep. "Well, what the hell?" said Miss Felicity, standing at the front door, looking through the peephole. She slowly opened the door, and I approached behind her.

"What the . . . ," I asked with my jaw dropped down to the floor.

"Blaze," said the familiar voice on the other side of the screen door.

"Shit," I whispered as Miss Felicity backed away from the door, and into full view came Ms. Aliyah James Willow.

She looked as radiant and beautiful as ever, untouched by the five-plus years since I had seen her last. She looked even wealthier than she did before, all the way down to the velvet of her deep cocoa tanned skin. A good fifteen pounds heavier than I remember her being, she was still the most beautiful woman in the room.

"May I come in?" she asked with no visible trace of a Southern accent anymore. She had dropped her entire Southern identity in the City of Angels. As she entered, adorned in the finest tailored two-piece linen suit with matching hat, straight A-line skirt, and stunning rhinestone heels, she was a sight to behold. Even Miss Felicity backed up in awe of her aristocratic appearance.

"Blaze," she said again, entering and directing all of her focus on me. I stood under heavy scrutiny as she looked at me, shocked by my short hair and slovenly appearance in comparison to her own. "Get your things—you're coming home."

Immediately, rage shot through the back of my spine. Whoever did she think she was to demand such a thing?

"I beg your pardon?" I said.

"There's no need to beg of anything," she said with a bite. "Get your bags—we're going home."

"This *is* home," I said with a hard stance.

Aliyah James looked hard at Miss Felicity, who was inching her way back from the scene, which looked as though it had great potential to become explosive.

"You have made an embarrassment of yourself," Mama said to me, "and a mockery of our family name. Now get your things."

I shook my head and laughed. "Some things never change," I whispered under my breath.

"This whole town is laughing at you and this woman," she said, pointing to Miss Felicity. "Word has gotten all the way back to California about the way you two were carrying on at her shop."

That was all Felicity Hardaway needed to hear. She looked as though a tram had run her over without warning that it was coming full speed ahead.

"I don't care," I said with conviction. *Who did she think she was, coming up in here like she owned this city?*

"I care," she said. "You're still my child."

"Yeah," I said with a shrug, "and what did that ever mean to *you* or to *me*?" And with that, she smacked me as hard as her hand could hit the side of my cheek without breaking the skin. It stung to high hell, but I was too bold, too cold, and too grown to show it. I didn't flinch, not even an inch.

"I want you out of here," I said to her. She shot the ugliest stare at Miss Felicity and began to spew venom across her living room floor. "Are you pleased with yourself?" she asked Miss Felicity, who did not respond but simply lowered her eyes into the living room floor. "You should be ashamed of yourself, raping a child. I should have you arrested!"

"I am NOT a child!" I screamed into the harshness of her words.

"You don't know a THING about life, Blaze!" screamed Mama. "And you've gotten yourself all mixed up with this . . . this . . . ," she said, eyeing Felicity.

"This what?" asked Felicity, who looked as though she had taken just about enough of Mama's crap.

"How old are you?" Mama asked Miss Felicity. "You're about my age, right? In your thirties . . . What could you possibly see in a little girl that could interest you? Sick and perverted, you are."

"Mama, stop it!" I screamed.

"Down here, doing the devil's bidding in your sleep," said Mama to Felicity Hardaway.

"You don't know a damn thing about me, lady," she said. "Just 'cause you're wearing a fancy suit doesn't make you qualified to come up in here, in my house, as a judge or a jury."

"I know plenty about your kind," said Mama to Miss Felicity.

"And I know plenty about *yours*," said Felicity to Mama.

"Blaze," said Aliyah James without taking her eyes off Felicity Hardaway. It did seem as though we had us a standoff going on right here, right now.

"I'm not leaving without you," said Mama.

"Then you're going to have to stay the night, 'cause I ain't going anywhere," I said, eyeing her down to the floor with the bitterness of my own stare as I made my way to the bathroom and shut the door. Something had to give, and somebody had to go. But at this point, no one knew who it was going to be, how much they were going to give, and where in the hell they were going to go. At this point, it was anybody's game and anybody's good guess, or good bluff.

I sat it out on top of the commode for two and a half hours, and there wasn't a sound that squeaked from the other room. I imagined one of two things had happened—Aliyah James had left empty-handed or had opted to murder Felicity Hardaway on the front porch. Both were a strong probability, and whichever one she chose, I could rest assured that she would return someday, if not *sooner*.

Upon exiting the bathroom, I found Felicity sitting in the dark, smoking a cigarette. All I could see was the flame from the cigarette, nothing else. She was sitting on the edge of the sofa, hands shaking, smoking.

Aliyah James was nowhere to be found, and only the scent of her expensive perfume lingered faintly beneath the fumes of Felicity's smoke, flames, and rage.

"She gone?" I asked, feeling as though I were stepping into a den of vipers. The mood did not seem inviting or friendly, and Miss Felicity looked as though she had been broken entirely in two.

"What?" she asked. "You think she's been out here playing hopscotch with me while you been locked away in that bathroom? You piss-ass scaredy cat," she hissed. "I'm sorry for the day I ever laid eyes on you again."

Her words stung harder than Aliyah James's slap. I looked down.

"You think that shit's funny?" she asked. "Your mommy comes up in here and calls me a fucking child molester, some kind of fucking psychopathic rapist?" She stood up, in a terrible breath of anger. "Did you see the way she looked at me?"

"Yes," I said, "I did."

"Did you see it?" she asked again, louder. "No, did you see it?" "'Cause . . . 'cause . . . she looked at me like I had violated you. She looked at me like . . . like . . . I was dirty and sick."

"She didn't mean nothing by it," I said faintly.

"Don't tell me that bullshit," said Felicity, getting off the couch and coming into the dim light in which I stood against in the hallway. She looked a frightful sight indeed, pitiful, as though she had been crying the whole night. She looked drunk and high, but the sad thing about it was, she hadn't smoked a joint or had a drink or done anything except chew her fingernails down way past the skin. Her hands were bleeding all over the place, dripping blood all over the top of her cigarettes.

"My grandmother confronted my father back when I was a little girl," she said, remembering, "and she called him a sick fuck. And I'll never forget the look in her eyes when she asked my daddy if he had been fucking me at night after my mama went to sleep."

I looked into Felicity's eyes, and my own began to fill with tears, for she had been through more than I would ever understand in a single lifetime. And truth is, I didn't want to understand that kind of horror in this lifetime. I didn't want to understand, or know it, or feel that I should be familiar with it. I didn't want to talk about it or listen to it or make peace with it or war with it. I didn't want to rage with it or forgive it. I didn't want it to exist at all, but Felicity Hardaway wouldn't let it go— for love, peace, sex, or God; in the name of all that was good and decent, holy and unholy, she just wouldn't allow herself to let it go.

"And my grandmother looked at my father, just like your mother looked at me . . . like a sick fuck."

"I'm sorry," I said faintly.

"And in that moment, I felt like my father . . . I felt like a dirty sick, bastard of a fuck . . . criminal . . . rapist, fucking pedophile for touching you," she said, staring into space. "And to this day, I still think about cutting his throat."

I paused, alarmed. "You think about what?"

"Slitting his throat," she said again without hesitation.

"I thought he was dead," I said.

"Whatever gave you that crazy idea?" she asked.

"When I was a kid, you told me he was dead," I said, "You said he died when you were thirteen years old and that you didn't shed a tear at the funeral. . . ."

"You believe every goddamned thing you hear?" she asked with attitude.

"Not anymore," I said flatly. "Why did you lie?"

She didn't answer.

"Why did you lie?" I repeated.

Still no answer.

"You're a liar!"

Miss Felicity grabbed hold of my throat and wrestled me down to the floor as I fought against her with my body weight, pulling her down on top of me on purpose, where she would lie screaming, crying, and pulling my hair. And I would smack her in the face, and she would slap me back but harder. I slapped her again, and she slapped me back, till we ran out of anger and energy to abuse each other. Until we had run out of room to hurt and all that was left was to heal and love each other back to life. And then we kissed each other's forehead passionately and with healing intentions. We kissed the angry marks we had made with our fists, with our slaps, our words, our curses, and with our anger. And we held on to each other as though we were the last two people on earth, and neither one was willing to let the other go, for life, for breath, for air, for death, for nothing, and for everything at all.

Chapter 26

Pussy Lickers

The next day, we would be shaken awake at dawn by the commotion. Trash cans were being knocked over in the back of Felicity's house, and beer bottles were being thrown against the back patio. Disoriented and heavy with sleep, Felicity would almost stand to her feet without even being aware of what had awakened her or why she was standing in the middle of the room.

Dazed, I was the much slower of us to react, and by the time I sat up, Felicity was already in her bathrobe and somewhere in the vicinity of the patio, where she swore off a group of youngsters who were ransacking the backyard for sport.

"Get out of here, you little fucks!" I heard her scream from outside. As I made my way to the patio, I saw her through the glass making unfriendly hand gestures at the kids, who hauled themselves away on bicycles at top speed from her backyard's view of the city trash dump.

Not a productive way to start the day, I imagined. And as I turned my attention to the front window, I noticed an entirely different drama unfolding on the front lawn, being carried out by mischievous boys wearing baggy pants and baseball caps, carrying giant bottles of red spray paint.

Uh-oh, I said to myself, only imagining what trouble lay ahead under the breath of such mischief. As I walked to the front door, with an eye steadily fixed on the back where Felicity was still cleaning up one mess made, I could not help but feel leveled to the ground when I opened the front door and saw the entire driveway covered in freshly painted letters that were dripping bloodred: **PUSSY LICKERS**

I lowered my head, disenchanted, knowing that Miss Felicity was destined to lose it now. I could see the neighbors peeking through curtains, gawking and pointing. And as I ventured outside, I could feel all eyes on me, even eyes I couldn't see.

The boys who had done the deed were more than halfway down the street, but I could still hear their jeering, shouting, and laughing. They probably felt like grown men for writing such big words in permanent paint that lay streaked and bleeding across the concrete for the whole world to see. I shook my head, and before I could even finish cursing them under my breath, I could feel Felicity's body heat behind me as she stood with hands on her hips, staring with a bleak expression into the red, bleeding driveway.

"Where did they go?" she asked, looking around.

"Took off down the street," I said.

She just stared expressionless in the direction of the cheering, which was at a distance and slightly isolated.

"I'll help you get it off," I said, turning on the water hose and saturating the ground with gallon after gallon of water, which only helped to bleed the words deeper into the driveway, making them bigger and easier to read to strangers passing by. Only thing, there was no more such a thing as "strangers," because everybody passing by knew us now by name: *Pussy Lickers.*

"It's only getting worse," said Felicity in a huff. "Just stop," she said, "and I'll back the truck up over it and try to cover as many of the words as I can."

"Okay," I agreed, thinking that might be best.

Within moments, Nathaniel Wheaton drove down the street and cut sharp eyes in my direction. He looked down at the driveway and read the words with heaviness looming about him. It was almost as if he needed clarification:

Oh, now he understood.

Miss Felicity backed her truck over the top of the words, and we went about the rest of our day pretending nothing had ever happened. Though at the same time, we knew that nobody could leave the house till after dark, lest we pull the truck out of the driveway and the neighborhood see with their own eyes that the two ladies who lived up the street weren't just ordinary girls, but *Pussy Lickers*.

"I need to go into town," said Felicity, coming into the bathroom later, where I was resting in the tub.

"For what?" I asked.

"I have a business to run," she said.

"You think you're going to have any customers today?" I asked.

"Don't have any appointments on the books," she said, "but somebody will be needing a haircut before the day is out. It's Friday—my busiest day."

I just looked at her but didn't say anything. For her to be the so-called smart one, at times she seemed so damn naïve. In my humble opinion, Shreveport wasn't ready to forgive her for being a lesbian. And if they weren't ready to forgive her licking the ladies, they damn sure wouldn't be ready for a haircut.

"I'd like to come . . ."

"It's best you stay here," she said in a quick panic. "Just till things blow over."

"When you think that might be?" I asked.

She didn't answer.

"When do you think this little shit, no-nothing town is going to get over themselves?" I asked with a whole lot of attitude.

"When we get over it." she spat.

"And stop being dikes, right?" I asked.

"You're such a bitch sometimes," she said, sliding down to the floor, lighting a cigarette. She was looking more and more tired each day. The woman I had fallen in love with had all but disappeared, and in her place emerged the shadow of a brazen spirit I once knew.

"I just want to go with you," I said. "That's all."

"Do you *really* think it's a good idea?" she asked, looking at me as though I were stone crazy and out of my mind.

"Yes," I said confidently. "Why not?"

"Because your mother's in town, and she's probably causing chaos in the city, raising hell about you being raped by a pedophile," said Felicity.

"Can we please not go here again?" I insisted.

"We're already here, darling," she said, taking a long hit off the cigarette.

I got out of the tub and dripped dry in front of her as she sat on the floor looking up at me. I slid my wet body between her legs and took the cigarette from her hand, putting it out in the sink; then I returned to give her all of my undivided attention, kneeling before her and cupping her breasts in my hands. They got so hard, her breasts, and swelled to double their size, allowing each nipple to stand at attention, prior to me dropping down and licking them like a good ice-cream cone, playfully rolling them in and out of my mouth and around my tongue.

She resisted a bit at first, citing as an excuse, "I have to go."

"Not yet," I whispered, pressing her back against the wall. "Not till you fall in love with me."

"You'll be waiting for the rest of your life," she insisted, "and then at the end of it, you'll be disappointed."

"How can you be so sure?" I asked, slowly kissing her nipples, teasing and rolling them around my tongue.

"Damaged goods," she said.

"Why are you so hard on yourself?" I asked.

"It's hard being me, Blaze," she said.

"Then be somebody *else*," I offered.

Later, I would talk Felicity into letting me go with her down to the shop. When we arrived, it was the beginning, or should I say the continuation, of more chaos. The front of her barbershop window had been busted out, with a brick or something heavy.

"Shit," she said, pulling the truck to a quick stop and jumping out with a certain hysteria. "No!" she said in front of the shop. "No!"

Upon exiting the truck, I could not believe what my eyes were seeing. The shop had been vandalized something gruesome. The front window was broken, and glass was everywhere, inside and out. The chairs had been cut with razors and the floor was filled with urine.

The walls were spray-painted with obscenities: **PUSSY LICKERS, PUSSY LICKERS**

"Who would do this?" I asked as we stood atop broken glass.

"You still don't get it, do you?" she turned to me and said.

"I'm calling the police," I said.

"For what?" she asked.

"We should report it," I said.

Within thirty minutes, two disinterested police officers had arrived, wearing badges and bad attitudes. They came into the shop, milled around without grand concern, and cast heavy eyes of judgment on Felicity and me, and in between pauses, they exchanged looks between themselves.

We stood in the center of the shop, and I could tell that Felicity was growing more and more humiliated, especially when the cops read the walls, then looked at us, then back to each other, and then back to the walls again. It seemed to be some kind of sick, ritualistic mating dance.

"Okay," said Cop #1, with bad skin and a big belly. "We got what we need."

"So, what are you going to do?" I asked them, and they both just looked at me but offered no response.

"What are you going to do?" Felicity asked, clearing her throat as though she demanded an answer.

"Looks like it's already been done," said Cop #2, the short, sarcastic, balding one. He removed his hat and scratched the top of his shiny, round head.

"Are you going to actually do something about this, or did you just come down here to add your piss to the puddle in the middle of the floor?" I asked.

"Girl with a mouth like that," said Cop #2, "could come up missing and wouldn't nobody come looking for her."

"You threatening me, cop?" I asked.

"Blaze," warned Felicity, "let it go."

The cops and I had a silent standoff with our eyes. "You ain't big enough to play with us, lesbian *girl*," said Cop #1.

I looked at his face hard, then his left hand, which bore a shiny wedding band. "That's interesting," I said, "'cause your wife told me last night in bed that I had bigger balls than you do."

"Blaze," snapped Felicity.

"I'd squash you like a bug," he retorted.

"Don't count on it," I said. "You'd have to catch me first," I said, staring down at his big, fat gut; then I burst into laughter.

"We're leaving," said Miss Felicity, grabbing my hand. "Call me if you catch a lead."

They nodded and Cop #2 looked at me real hard and said, "Likewise," he said. "Call us if you catch a bullet."

"You threatening me?" I snapped. "I will have your badge."

Miss Felicity put her hand over my mouth until we got in the truck.

"Don't you *ever* do that again!" she scolded. "Ever."

"What?" I asked her, under the pretense of being innocent.

"These crooked cops down here will cut your throat and leave you to bleed to death in the middle of the woods some-where—do you understand me? This ain't California, this is the backwoods South."

"So," I said, "they ain't got laws in the South?"

"They got *their* laws," she said, "and they make 'em how they see fit to play 'em out."

"I don't care, Felicity," I said, arms up against my chest. "I can't live like this . . . this is some bullshit."

"It is what it is," she said. "It's their games, their rules, their world."

"Sucks," I said.

"Blaze," said Felicity, "we're pretty much at of the end of this rainbow."

"What do you mean?" I asked in a panic, hoping it didn't mean what I thought she meant.

"You really should call your mother and head on back to California."

No.

No.

I just want to be with her. Why can't she accept that?

"What about you?" I asked.

"What about me?"

"What are you going to do?"

"I'll manage," she said flatly.

"Don't you want to do more than just manage, Felicity? You really should raise your expectations of life. Don't you want to be happy?"

"Who says I'm not happy?" she asked. "You saying that?"

"Yeah," I shot back, "I'm saying that."

"You're a pain in the ass," she said to me.

"And so are you," I offered the same in exchange. "But I love you."

"Don't," she said. "Somebody could get hurt."

"Somebody already has," I said.

Chapter 27

God Does Not Live Here

I would stay with Felicity Hardaway another day, then two, and three. The days would roll into months, and the months would roll into a year. It was ironic, I know, but I just never got around to leaving.

Aliyah James would return to Felicity's front step at least two more times within our first year together. She would come announced and sporadically, making several trips from California back to Shreveport to "talk good sense into me." And each time, her return would be met with silence, as I would stand on the other side of the door and not even bother to open it.

"Blaze," she would call out each time, "I know you're in there."

She was always right. I was always *in there*, but it would do little to secure a conversation and open up a dialogue between us.

Instead, each time she would stand at the door for a good six, seven minutes and knock relentlessly. She'd knock, then stop, then pick back up to knocking again. And ultimately, she would turn away in frustration and return to the chauffeured town car that had delivered her to the doorstep, to return back to the world from whence she came. And interestingly, I never felt guilty watching her go, even knowing that she had flown several thousand miles just to stand on this step and have a conversation with me.

No, I would never feel bad or be pressed with an urgency to

apologize for wasting her time, her money, her days, her expense, and her breath. I never had an inkling to open the door and reach out with a fierce embrace and welcome her into my arms unconditionally and thank her for coming this long distance, all the way back down to the slums in a last-ditch, desperate effort to reach out and rescue me.

"You ever gonna talk to her again?" asked Felicity one morning as we took a bath together, and Aliyah James Willow appeared on our doorstep again, knocking with a vengeance.

"I suppose," I said, resting my naked body against Felicity's "Someday there'll be reason enough to have a conversation."

"It must be crazy having a kid that you can't even talk to," said Felicity.

"Yeah," I agreed, "it's about as crazy as having a parent that won't listen." And I laughed, and she laughed too.

What else could we do?

Life had changed so much since the first embrace of me and Felicity Hardaway. As she had promised, it was not a journey for the faint of heart.

Miss Felicity repaired her barbershop from the vandalism that had occurred months back, but business would never be the same again. And though she would go to that shop five days a week, in hopes that the town would ultimately forgive her indiscretions or simply break down because they needed a good haircut, it never happened. All of her regulars and strangers seemed scared to come because of the rumors.

Felicity Hardaway, the best barber in town, hadn't cut a strand of hair in almost one year, with the exception of her own head, and mine sometimes.

"Times are bad," she said one morning upon waking at 3:00 A.M. because she couldn't sleep. "I've run through all my savings, and there's nothing left, Blaze."

I, too, was feeling the backlash of a backward town, where everybody was too close up and personal on everybody else's business.

Everywhere we stepped on solid ground, we were called SINNERS in the eyes of another. Silent words that rang out so strong, you could hear deaf echoes in the back of your head and high whispers in between all of the words they were too scared to say to your face, so reserved for that special place, the one you'd stand in when you turned your back on them, and they mumbled, "You're going straight to hell . . . don't you know? Don't you know?"

Newsflash, baby, I'm already in it. And funniest thing of all is, *so are you.*

"I have fifteen hundred dollars left to my name," I said, sitting up with her that morning. "It's yours if you need it."

"I need it," she said, "but so do you." And she was right in her summary, as I couldn't sell so much as a pair of panties in the open marketplace these days, and I was beginning to feel like a fish encased in a glass bowl, on display for public consumption and opinion.

I felt as though I were wrapped in the chains of other people's ignorance. I could not bend my mind around the insanity, in that an entire society would shun another person on the basis of their sexual preference. Every time we went outside, people would stare and gawk. We were human oddities, in a city that pretended not to know about us lesbians. We were freaks of nature, the outsiders, condemned to walk upon unholy ground. It was as if every step was followed by a trail of unpleasant odor. We were regarded as community lepers, disease-ridden and highly contagious, terminal, flammable, combustible. Women did not allow their children close to us lest they brush up against us and our disease rub off on them.

Hush your mouth.

What do you say?

A fate worse than death itself? To be a self-declared lesbian condemned to a life of pussy licking and breast groping. However will you procreate and carry out the most basic of all God's commandments, go forth and multiply?

There would be no Sunday-morning greeting from the church, the minister, the choir, and the parishioners.

How could they judge us, treat us like criminals, and yet still hold themselves under the dim light of all that they would call holy? Isn't that the very declaration of hypocrisy itself? They would call themselves Christians, and me and Felicity sinners. What sets them apart from us and who are they, that they have the final word in our destiny? I did not for the life of me see their lives so grandiose and worthy of praise, and ours of condemnation. And God knows I would look. I would look high and I would look low, and then lower than that. I would search with all of my might and breath, life and death. I would search beyond and behind the bias, through and beneath the ignorance, over and atop the self-righteousness, indignation, and holier-than-thou display of fundamental Christianity, which was riddled with holes and insecurities, prejudice and judgments, harshness and ridicule, and I would decree in my own way, my own time, my own day, and my own words, **GOD DOES NOT LIVE HERE** entangled in all of your madness. And if by chance he does, then perhaps he is in the greatest need of his own salvation and mercy.

"Why don't we move out of Shreveport?" I asked.

"And go where?" She put it back on me.

"Anywhere," I said, pulling on the words in exaggeration.

"I don't belong anywhere else," she said to me.

"Goddamned Felicity Hardaway," I said in frustration, getting out of bed and walking over to the window to look at the night sky, "if you don't stop playing life so small, one day it's going to leak itself right out from beneath you."

She didn't answer me. I turned in the direction of the black night and pointed up toward the sky. "Do you see how big God made this sky?" I asked her. "What makes you think he does anything on a small-time basis?"

"You're so young, Blaze," she said to me. "When you've lived as long as I have and seen what I've seen . . ."

"But that's just it!" I declared. "You haven't lived and you haven't seen, and I'm here to tell you that life is SO big, and you've squeezed yourself down to something so small, I need a magnifying glass to find you these days."

"Well, to hell with you," she said in a bitter scoff. "You get that fucking magnifying glass of yours and you find the rest of my goddamned life that's been ripped apart, from end to end, and lay bleeding somewhere in the middle of the dirt road—you find it, bent ear to ear."

"It doesn't have to be that way," I contended.

"Do you see my barbershop in that little glass of yours?" she asked, shaking a fist at me from across the room. "In that little, itty-bitty microscopic telescope you're looking in, do you see my fourteen years of blood and sweat to build a business by the seat of my ass, only to have it ripped out of my gut, while still attached to every inch of my bowels? Do you see that in there, girl?" she asked. "Or what about my childhood—do you see that in there too? Can you find my rape and document it in there just for good measure? A nine-year old virgin whore."

"Stop it, Felicity," I snapped. "Just stop it."

"What about my sexuality?" she asked. "You see that in that scope of yours—a little girl who had been raped so much by the time she was eleven years old by her own daddy that she made a promise to NEVER allow ANYTHING with a penis to so much as breathe beside her again?"

I looked at her in horror, for I had no words to say.

"So what's your excuse?" she asked. "WHY would you for NO good reason waste your good life condemned as a lesbian if you had a choice to go another way?"

"I don't have a choice!" I blurted.

"You always have a choice!" she screamed at me.

"I don't have a choice," I defended. "This is who I am."

"Then you're STUPID!" she shouted. "You're fucking beautiful, Blaze. You could set the whole world on fire with your beauty and have any man you so much as turn your sniveling nose up toward, and he'd be on all fours, lapping up your piss, but instead you chose . . . you chose . . . *this*," she said, her voice trailing off into nothing.

"I didn't choose *this*," I said. "I chose *you*. Because I think you're fucking worth it, even if you are hell bent on destroying yourself, Felicity Hardaway. There will always be a grace that lives within you that I'll always love, and you can't destroy it, and you can't wish it away, and you can't overlook it, and you can't overshadow it, 'cause it doesn't come from you—THANK GOD—it comes from God, and what HE gave you can't nothing take away," I said with tears rolling down my face, and my heart beating out of my chest and pouring blood, rage, and compassion into my bloodstream by the gallons. "So, you can blow yourself up into a thousand destructible pieces, and I imagine that one day that's just what you're going to do, Felicity. But good news is, you can kill yourself a million ways to Sunday, but you ain't never really gonna die. So you might as well make up your stubborn mind and get on with the business of living!"

And with that, I got back into bed, put the covers over my head, and went back to sleep. Enough already. It was only daybreak, and, Good Lord, it was only Monday.

Chapter 28

"I Have Danced with Her There . . ."

One Year Later

And that is what we would do for a period of time, go on living. Felicity began to set up new connections two hours away in Baton Rouge, where she was virtually unknown. This led her to a certain peace, easing into the cracks of an ambiguous lesbian lifestyle. On the weekends, she would cut hair, and I would accompany her to sell fashions.

It was humble.

It was honest.

And it was *decent*.

And it would seem that, for a while, Felicity Hardaway was happy. We rarely conducted any business in Shreveport, and everything from washing the truck to going grocery shopping was done in Baton Rouge on the weekends. We were unmarked women there, and no one suspected a thing, so we blended into the good vibration of everyday, ordinary living. From time to time, I would receive lengthy letters from Aliyah James, and these would go unopened by me, but Felicity would open them, because usually between the pages, there would always be a check.

The checks would go uncashed, and no matter how desperately we needed the money, I never allowed Aliyah James Willow to contribute to my life. But she was stubborn just like me and would not allow her wishes to be ignored, so eventually, she stopped writing checks and started sending cash. And the crisp, green bills would lie beneath the same note that always read, *Don't be a fool. Take the money.*

"You heard your mama," said Felicity on one such occasion, forcing the $500 into my hand. "Don't be a fool. Take the money!"

"I don't want the money," I said.

"Just take it," she said, "and quit being a stubborn ass. Life doesn't always have to climb uphill, you know."

"That sounds mighty funny coming from somebody who only knows the meaning of an uphill battle."

"Yeah," she said with a curve to her mouth, "and just 'cause I'm a goddamned fool doesn't mean that you have to follow suit."

There were times when I would learn from Felicity, and then there were times when she would learn from me, but whatever the times were, I cherished them all. I had fallen deeply in love with this woman, who had all the potential in the world to be a real-life angel if she would only just give herself permission to sprout real-life wings and fly.

My twenty-first birthday was right around the corner, and we had decided that this weekend, instead of working in Baton Rouge, we would go out to the swampland and go fishing.

"Fishing?" asked Felicity. "That's what you want to do on your birthday?"

"Yes," I said. "I used to go when I was a little girl, and it was so peaceful there."

"But fishing?" she asked.

"Yes, fishing," I flat declared. "My mama sent some extra money this week, so we can make a nice day of it."

"Okay," she agreed, "it's your day. We can blow it doing whatever kind of craziness you feel so inspired to do."

"Thank you for your kind indulgence," I said in jest, and she just looked at me on this day with an eerie set of eyes, which made me wonder sometimes what she *really* thought about all of this. "What?" I asked.

"Nothing," she responded, shaking her head. "Sometimes I ask myself," she finally said, "if you really are happy."

"Of course I am," I said with a smile, which almost seemed forced at times. Not sure why, I just wondered if she could see something in me that I couldn't.

"You wouldn't be happier just being normal?" she asked, brushing the sides of my face against her hands.

"I *am* normal," was my only response. And she laughed before looking at me again with a heavy query playing out in the recesses of her mind. And by virtue of the fact that I could see it, I knew it was there.

"No regrets?" she posed to me.

"About what?" I asked.

"Being gay?"

"No regrets about being *me*," I said. "None ever." Then I flipped it around to her. "And you?"

The question went unanswered by Felicity. It always did. But on this particular day, as we prepared for our journey to the swampland, I brought it up again. "You never did answer my question," I said, reminding her of what she had not forgotten as we rode in the truck on the way to the swamp.

"What question was that, darling?" she asked.

"You have regrets about being gay?" I asked, and there was a long pause that fell over the top of all our communication.

"I have regrets about being *me*," she said, lighting up a cigarette, "and let's just leave it at that, okay, Blaze?"

I nodded. "I want to ask you something," I said to her.

"Shoot," she said.

"Why did you lie about your father being dead, Felicity?"

"It's just easier with him being dead," she said.

"But he's not *really* dead, right?" I asked.

"No, he's not *really* dead," she said, "and I don't want to talk about it. I don't want a long, drawn-out dissertation from the Blaze James School of Theology and Philosophy."

"Whatever," I snapped.

"I'm serious," she said. "I just want to go hang out on the water, drink a couple beers, eat some fried chicken, be eaten up by some big ol' fat mosquitoes, spit out watermelon seeds on top of the water, and fuck my brains out when the sun goes down!"

I burst out laughing. In Felicity's own psychotic way, she really was one of the most charming people you ever would want to meet on an off day. Filled to the brim with God's good grace, the spirit that lit up those eyes was incomparable to anything I had ever known, and I loved her so. That honorary, stubborn, bitter woman was clutched right in between my beating heart, and I loved her with a passion unequal to another.

"Maybe we'll do it right here in the back of this truck," she said with a laugh.

"Wouldn't be the first time," I whispered beneath my breath, "wouldn't be the first time."

The water was murky and puke green. It looked like vomit on a good day, but it was the most peaceful place I do believe I had ever seen. With trees that touch the sky, adorned in Spanish moss that dripped its tears upon the earth, there is something that lives in the swampland that speaks of its own glory, and it need not be validated by anything else.

It is not waiting for you and I to come and dance along its muddy edges and call it *lovely*. It need not wait for something outside of itself, like a pretty blue lake or a cascading mountain or a waterfall, to look upon it and authenticate its beauty. Its beauty is hidden in the fact that it *knows* it is beautiful. And if that be the case, as I have just presented it, then we all do well to sit in session upon the humble waters of a murky swamp and learn from its greatness and pray that someday its lessons become our own.

We rented a small private boat and took to the waters under the reassurance of our own navigation. Neither one of us really knew our way around the swampland, but it was easy enough, one way in and one way out.

We had packed a picnic that included fried chicken, watermelon, beer, and dessert, and we sailed adrift on top of the water for what seemed like hours. We also had fishing rods, but that idea seemed like little more than a notion, as we hadn't so much as baited the hook; instead, we traded fishing for each other, basking in the glow of each other's company.

"It's nice to get away," I said to Felicity as she kicked back in the boat, opening another beer.

"Indeed it is," she agreed with a loud beer belch bubbling forth from her throat.

"How many beers have you had?" I asked her.

"How many we start with?" she asked.

"Twelve," I said, looking in the cooler.

"How many we got left?" she asked.

"Two," I said, "and I don't drink beer."

She just looked at me and smiled.

"Ten beers, Felicity?" I questioned. "Shit, guess you ain't driving back home."

"Hell," she said with an obnoxious burp. "I'm not even fit to drive this boat."

"You are so goofy," I said to her. "What am I going to do with you?"

"Love me, I hope," she said with the innocent expression of a child, which surprised me, because Felicity *never* spoke like that. She never asked to be loved or dare pretended to be vulnerable.

"Always," I promised, moving in for a kiss. "I'll always love you."

She smiled, but beneath the smile, I could see sadness brewing. I wasn't sure why, but it always seemed in close proximity to Felicity Hardaway, and wherever she was, sadness was never too far away.

I turned my attention from Felicity and back to the cooler, where I searched for our dessert and something decent to serve it on. In that moment, I became absorbed in the hunt for proper utensils.

"Now I know I bought us some dessert plates," I said in frustration, shoving food to the left, to the right, trying to figure out why we had brought so much food in the first place. "Felicity, have you seen the plates?" I asked.

No answer.

"Felicity," I repeated a little stronger, "have you seen the plates? Stop playing," I suggested, but when she did not answer again, I felt something eerie in the silence. I quickly turned around and she was gone.

She had disappeared into air that was not so thin at all.

"Felicity!" I screamed, alarmed, making my way to the edge of the boat. I looked over the sides to find her but did not see her.

I panicked.

"Felicity!" I screamed again. "Felicity! Felicity! Felicity!" I shouted out her name again and again, running frantically to each end of the boat, nearly throwing myself overboard in search of her.

The waters held an unsettling calm, for they did not look disturbed or rippled. There was no sign of her anywhere! It was as if she had never been on the boat at all. It was truly bizarre and one of the most frightening moments of my life.

"Felicity!" I screamed in the rage of blood-curdling desperation. Within a minute and a half, I was in an all-out desperate panic, and a violent sweat broke out against my forehead. I began to spin around and around and around in circles on the boat, calling her name more loudly, more desperately, more violently and passionately till eventually I removed my jacket and leaped headfirst into the murky, dirty waters of the swamp. Upon entry, it was not a pleasant sensation, as there were weeds, husky branches, scaly critters, and creepy crawlies rubbing against my skin.

I choked and gagged on the thick mud bubbling forth from my disturbance in the swamp. I went deep, into the bottom of the swamp, and dared to open my eyes as best I could, given the desperate circumstances at hand.

I searched beneath the boat and the surrounding area, swimming fast, hard, deep, and long into the swamp, looking for Felicity.

"Felicity!" I screamed, till the sound of her name echoed off the trees and returned to me, untouched by her response. A boat carrying a local tour group heard all the commotion, and made their way to where I was, still in the swamp, screaming and crying. From their radio, they called for help, a search party, under the code that someone had fallen in the swamp and had gone missing.

I was helped out of the water by someone, I don't remember who, but as I boarded the boat of tourists, these foreigners, mostly from Japan, stared at me in horror, dripping in Spanish moss, the residue of murky dirt, and heavy tears. It was a frightful sight indeed.

Within an hour, there was an all-out search party consisting of the local sheriff and law enforcement, special-unit volunteers, and even a swampland native, who was an expert on the murky waters.

"How long you girls been out here?" he asked.

"Few hours," I said, standing by this time on the edge of the bank wrapped in a blanket.

"Was there any alcohol involved?" he asked.

"What do you mean?" I asked. "She just *fell* out of the boat?" he asked, carrying suspicion in his voice.

"What are you insinuating," I asked, offended, "that I pushed her?"

He lowered his head, and no one said a word.

"What's it look like, Chief?" one of the law enforcement officers asked as the sun began to go down.

"It's been three hours," said the expert, "and there's no sign of her anywhere. At sundown, wherever she is, she'll just be food for hungry gators."

I burst into tears and began to scream, *"Noooooo!"*

Someone tried to comfort me; I was not sure who it was, if they were male or female, black or white, law enforcement or volunteer, but I could feel the presence of human arms around me, trying to pull me away from my grief, into their bosom for comfort.

There was a deep pit that rested in my stomach that grew more hollow, more shallow, and more fiery with the passing of each minute as I began obsessively checking the position of the sun against the dusk-ridden sky. And I called on the sun for a favor, with all of the strength in my body, begging it to not go down and bring the night sky upon the land without the presence of Felicity Hardaway But there would be no pardons today, and without my consent, the sun did go down and darkness arose in its place. One by one, the searchers in the volunteer party dispersed and went home. And with each person leaving, my heart sank a little bit deeper. It was like one by one, they were saying, *Rest in peace. We're all done here.*

"Ma'am," said the local sheriff, approaching me looking very official, "we have to call the search off for tonight."

"No, please," I begged, "please . . ."

"There's nothing more we can do tonight," he said. "We've been out here six hours and have combed every square inch of these waters up to twenty-five miles out and . . ."

"And what?" I asked desperately.

"There's no sign of her anywhere," he said.

"We'll pick it back up at daybreak," said their residential expert.

"Daybreak!" I said, panicked. "Daybreak—"

"We'll go back in the A.M., and try to scoop out a body," said the expert to the sheriff, "if the gators leave anything for us to identify."

At hearing the words, I collapsed onto the ground.

I came to in the back of a patrol car, with two police officers staring into my eyes and down my shirt with a bright light.

"You have anybody you can call?" they asked.

Zombie-like, I stared ahead and slowly responded, "There's no one to call."

I didn't even know if Felicity Hardaway had any living relatives. Well, I had just recently found out her supposedly dead father was alive, but God only knows where he lived. I knew nothing of Felicity's mother or any other extended family.

She never spoke of anyone. She had lived her life as a loner, with the exception of the foreign lovers she took to her bed every now and again. She had no external connections to the outside world. She had a business that went under and clients who had walked out on her. So, no, there was no one to call.

She had no family.

No friends.

She had me, and that was the way she wanted it.

As the patrol car drove away from the swamp, we pulled alongside Felicity's truck, and in staring at the empty driver's seat, I felt a sharp pain in the center of my chest. I lingered somewhere between horror and absolute horror, without pause and breath. I started to hyperventilate before bursting into tears.

The officers looked at me with compassion, sorrow, and a bit of confusion. They knew not what to say, do, or how to be. "Where can we take you tonight, miss?" one of the officers asked.

"Hotel," I said.

They obliged, taking me to one of their local spots, where I got a room, showered, and eventually passed out under the weight of exhaustion, naked on the bed. I awoke early the next morning to resume the search with volunteers and local law enforcement.

The next three days would be an all-out exhaustive search for Felicity Hardaway, but at the end of it all, it would turn up nothing.

No-thing.

Nothing.

By the third day, heavy under the weight of emotional hysteria and sleep deprivation, I began to beg that something be found, even if it was something as dreadful as her body.

But nothing was found.

No-thing.

No trace of Felicity Hardaway.

No evidence of her death and even less of her life.

There was no body, no clues, no foul play, no indication that she was anything more than a figment of my imagination. There were no shoes, no clothing, no articles of personal belongings, no strands of hair, no loose and unattended body parts, no sign of struggles or blanket of surrender.

Nothing.

No-thing.

On the fourth day, the state of Louisiana declared Felicity Hardaway deceased and labeled "accidental drowning" as the official cause of death. Law enforcement presumed that her remains were "disposed of naturally by the forces of nature." It could have been in reference to anything from natural decay in the murky waters to consumption by alligator. And on the edge of this announcement, there were no words to describe the heavy anchor pulling from the bottom of my heart.

There were no words.

No-thing to say at all.

I was exasperated and grief-stricken beyond all verbal description.

There are no words.

No-thing to say at all.

I returned to Shreveport by way of police escort. News from the local media had traveled fast. As we drove through town, I will never forget the distant looks of strangers who stood in the street, peering at my reflection in the backseat, through the hollow glass of the patrol car.

When we arrived at Felicity's house, I sat in the back of the car and stared into empty air. I wanted to break down and sob, weep, cry, shout, scream, holler, yell, beg, plead as I stared into the front window longingly, hoping to see her beautiful silhouette gracing the front porch in high heels and short shorts. I wanted to see her brilliant embodiment, larger than life, parading through the yard, shooting nasty looks to anyone who dared to question her as to why she lived her life in the way that she did. I wanted to crawl up into Felicity's arms and have her throw herself around me and reassure me that this was some kind of nightmare. *I'm not dead.* I wanted so desperately to hear her say that, as well as, *This was all just one big, gigantic, lame misunderstanding.*

But there were no words, only silence, as I made the long walk up the driveway, as I had done so many times before, but NEVER did the walk ever feel this long and this hollow, this lonely, and this gigantically, monumentally difficult. Each step felt like miles, and the anchor upon my heart pulled heavier and deeper, the closer I came to the front door.

I slowly opened the door, hands shaking, expecting in some

strange way to see her there, and though I knew she would not be, I could not have imagined my own disappointment not to see her. I almost fell ill with a shaking that overtook my body as I made my way across the living room, where everything had gone untouched and lay just as Felicity had left it.

Her slippers were by the front door, and for the first time, I noticed every detail of them: the fur, the color, the pattern, the stain to the left, and the wear on the sides and the heel. Her nightshirt, the flannel thing she slept in sometimes, lay in the middle of the floor.

I walked to the flannel shirt in order to inspect it for content. I examined its fabric, its scent, its coarseness or softness, its very essence.

I could feel Felicity in the shirt. And as I clutched it between my hands, and then my fingers, I held it against my face, my neck, rubbing it against my nose and into my nostrils, where I grabbed hold of a scream that, with its bleeding intensity, lay me out in the middle of the floor, where I sobbed so loud that even the walls bent to absorb my grief. I cried out to find pure understanding.

Why, dear God, had she left me when I loved no one but her and could not see myself against the reflection of any other, including my own, without her? She was the other half of my beating heart, and how I had managed to find my next breath without her was beyond my comprehension.

I stayed on the floor for two days without moving. It would appear that for a time or two, I, too, had shuffled off the face of the earth, taking to dreams and places so vivid and colorful, where Felicity and I would meet on the inside of lyrical song, and I would eventually awake knowing that she was one lesbian who had gone to heaven and not to hell as the Christians had tried to convince her of when she was alive.

How do you know she's in heaven? I could almost hear them asking me.

Because, I would say to their smug expressions, *I have danced with her there.*

I have danced with her there.

Chapter 29

What God Would Do

Seven Days Later

Rain poured from the sky so heavy upon the day, I knew that it was only a declaration of God's tears. Though she was well known throughout the city of Shreveport, Louisiana, and word had spread like wildfire of her death, on the day of her memorial service, which was held at a famous local funeral parlor, the guests in attendance were minimal—two to be exact, me and a stranger.

The stranger was a man who seated himself boldly in the front row, and I took a seat in the second. And as the makeshift pastor (i.e., owner of the funeral home) conducted a brief service, seven minutes to be exact, I sat in awe that the townspeople could not find within their unforgiving embrace the common decency to come to this humble gathering and bid Felicity farewell. Most of the Christians felt as though they would go to hell to pay respects to the life of a lesbian. In fact, most of them would contend Felicity was already there, and they were trying to protect their own souls from any unexpected detours on the way to their own salvation.

I sat in my seat, numb, and to be honest, I did not collect much of the seven-minute presentation from the funeral director. I noticed more along the way of details regarding his bad toupee than I did the presentation of Felicity's life in his one-size-fits-all eulogy, where he spoke NOT a bit of relevant truth in regards to the woman I knew.

Eventually, I turned the bulk of my attention to the man who sat in front of me, with a head shaped like a bowling ball, balding on top in the curve of a U. Small patches of salt-and-pepper hair made their way graciously around the sides of his head. *He is a withering man*, I thought to myself, *who seems small in his presentation.* I noticed the colors of his jacket and the width of his lapel, which indicated that his suit was outdated by years on top of years. His dress shoes, probably his best shoes, were scuffed and scratched on the sides, and his pants resembled what a child would tease and make fun of and call *flood waters.*

Perhaps he was the one decent citizen in a town that bled no mercy for a lost one of their own. And even though they would cry out in the midnight hour that she belonged not to them, she had come from Shreveport's womb, so to Shreveport, she would always belong. As did I, but I just gave a shit less about it than she did.

He was calm in demeanor and passive in presence. He did not look up or around, just sat still and stared straight ahead at the beautiful, enlarged photo of Felicity, boasting her glorious smile.

Life was just too big to die.

Too goddamned big not to be anymore.

And this was my conversation with God, because it didn't matter what the good people of Shreveport thought; I knew within my bones that God didn't work like that.

She's still got to exist somewhere.

As the service concluded, the funeral director nodded and said, "Take your time, folks," before making a quick exit to catch lunch, which he purchased just off to the left of the funeral parlor, where a taco catering truck was awaiting his patronage. His stomach had been grumbling with the sound of thunder all seven minutes of his sorry-ass service.

I just shook my head in apology to Miss Felicity. *These have got to be the tackiest motherfuckers on the face of the planet*, I thought.

The man in front of me stood and turned around, and it seemed only right that we speak and acknowledge each other by shaking hands. When his eyes met mine, my hand almost dropped to the floor, right alongside my jaw. His piercing green eyes were ones that I knew.

I knew him.

Very well.

"My name is Buck," he said quietly, extending a hand.

I was barely able to return the shake. "Blaze," I said, almost floored as we proceeded to stare at each other. And though neither of us had ever met before this day, it was obvious by all accounts that we knew who the other was. He knew I was her lover. And I knew that once upon a time, she had been his lover by force. I knew not what to say.

It was one of the moments where words were an unworthy symbol to express whatever it was that either of us would dare speak into existence.

"I have to be honest with you, sir," I said. "I don't know whether to embrace you or pull out my pocketknife and slit your ugly throat."

He looked at me, guilty by the confession of his eyes. And with that, I was prompted to say, "Perhaps I should ask the Good Lord what I've come to know about in this lifetime—to have mercy on your wretched soul."

He looked down, but again, there were no words.

What in God's name could he say?

"I didn't remember your name," I said to him, "only your deeds." And still, his head was low as his eyes filled with tears, and one by one, they began to spill out upon the floor. It was in this moment that I saw what most will never see—human remorse taking form, right before my eyes. He began to weep as inconsolably as a newborn baby with colic, and painfully so. I could not help but to reach out and extend myself by wrapping my arms around this pedophile, child rapist, molester, and thief of all that had been innocent, Buck Hardaway, Felicity's father. I held him for a moment in my arms, because I do believe that is what God would do—not a Christian, *but God.*

Chapter 30

A Pusher

The next morning, I was awakened by a strong steady knock at the front door. I was passed out on the bed in between altered states of consciousness searching for Felicity in a dream.

Knock.

Knock.

As usual, I awoke with a break in my heart, pining for the love of Felicity Hardaway. But there would be no time to wallow in pity, at least for this moment, because the knock on the front door came again, this time harder and with a much greater force. It came with an urgent calling to be answered.

Knock.

Knock.

I quickly roused myself awake and sluggishly made tracks to the front door, where I saw the silhouette of two shadowy figures. Slowly, I answered because I knew that eventually I would someday answer the door and meet them *both* again. But I had hoped, as I had always hoped, that it would be on my terms. As I opened the door, there stood the past *and* the unfinished business of my life, Aliyah James Willow and Aerial James.

"Blaze." Aerial spilled from the doorstep with tears in her eyes.

I felt pleasantly detached, though I did feel a hint of affection for her. The remote feelings drew deep upon what I had loved of Aerial from childhood, prior to the loss of all that made us ourselves.

I had not seen her since I was thirteen years old, and time had done better by her than I had expected. For it did appear that she had undergone several more surgeries in the advancement of curing the scars from her face. *Willow's money has come in handy*, I thought in observation. I wanted to break down and weep when I saw her, giving way to vulnerability and relief. My life had come full circle, and my twin had returned to me, in much kinder spirits than our last meeting, it did appear.

Aliyah James looked as well kept as she always did, pristine in appearance and immaculate in the conception of her flourishing image. "May we come in?" she asked, rather formal in her presentation.

I said nothing, only opened the door wide in acceptance. They entered, slowly passing me in deep inspection as they searched my exterior walls for flesh wounds. "You won't find them there," I told them.

"What?" asked Aerial, slightly confused.

"My battle scars," I said. "You won't find them on the outside."

They did not respond, only stared as I closed the door tightly behind them. They stood like strangers not knowing what to do or where to sit.

"There's only one couch," I said, pointing to the sofa. "Feel free to make yourselves a part of it."

They slowly walked to the used and tattered piece of furniture and sat down stiffly, like statues, as though the couch might actually *bite* them or spoil their fine apparel if they were not careful.

Aristocrats.

Or better yet, *snobs*. Even Aerial, the burn victim, had grown into a snob. They were both dressed very well, in the manner in which wealthy people tend to dress. Aliyah wore a two-piece skirt suit, and Aerial wore a two-piece pantsuit. They were matching aristocrats, both wearing crème colors and both made of fine linen. Aliyah's hair was swept into an updo, and Aerial's hair hung down to the middle of her back. I was deeply impressed at how well modern medicine was able to put Humpty Dumpty back together again. Aerial's disfigurement looked minimal, in comparison to how she appeared last time I saw her. In fact, she looked almost *human* now, wearing fancy hair, fine linen, and attractive makeup.

"We heard about what happened to Felicity Hardaway," said Aliyah, her voice trailing off into silence. She could not even bear to say the words. Tears swelled in my eyes, as the "subject matter" itself was difficult for me to digest. I was still in the raw, sensitive stage. "We send our condolences to her family," concluded Aliyah.

"She didn't have any family. I was her family," I blurted before quickly changing subjects. "Do you want some juice?" This switch rather surprised them, and they shot eyes to each other as I continued. "Orange juice, apple juice, carrot juice, lime . . ." I said quietly.

"Water would be nice," said Aliyah.

"Yes, water," agreed Aerial.

I walked into the kitchen and retrieved their request. As I stood at the refrigerator pouring water, I don't know why, but I felt an overwhelming urge to fill the glasses sky high, then run into the living room and dump it over the top of their heads, ice cold and wretched against their skin, causing them to yelp like small, wet dogs. I don't know why I fantasized about being so cruel, other than the fact that I viewed them as hypocrites to come here when I knew that they deeply disapproved of our relationship, especially Aliyah James. I could not bite my tongue from the expression of my own displeasure of their hypocrisy.

Or could I?

"Thank you," said Aliyah with such eloquence when I gave her the water.

She responded with such gratitude, it was as if I had poured her a hundred-dollar glass of champagne. *Hell*, I thought, *it's only a cheap-ass glass of tap water over ice. You'll be lucky if you don't die in your sleep from the raging bacteria contained within it.* I sat across from them and stared and waited. I knew they had come here for a reason, and I was preparing for the bullshit.

"You look good," I said to Aerial.

"Thank you," she said with a tender smile.

"So," I asked, "what did you end up doing with your life, Aerial?" I asked with obvious exaggeration in my voice. "Did you become something grand with Willow's money at your feet?"

"Blaze," cautioned Aliyah.

"I'm a student at UCSB," she responded. "University of California—Santa Barbara. I'm studying to become a teacher."

"Of course," I said, "I should have guessed—something noble . . ."

She lowered her head almost in shame, because she knew as well as I that her life's direction was heavily influenced (*translation: dictated*) by the command of Aliyah James. And seeing as how she was dressed so nicely, I had no doubt that rich rewards and heavy bonuses were distributed in direct correlation to the obedience she displayed.

"And how is your doting husband?" I asked Aliyah with a smile. I could almost see her blood boil beneath the sarcasm of my words, and it did give me pleasure.

In that moment, Aliyah and Aerial exchanged looks. I came to realize they were very good at communicating entire blocks of thought in a single, purposeful glance.

"So," I said rather flatly, "let's get on with it."

"Get on with it?" asked Aliyah, taken aback by my rather direct approach.

"I'm sure you didn't fly all the way across the country for a glass of chlorinated tap water, did you?"

"Blaze," said Aliyah, leaning in toward me, "we want you to come home."

I was silent.

"What are you going to do—stay *here*?" she asked with heavy reservation, looking around the room in judgment.

"What's wrong with *here*?" I asked, looking into her eyes and uppity stance. "Is it worse than being *there*?"

"I do believe it is," said Aerial as smugly as her mother would have said it.

"How will you continue to support yourself?" injected Aliyah.

"I've done all right up till now," I said with fierce determination.

"But now you're alone," said Aerial, "and you don't have to be. You have *us*."

I laughed out loud a bit, then dropped my voice. "Forgive my brutal honesty," I said, "but I'd rather be alone."

"You're so goddamned stubborn," said Aliyah James, sliding her expensive gloves over her hands, which captured the essence of her rich, snobby appearance. "Let's go, Aerial." And with that, they both stood at once, but I remained seated, as I saw no need or purpose in getting riled up. "You haven't changed a bit," said Aliyah to me, shaking her head.

"Now, why would I do that?" I asked, finally standing up. "It would be so out of character."

"Why did you cut your hair off?" she asked, looking so beside herself. "It was *so* beautiful."

"Beauty has more than one look, Mrs. Willow," I said with words that were so sharp they probably punctured a lung.

"You've thrown your life away up to this point," she insisted, "but you're young enough to get it back."

"And how would you know that?" I asked.

"How would I know about throwing my life away?" she asked, so prepared to give me her ready-made speech on the rags-to-riches story of a poor Southern Negro woman.

"No," I interrupted her, "not throwing it away—*getting it back*." Her face twisted with displeasure, and Aerial's eyes widened at the insinuation.

"I don't see your point," said Aliyah ruthlessly.

"Exactly," I said, "and that *is* my point."

"I'm interested in what's best for you," she said harshly.

"You're interested in what's best for *you*," I clarified, "and, as usual . . . that has nothing to do with *me*."

"You are the most ungrateful—" she started.

"Why don't you save it, Aliyah James?" I snapped. "Save your charity work for one of your causes. I'm not it. I don't need your pity, your sympathy, your guilt, or whatever synthetic emotion you're manufacturing in this very moment. I've had my fill, really I have, and I'm not in the market for a pusher today. So, please, take this drama to another stage for production."

Aerial shook her head in disbelief.

"I've just lost the love of my life," I said quietly, "and frankly, I just don't have the energy for the theatrics, so, if you'll excuse me," I said, dismissing myself from their presence and going into the bedroom, where I shut the door and left them standing alone with my words. I had no regret for my dissertation. I left them there to be with themselves, which probably seemed like an empty venture in and of itself. They could be cohesively bound together in all of their aloneness.

Two empty vessels pretending to be full.

Good-bye, Aliyah James.

Good-bye, Aerial James.

Felicity would be so proud.

Chapter 31

In the Heart

I knew the day would come when I would have to leave Felicity's house. It came sooner than later, as she was already several months behind on her mortgage at the time of her death, and I did not have the funds to keep the household going. What was left of my meager monies dwindled in the aftermath of the accident, and I was no longer accepting funds from Aliyah James. Actually, she was no longer sending money to me, so it worked out just fine. It was a mutual stance of stubbornness of one bull-headed person to another.

Down to my last $300, I packed up all of our things and gave a local charity the bulk of Felicity's personal belongings. It felt like a separation at the hip and a pulling apart of something priceless, saying good-bye to all of her belongings as they were loaded upon an impersonal truck and hauled away to share with strangers, people who did not know her at all. I could not keep the bulk of her belongings, for it would serve only to make my load heavier, and by now, trust me, it was heavy enough. Upon clearing out the house, I did one more walk-through and bid farewell to the end of innocence. I would leave the unpretentious, raw and honest lifestyle of a Southern lesbian and head out into the "real world," so to speak, and make a go of it.

But where would I go?
Back home.

Again?

It was Nathaniel's house, which sat upon my land. It was the sacred and holy ground that we lived upon and ultimately died upon. I slowly walked up the pleasant walkway and stood on the welcome mat with one large suitcase. I simply stared at the word **WELCOME**.

"Welcome," I whispered. "I wonder if he still means it."

I knocked lightly and waited with a heavy heart. Eventually, Nathaniel opened the door, and it was déjà vu, happening all over again as I stood on the welcome mat, looking down. "Those words still mean something?" I asked, pointing to his **WELCOME** on the mat. "Can I come in?"

He did not speak, simply opened his door wide, extending himself, and I entered. Once inside, I stood awkwardly in the center of his floor.

"Have a seat," he suggested.

"Thank you," I said, walking stiffly to his couch, where I sat down. He sat across from me, looking about as uncomfortable as I did. Perhaps it was bizarre to return to Nathaniel's house, and maybe I shouldn't have. Maybe it was wrong to regurgitate the past. "I'm sorry about your . . ." he said with pause, "*friend.*"

I nodded.

He looked away for fear that I would see just how much he had retained his "like" of me, which he had, and of course I saw. It was obvious as it flowed through him in full capacity.

"You moving on?" he asked, looking at my suitcase.

"Yes," I said, nodding quietly, "just wanted to say good-bye."

"Oh," he replied, "okay."

"Well," I said, standing up in such a hurry that he stood up with me, "guess I better be going."

"Okay," he said with a polite nod. "You okay?"

"Yes," I said, "why wouldn't I be okay?" And before I could finish the question, I burst into tears, sobs, wails, and, moaning, I fell to the floor, covering the top part of my face with my hands. And Nathaniel took to great concern, which was reflected through his eyes as he moved close to me and poured himself around me in the fashion of a human cloak, shielding and covering me. It was the first set of human arms that would embrace my pain since Felicity's passing. It was the first set of hands I would allow to touch the deep well of my sorrow. It was the first bond of affection I would accept. It was the first stirring of compassion that I would entertain. It was the first of what would become the *first* of many with Nathaniel and me. And this is where my life would undergo a rebirth, and the old would pass away like the dying husk of a freshly grown ear of corn that was destined to shuffle off its outer layer to make room for growth. And it was time for the regeneration of all that had withered and perished in the harsh season of unforgiveness.

"I would like you to stay," he said to me that morning.

I did not respond, simply nodded in acceptance. I would stay because here is where it felt like healing would take place, and here I did return to be healed.

Nathaniel stayed with me the entire day, and we slept, laughed, and sometimes, I cried. He and entertained ourselves as though we were the only two people in the world. In fact, it felt very much like we were. And from time to time, I made my way to the front window and stared out longingly across the way, and four houses down. On one such occasion, Nathaniel came and stood beside me, and also looked upon Felicity's house, which bore a **REDUCED TO SALE** sign in the front yard, courtesy of the bank that had foreclosed upon the tiny piece of property. "What do you see?" he asked, looking at me as I stared at the house across the street.

"My past," I said without emotion.

"And how does it feel?" he prodded further.

"Old," I said flatly before moving away from the window and to the table where Nathaniel had prepared our supper. He was an extraordinary cook, and his meals were always prepared, not only with the best of seasonings, but also in the season of love. His eyes danced a radiant flame every time he cast them in my direction, and as we sat at the table, I began to feel weighted by his heavy stare.

Why can't he stop looking at me? I thought to myself, but no longer did I wish to ponder this within the confines of my own head, so I spilled it out to him.

"Why can't you stop looking at me?" I inquired of him directly, which threw off his gaze in that moment, forcing him to look away.

"I don't know," he said shyly.

"I'm curious," I said. "I want to know why you stare."

He smiled, and he was such a beautiful man that when he did smile, his beauty rippled through his expression and beyond. Any woman, no, every woman, could appreciate the beauty of Nathaniel Wheaton. And as I had always thought, had I not been a "certified lesbian," perhaps I would have been more inspired by what my eyes beheld, but my heart was in no position to pay it any mind.

"I see *you*," he said, fluttered with emotion.

"And who am I?" I asked him.

"Well," he said, rather uncertainly, "that would seem best answered by you."

"Obviously," I said in my matter-of-fact voice, "you know that I'm a lesbian?"

And with that, he nearly choked on his pork chop. "Yes," he replied, "I heard rumors . . . but I never expected you to up and admit it."

"Why?" I asked. "Did you expect that I would lie to you or hold off on telling you the truth?"

"Neither, I guess," he said, drinking a whole lot of Kool-Aid to cover his unease. "Just didn't expect to have a conversation about it."

"It would make things easier, Nathaniel," I said, "if people told the truth. Most people never speak their real mind, which is probably their right mind, because they can't bear to hold themselves up under the weight of what other people think about them. Now, how much good sense does that make?" I asked.

"Not much, I reckon," he said.

"Exactly."

"I like you 'cause you're different," he said, then shifted his eyes elsewhere lest he have to hold the honesty of my stare. "You seem like you don't follow anybody's way; you just make your own. That's different. Maybe that's why your mama named you Blaze—you make new paths in life."

"I like that just fine," I said with a smile.

Nathaniel smiled again and nodded. I looked at him and wondered how such a handsome man with a decent-wage earning job and his own piece of property could still be single amidst all those desperate women with sticky hands trying to snatch up a husband into their back pocket. "How old are you?" I asked.

"Twenty-six," he said, proudly beaming, as though he had lived a million years plus some. "And you?" he asked.

"Twenty-one," I said with equal pride, and knowing that I *had* lived a million years plus some. "Where's your wife at?"

His eyes widened like fine china dinner plates. "Wife?" he asked, confused.

"Wife," I repeated loudly. "You ain't gay, are you?"

"Of course not," he regurgitated, stuttering and stammering all over the place.

"Well," I said, "I never see you keep the company of any women around here."

He frowned on the heels of my last statement and replied in his defense, "Most of the city women come wearing a tag on the front of their aprons—it says *buyer beware*."

I burst into laughter. "Nathaniel Wheaton, you are some kind of retarded."

He laughed, too, because it was funny. "I don't know," he said with a smile, "seems like most of the women in this town seem to be interested in catching me, instead of *knowing* me. And seeing as how I don't see myself as a wild animal or something in need of being caught, I keep mostly to myself."

Actually, it made good logic what he said, so I nodded in acceptance of his argument. I was fast coming to realize, as I had always known, that I did adore this young man, Nathaniel Wheaton. I liked his good heart. In fact, his sympathetic spirit poured itself out all over this kitchen, right down to the mashed potatoes and pork chops he had made us for dinner.

He was a gentle beauty, and with him, I felt comfortable, so comfortable in fact, I would be utterly shocked with the next set of words that came out of my mouth. I was unpredictable at best, even to myself at times.

"Are you a virgin?" I asked him.

And with that, his mashed potatoes left his mouth and landed on the table, with apologies, of course. "I'm sorry," he said quickly, wiping the spill.

"A virgin?" I repeated.

"No, I'm not," he said rather unconvincingly.

I started to laugh. "As beautiful of a man as you are, you've never been with a woman?"

"Of course I have," he said, his voice rising an octave or two.

"Pity," I said, shaking my head.

By now, he had started shoving food in his mouth to avoid the uncomfortable topic of his virginity. And again I laughed and removed my dinner plate from the table and put it in the sink, as I was finished for the evening. On my way out of the kitchen, I leaned into him and kissed his forehead gently.

"You are one of the most innocent spirits I've ever known," I said to him as his eyes closed and his long eyelashes blinked against my skin. I kissed his forehead again, and I could feel the heat rise from his body. He laid his head against my chest, where it would rest a beat before he looked up and kissed my cheek.

It felt nice.

It felt human.

So I kissed him back. And ultimately, our lips touchd again and again, and our lips locked, intertwined with each other's. His breathing increased till the point where he almost started to pant, and I could tell that he was reaching a peak of excitement. His heart was beating out of his chest, and the extremities of his limbs felt *very* hot. I liked it because I wanted to be close to someone, but it did not feel the same as it did with Felicity. It did not feel as natural, or as organic, but it did feel human, and I wanted so desperately to feel human. Within moments, he had led me to his bed, where I stared at it momentarily, pondering whether or not I was willing to lay with him.

Should I?

Shouldn't I?

Would I?

Wouldn't I?

I looked into his eyes, and I knew how much he wanted to be with me. I knew how much he longed for it. He ached for it in the same way that I had longed for Felicity. So I surrendered, letting go and allowing myself the privilege of loving him right here, right now. And though I did not love him at all, I liked him enough to pretend that in this moment, love was a conceivable option between us.

He kneeled at my feet and took my hand in his and began to mumble words, but he uttered passages I would not allow him to finish.

"No," I whispered. I did not want to hear his words, nor did I want a verbal covenant between him and myself. I did not want to breathe something into life that one of us would be forced to honor in the morning. It was for all intents and purposes *temporary*, our arrangement, and it was not meant to last forever or any longer than beyond now. But that's how ALL great relationships come into being; they start off in a moment that seems to bleed its way into eternity. And as he laid me down gently upon his bed and began to caress and fondle my body with great pleasure, I was indeed surprised that I was able to produce vaginal grease between my legs that would allow him easy entry, though not the *easiest* of entries, as I was myself a virgin when it came to the direct experience of intercourse. I had never been penetrated by Felicity.

I gasped in between a breath, or moaned twice after the fact, and he stopped instantly. "Did I hurt you?" he asked.

"No," I said.

"Are you sure?" he questioned further.

"Yes," I said, annoyed.

"Then what was the sound that you made?" he queried.

"*Pleasure*, retard," I said with a laugh, and he laughed also, and it eased the awkwardness of us. We were two virgins who lost ourselves in each other, flesh against flesh, heartbeat against heartbeat.

When he began to run his kisses along the side of my neck, at first I pulled back, squeamish. For it did feel rather odd for a man to kiss me with such intimate intention and direction.

"Are you okay?" he asked, feeling my withdrawal, weighing heavy on top of me as he straddled me.

"Yes," I said.

And then he kissed me again, but it didn't feel good. Didn't feel good at all.

"Are you okay?" he repeated

And this time I responded, "No."

He stopped and rolled off of me and onto his back, where he spent the next five minutes in silence staring at the ceiling. I laid down beside him, also staring at the ceiling.

I sighed deeply, taking in a giant gust of air. It was exhausting being me, a lesbian who in the blink of an eye opted out of the lesbian lifestyle in exchange for a "normal life." As far as I could see thus far, normalcy was highly overrated.

He was so beautiful, that perhaps I should have enjoyed it more, but I just wasn't *into* it like he was. His craftily sculpted frame and masculine body bulging with muscle and vigor did little to entice me in the direction of physical stimulation.

"I'm sorry," he said, staring at the ceiling.

"For what?" I asked, puzzled.

"Being a guy instead of a girl," he said with laugh.

"If you were really sorry," I said sarcastically, "you'd cut your dick off to appease me."

He sat up in bed and looked at me in fictitious horror.

"Of course you know I'm kidding!" I spat.

"No, I'm serious," he said earnestly. "I wanted you to like it."

"Who says I didn't like it?" I asked with a frown.

"Did you?" he asked with a smile.

"No," I said, "but it had nothing to do with you."

He lowered his head, disheartened. "What does it have to do with?" he asked.

"Me," I said. "I'm a lesbian, Nate."

"What made you a lesbian?" he asked.

"I don't know," I said, frustrated.

"Were you born like that?" he asked with an innocent query.

"I don't know," I said in a huff.

"When did it start?" he asked.

"You talk about it like it's some kind of disease I picked up along the way," I said, getting up off the bed.

"I don't mean to be ignorant," he said, coming up behind me like a little scolded boy. "I just wanna understand."

"What do you want to understand, Nate?" I shouted.

"You," he said with such a sincere appeal that it would be difficult for me to stay angry with him and because he was so dog-gone cute.

"Why are you so obsessed with me?" I asked.

"I'm not obsessed," he said. "I just think you're the most beautiful woman I have ever laid eyes on." There were tears in his naked eyes. "And I would do *anything* on earth to . . ." His voice trailed off.

"To what?" I inquired, because I had to know what he dared not finish.

Silence.

Silence.

Silence.

"To what, Nate?" I asked.

"To change your mind about me," he said quietly.

And with that, I felt a surrender of compassion toward him, and I gently reached for his hand and laid it against my chest.

"It's not in my mind," I whispered. "It's in my heart, Nate."

Chapter 32

Loner

And into my heart Nathaniel would find his way. It would not be a traditional love affair with stars and stripes, fireworks, and multiple orgasms. No, instead it would be a quiet friendship with kindness, respect, and adoration. And it would be he who would adore me in a way that I had never known.

In years past, I had not allowed someone to care for me so thoroughly and completely as he did, and so unconditionally without receiving like for like in return. He would not receive from the depth of what he gave, though I would sincerely make every effort known to man to offer him such. I would give as much as a lesbian could; therefore, we continued to make love to each other, but it was more along the lines of a friendship gesture on my part, versus a means of sexual gratification. It was my way of saying, *Thank you for the camaraderie.* It was his way of saying, *God, I love you so much, Blaze James, that when you step out of the room, the air is sucked out and I can't breathe!*

Needless to say, we were NOT on the same page as lovers. And I knew that we never would be. After all, I was gay and he was straight. This made for the most unusual coupling.

But Nathaniel would find his way into my heart, because there was a gap as wide as the New York skyline, in the place where Felicity once lived. She remained there, too, but her occupied room had to be economized and scaled down to size to make room for healing, lest I be able to go on with my life in the wake of her death. Otherwise, I would have shriveled into nothingness in the absence of her presence in my world, staring out of Nathaniel's front window for what seemed like hours each day, eyeing Felicity's empty house void of life and love. It had all died now, so in a miraculous kind of way, Nathaniel Wheaton saved my life and had conveniently managed to sweep up all the scattered pieces of my sanity upon Felicity's passing and glue them back together again.

It all seemed a perfect arrangement till the morning I threw up on the bathroom floor.

"Are you okay?" asked Nate with great concern.

"Fine," I said, "just need to lie down. I feel queasy."

"Okay," he said, helping me back to bed.

And it is there I would stay for days on end, throwing up each morning and each night like clockwork, and battling the most heavy burden of fatigue I had ever known.

"Blaze, what's going on?" he finally asked after day four, or maybe five.

"I don't know," I said, curled up in a ball on the bed. "Feel like I got the worst kind of food poisoning that just won't go away."

He looked at me long and hard. "Uh-oh," he said.

"Uh-oh, what?" I asked.

"Your face is shining," he observed.

"It's dehydration," I insisted.

"No," he said, "you look pregnant."

"Pregnant!" I snapped. "You're out of your mind."

"No," he mumbled, "I don't think so."

Within thirty minutes, I had sent him quickly to the local market to purchase a home pregnancy test. And in great angst, I peed on a strip of nothing and waited for something to give me a verdict on the rest of my life. It took three minutes to obtain the results. It was the longest three minutes the universe had ever recorded from here to infinity.

And the test would scream out loud, *Positive*.

That means yes.

That means hell yes.

"Oh God," I said, throwing up again, right on top of the bed. I don't remember much about the rest of the afternoon except Nate trying to talk over my loud sobs.

"Blaze," he said, "I'm not upset. I'm so happy!"

Of course, I thought to myself, *why wouldn't he be?* He was in love with me. But as for me, this was temporary, remember? A baby seemed some kind of permanent to me.

I loved Nate, truly I did, but in a favorite-stuffed-animal kind of way, not in a let's-make-a-baby-and-stay-connected-at-the-hip-forever kind of way. One way felt sweet and endearing, whereas the other felt like a violent hostage takeover.

"Blaze," he said, on his knees, "I want you to have my baby." I looked at him, numb, but there were no words to say. "Are you sad it's mine?" he asked.

"No," I said, "I'm not sad that it's yours, but I am devastated that it's *not* Felicity's. And I don't know how NOT to feel that, Nathaniel. It's who I am. I been telling you that the whole time."

There was nothing to say on the heels of those words.

What could he possibly say to me in that moment? *I'm sorry. I didn't realize you were serious about being a lesbian?*

What could he possibly say to me now?

Silence.

Silence.

"Let's get married," he spilled out of his mouth, splattering the words hard onto the ground, where they would lay dismantled. I should have imagined he would come up with something grand and borderline horrific to fill in the gaps of silence.

Shit.

"Surely you're not thinking of . . . ," he said, hinting around the devastation of a purposeful termination.

I shook my head for all the wrong reasons, not because I had a problem with it at all, but because I felt that he had been too kind to me that I should slap him in the face and bring his empire down by taking his namesake out. I felt that would have been a direct statement saying, *Your seed ain't worth a shit*, and I just couldn't do that to him. I loved him too much as my friend, and as much as it was breaking me down, I didn't have the heart to suck this fetus out of me, though God and every angel watching knows for sure that was my most sincere intention, and to hell with what the Christians thought, 'cause they didn't know my life like I did.

They didn't know my life.

"You're going to have it, right, Blaze?" he asked, scared to death that I would say no.

"Of course I am, Nate," I said. "After all, that's what friends are for."

Fuck.

I should have stayed a loner.

Chapter 33

Bystander

Nathaniel Wheaton and I married eight months later in a civil ceremony. I waddled into the county courthouse and said, "I do." And even though the bootleg minister mentioned something in his presentation about "till death do us part," I felt like saying, *Now, let's not get carried away with ourselves, 'cause I just might outlive all these bullshit promises I'm about to make in here today.*

I was dressed in a simple maternity dress and beamed with the glowing radiance of cellulite, which was spreading like wildfire on the back of my thighs. Between that and the unnatural sensation of having to pee every two seconds, I was hard pressed to locate the sunny side of my natural disposition, which was getting shadier and shittier by the minute. In some ways, I felt like Nathaniel paid dearly to have this baby. And he would be called upon again and again to overlook my poor attitude and the constant complaints of this pregnancy's toll on my body.

He would cater to, bend around, lean into, and extend himself in every conceivable human way to accommodate my misery, without participating in it himself.

On our wedding day, Nathaniel was handsomely adorned in a navy blue suit. I have never seen him look so proud and smitten in all of his days. It was almost as if *this* moment was his greatest accomplishment in life. As for me, I felt removed from the details of it all. It seemed like a natural state to me these days. I didn't have to like it; I just had to show up and *look* like I liked it.

Everything was different now, but nothing had really changed. At last, my life looked normal to those around me, and the good people of Shreveport would find their way to forgiveness in the fact that now I looked like *them*—miserable. I was a common housewife whose womb carried the fruit of a new generation. I had a handsome husband with a good-paying job and a lovely home painted in pleasant colors and an attractive front lawn.

My husband went before me and nearly polished the concrete itself where I was to lay my next step down with my foot. And with that, every common housewife who took notice of his generosity silently envied me, but they did it out loud and with eager stares that lasted too long when they rested heavy eyes on Nate or cast eyes down toward me. After all, they had only *forgiven* that I was a lesbian, not forgotten it. And so here it was that I stood, taking a vow and making a promise upon ground as soft as sand. And all that I could do was pray that no wave would crash against this weak and brittle castle and damn it all to hell and wash it all away. And all that I could truly conceive upon this day was the fact that I missed Felicity Hardaway more than breath itself, and almost one year since her death, I questioned with feverish intensity whether or not I would *ever* get over her passing. All of the grand experiences that I was having with Nate—a wedding, a baby, decorating the baby's room, picking out a name, et cetera, et cetera, et cetera, I longed to have with *her* instead of him, because at least with her I would feel real in the experience, and not just a bystander.

I felt as vacant as my grandmother's old attic and, more, as though I had lent my womb for rent—one, for a man and his penis and, two, for a soul that wished itself to be born.

I was just an innocent bystander.

Our simple wedding ceremony was not attended by family or friends, because neither of us had much of either. I had not shared the news of my pregnancy or wedding with Aliyah James, lest she lose herself in dizzy joy that alas she had won, and I had decided to be boring, bland, and ordinary.

Nathaniel's only living relative was his mother, Savannah, who had been quietly tucked away from civilization in a lovely little mental institution in Camarillo, California. It's funny how this stuff never comes up till *after* the wedding date and just prior to an unexpected visit.

"My mother's coming for a visit," he said to me casually the morning after our wedding.

"Your mother?" I asked, for he had only spoken of her briefly before that moment, and only in reference to her being "tucked away in a nuthouse."

"Yes," he said, "she's been released."

"When is she coming?" I asked.

"About four minutes."

"Shit, Nate," I declared. "Is she stable?"

"Stable enough," he said, trying to duck and dodge as far as I was concerned.

"Stable enough to visit?" I inquired.

"Stable enough not to be locked up," he said faintly, "I guess."

"Goddammed it, Nate," I said, slamming my hands upon the table, which came on the heels of the doorbell ringing. I cut a pair of very unwelcoming eyes in his direction as he smiled shyly and excused himself from the breakfast table.

"Nate," I cautioned as he made his way to the door, "you know this is some bullshit!"

He opened the door, and two seconds later, a 400-pound white woman with rosy red cheeks, wearing a bleached-blond afro, was standing in our doorway.

"Nathaniel!" she screamed, bigmouthed and wide-eyed. She was wearing a polka-dotted moo moo and dirty, stained white sandals, bearing crusty, dry heels.

Holy Mother of God.

I never knew his mother was . . .

Crazy.

Fat.

And white.

Holy Mother of God, *I'm married to a white man.* Well, I guess that explains the blue eyes. This seemed in the moment a lot to spring on a woman on the water's edge of giving birth.

"Nathaniel David," she said, just as loud as the great outdoors as she waddled her way inside the house, tilting more than I did at nine months pregnant. He smiled and they embraced, till she peeked over her shoulder and saw me; then she burst into a cowl, a laugh, or something that scared the bonkers out of me, and I jumped as she ran over to me and scooped me up in her big flabby arms and filled me full of kisses and prickled my face from the sharp hairs on her chinny, chin, chin hair.

Shit.

"Good Lord," she yelled, rubbing on my tummy, "what are you giving birth to? A whale?" she hollered.

"Pardon?" I asked politely, shooting Nate death threats with my eyes over her left shoulder. "You're about the most beautiful thing I ever laid eyes on," she belted. "Bet my son has a good time with all of your goodies!" she cackled.

Okay.

So this is the crazy side of his family.

His only living relative . . .

Who happens to be the grandmother of our unborn child.

Later that night in bed, Nathaniel could read between the lines of my not-so-friendly thoughts.

"You all right?" he asked.

"No, I ain't all right," I said.

"What can I do to make it better?" he asked.

Bring me a life partner with a vagina, I wanted to say, but that may sound a bit outrageous at this point, in the production of it all. *In fact, just bring me Felicity. Drudge her up from the dead, if you have to. Wash her body ashore, and bring it to me at once.* I no longer wished to be normal. Normal was killing me, and it was a slow, painful death.

*   *   *

The next morning at 3:00 A.M., I gave birth to a beautiful baby boy, Nathaniel David Jr. As unpleasant as the pregnancy had been, Nathaniel Jr. was born with ease and a certain grace; more than likely, it was a pardon or favor from God. Nathaniel Sr. did little more than weep throughout the whole ordeal and alternated between tears and kisses to my forehead. His mother was also present for the birth—not in the room, but in the hospital, which was still too close for my liking.

The whole, big event lasted the sum of thirty-six hours, and then I was back at home again, a new wife and mother, balancing Nathaniel's obsession with the baby and trying to dodge sporadic and frequent visits from his obese mother.

I still had not alerted Aliyah or Aerial as to the recent developments in my world, but I felt no particular urge to do so. Even though this was Aliyah's grandson, I could not imagine that she would have been much more bonded with my child than she was with me.

"I love you so much," Nathaniel said to me the first night upon my arrival back home.

I did not have the strength to respond; not because I was weak, but because I had grown weary of pretending.

I did love him, but it was *not* the same. And it certainly was no match against his affection for me. It was very different indeed, and I was not sure how a free lesbian spirit could have possibly ended up being the housewife of a common man, with a torn pussy and a real, live breathing human being to take care of for the rest of her life.

Where?

And how?

And why?

And what the hell had happened to my life?

"Are you happy, Blaze?" he asked me directly, looking into my eyes. "I want to know the truth of you."

I did not answer, and he simply turned away, because he could not bear the truth of me in his heart, and he and I both knew it. He stood up from the bed, and in the center of our bedroom floor, he began to weep and mourn for what he always wanted us to be. "I love you so much," he said, "so, so much . . ."

"I know, Nate," I said quietly. "I have never doubted your love. It has been the force that has sustained me through what otherwise would have killed me. Let that be enough . . . let it be enough, Nate, please."

"I want to know *you* love *me* back," he said, looking deeply into my eyes while making an unfair search of my soul.

"You know that I do," I said. "I do, Nate."

"I want you to love me like you love *her*," he said with a bite in his voice.

I had never heard him sound so sharp and bitter in all of my days. I did not respond, because he knew that it was an impossibility. I had stretched my skin far enough in the believability of a make-believe life.

"I want it, Blaze!" he shouted. "Your love!"

I was startled and taken aback. He had never raised his voice or his temper in my direction. And it angered me greatly, because he had no living idea what I had sacrificed to play the part of a heterosexual woman with a husband and a kid. And what a part I had played for so long, a stranger in my own skin and on the outside looking in, wearing the wrong costume. How dare he demand anything else from me, as I sat erect and upright in this gigantic bed bleeding from a shredded vagina and peeing through stitches.

How dare he.

"Do not *ever* raise your voice to me," I said in a low, eerie but direct tone, "or I will walk out of that door, and you will never lay eyes on me again. Ever."

His eyes widened in fear at the mere thought of it.

"I gave you everything I have by way of love," I said, "and if I ain't gave it to you, then you shoulda been smart enough to figure it out by now, Nate—*I ain't got it to give*." And just like that, Nate was reduced from a grown man to a baby boy. And his newborn son, who was sleeping in a bassinet only six inches from our bed, began to stir, and it would only be seconds before the baby would begin to cry out desperately.

I got up out of the bed and stood in the center of the room with one eye on Nate and the other eye on his newborn son. In that moment, I could not distinguish which one was more helpless, and in an authentic appraisal of who needed me most, I exited the room and left the two of them to take care of each other.

Chapter 34

Black and White

In a million years I would have never imagined that within a six-week period of time, Nate Sr. would have sold the house right out from beneath my feet. But he did and he did it on a day when I was least expecting such a bold move from such a timid man.

We had thirty days in which to pack of all our belongings and move. But it would not be as if we had nowhere to go, for there was *always* somewhere to go. And for us, we were destiny bound for Providence, Rhode Island. It was the city that held Nate's lifelong dream of owning a tire store.

His plan fell into place rather quickly, and before I knew it, he was bringing home boxes by the oodles to pack away our things. As you can probably imagine, I did little by way of assistance to help in the process. But it did not deter Nate; it only made him more determined to move me away from the bond I still held with Felicity. And as I stood in the infamous picture window as I often did for hours each day, staring at Felicity's front door, I could feel the cool stare of Nathaniel Sr. as he watched from the other room.

He always watched, and though he said little most of the time, I could feel waves of his resentment. He longed to be the object of my affection and replace my gaze upon a dead piece of property and put it on him where he felt that it belonged. And this would be the demon he would battle each day in a desperate attempt to swindle me out of loving a ghost.

It used to bother me that he watched, because I could feel his silent judgment and deep longing for my affections, but it bothered me less and less each day. In some ways, I felt as though I had done my part to repay him for his kindness by giving him a son, a precious little boy to radiate back to him the perfection he sought in me.

Find it in your son, Nate.

Find it in your son.

It's there.

Blooming and crawling with life, bursting out of its edges, and awaiting your consumption.

In other words, back up off me and give me room to breathe and to grieve for Miss Felicity Hardaway and love her from this side of the grave.

Give me that, I wanted to tell him so often. *It's all I've truly ever wanted from you—that you would allow me to keep Felicity alive within me. It's all I've ever wanted, and in return, I would be willing to comply as I always did with your wishes to consume me.*

Each night upon his entry into bed, I would allow him access to my private chambers, where he would revel in great, untold pleasure. And how he loved to caress my skin and fondle my breasts. And how he adored the closeness of his face pressing against mine with such a vigor that it barely left enough air for consumption. And how he longed to dominate me, turning me over on my back and mounting me like a horse. He was so desperate to break, bend, and command me into loving him. He would pry apart my legs with such desperation, it was as though he could not wait to enter me and give me something that Felicity simply could not.

His manhood.

He wanted me every night, and most nights I surrendered, with the exception of the nights that I was bleeding, and dear God how I awaited each month with an eager joy for menstruation, because in my own season of blood, I found peace from his constant consumption.

"What are you going to do without your precious window?" he asked with a hint of sarcasm in the background of my shadow as I stared quietly through the glass one morning before the sun had come up.

I always found my way to the window before dawn, for it was then that I could feel the deepest well of Felicity's presence. It was as though she roamed the earth before the sun came up so that she could wander peacefully, before man's ignorance could soar to its peak in the waking hours.

"Why does it bother you so, Nate?" I asked with my arms crossed against my chest and all of my attention fully focused elsewhere.

"It doesn't," he said. "I just wondered what you'll do to fill your time when you no longer have the front door of a dead woman to keep you company."

"This is tiring," I said to him. "Isn't it?" He did not respond. "Aren't you tired of being jealous of a ghost, Nate?" I asked.

"That's just it, Blaze," he said. "She's not dead to you. She lives *between* you and I—a dead woman separates the living. Don't you find that insane?"

"Do you know what I find insane?" I asked him. "If GOD allows me the freedom to be in my own head and think my own thoughts, then why can't you? Are you greater than God, Nate?"

"It's not right, Blaze," he declared. "It's not right."

"What's wrong?" I asked him.

"That you love a dead woman more than your own newborn son."

"Don't you do dare go there," I warned.

"It's true," he snapped. "You spend hours tending to that window. What about your son?"

"What about *your* son?" I asked him.

"I take care of him more than you, Blaze," he retorted.

"Good, then you'll deserve all of the fine praise that he'll give you for raising him up to be such a fine young man."

"I never realized how stubborn and arrogant you were," he declared, "how grand and special you think yourself to be!"

"You only see me that way because you can't have me, Nate," I said, "not in the way that you want me."

"You don't care about anybody but yourself!" he shouted.

"Who better to care about me than myself?" I asked. In that moment the baby began to cry from the other room, and for a beat of time, neither of us moved. I glanced in the direction of the commotion and then cut sharp eyes back to him.

"Your son is calling," I said quietly.

He looked at me with an exasperated expression upon his face before exiting in a huff to go and care for our son. And the second he stepped away, I returned my attention back to the window.

He was right.

I did give more attention to a dead woman than to my own living son. I was in no position to argue that against him, because I knew it to be a truth.

I gave Nathaniel Wheaton a son. *I did not want one.* I merely allowed my womb to be used as a passageway for entry. Now, do you expect me to feel cozy toward such a proposal? It was my love offering, a noble suggestion. Condemn me to hell for that if you wish, but it was my truth. It was my God's honest truth. And it was as real as the blood that poured through my veins and the H_2O that watered down my cells. It was as pure as the breath that exhaled from my nostrils and the waste I excreted from my bowels. And I had lived against this truth for so long, I could barely recognize its colors anymore.

What *is* the color of our truths, and do they fade in time if we deny their existence? Ultimately, do they end up bleeding into the background of a life that is washed up and dried out, till one day our whole world is a lifeless shade of black and white, where color lives no more?

Then tell me, how do you see a rainbow?

Chapter 35

Skin

Twelve Months Later

Rhode Island is the smallest state in the United States of America, and from the day we hit its doorstep, I felt squeezed down to size. It was almost as if I had taken it upon myself to open a bottle of ketchup, turn around, and smash my ass down into its narrow neck. I felt as though my butt was stuck in the middle of the bottle and my legs were dangling at the sides.

We settled into Providence after an exhaustive search for the perfect house, which of course Nate found on a beautiful, quiet residential street filled with charming homes and Kodak-captioned families.

Everyone was white and well educated.

Everyone had 2.5 kids.

Everyone had a white picket fence, a working doorbell, a golden retriever named Molly, a cleaning lady named Maria, a gardener named Jesus, and a minivan named Dodge.

Most of the women on my block were housewives who cooked seventeen-course meals every night just for the hell of it, and I bet every one of them offered their fat husbands sex upon command.

We fit in every well.

Nate's Tires was doing amazingly well, and he had captured

most of the competitor's business in and around the surrounding cities.

We had a bit of money coming in, and I could purchase just about everything I wanted. The only thing was, I didn't want anything but Felicity Hardaway.

We were upper-class black folks, and if the picture-perfect Caucasian neighborhood was to be sprinkled with bits of color, it would be the finest assortment.

A handsome stud.

Beautiful girl.

Gorgeous baby.

And perfect home.

It was a wretched lifestyle indeed, and if you thought I was a miserable little bitch in Shreveport, you could not have begun to imagine my mood in Providence, which lingered between mania, depression, hysteria, and downright schizo-mother-fucking-phrenia. And still, through it all, Nathaniel Wheaton would continue to love me as though I were the last breathing mammal on earth.

I continued to mourn for my beloved Felicity, and in this house I would find a new window to search for her soul. It had become our bedroom window, which fell into a sprawling, green backyard, and every time I looked upon the rolling hills of our spacious residence, I would capture her life in my breath. And though I grieved her absence in silence, Nate could always hear the silent doldrums of my heart, though he had long given up responding to their sound.

"Babe," he said one evening at the dinner table, "I bought a present for you today."

"Really?" I asked with little interest.

"You can go and pick it up tomorrow morning," he suggested, "if you'd like."

"I'd rather go tonight," I said almost desperately. "I could use some fresh air."

The days were spent in solitary confinement in the house taking care of an active one-year-old, who was just beginning to walk, see things, and study them with amazement by putting them into his mouth. It was an exhaustive endeavor, scrutinizing his activity.

"Okay," he said, staring at me with a peculiar look. "You all right?"

"Fine," I responded quickly, "just need to get out and breathe—Nate Jr. has been really cranky today, and I just need some air."

"I was hoping we could spend the evening together," he said with a pleading edge on his voice, but my displeasure only reflected back to him a sour expression upon my face. "But," he said, caving in, "if you need the air . . ."

"Thank you," I said without further ado, snatching my purse and keys from the table. He looked at me as if to say, *Hot damn, can't you even wait till I have swallowed my last bite of mashed potatoes?*

"Where am I going?" I asked him with a gigantic smile.

He slowly handed me a card. It was an antique jewelry store not far from the house. He had handed me the card with a hint of sadness, because he so desperately wanted my participation in this marriage. He would give and give and give, till he had no more of himself to give, and then he would buy *things* to replace what he could no longer provide by way of heart space. At only twenty-nine years of age, he had already begun to show signs of aging. His love, affection, desperation, and fondness for me had begun to send tiny wrinkles to his brow.

He could have purchased the item and brought it home for me to see, but he had long since stopped setting himself up for disappointment, because I always responded so ordinary to things that were so extraordinary.

I kissed him and the baby on the cheek and bolted out the door as though I had just received the governor's pardon.

I jumped in my car and sped off down the perfect little block, which open curtains revealed flawless families sharing supper in a picture-postcard paradise.

Fuck you all, I wanted to say.

Fuck you.

Fuck you.

All.

As I made my way down the street, I exceeded the speed limit by twenty-seven miles per hour, because at least in flying down a residential road, I felt mother-loving free.

I came upon the fine antique shop, which to my good fortune kept late enough hours that I could make the trip tonight. It was a great bargaining tool for getting me out of the house, and Nate knew that. This was his most honest expression of compromise. But somewhere along the way, somewhere between my home and the antique shop, my life would change forever, and this time it would be an irrevocable change, where even eternity could not change its mind.

I got out of my car and locked the door behind me. The antique shop sat along a quiet street with a string of quaint and charming cafés. I loved to look through windows in search of Felicity's soul, and as I stared at young lovers from all throughout the city, I noticed the distinct essence of a woman who dined with another woman in the far corner of a café by the name of Sam's Lot.

And I stopped.

And I stared.

And stared.

My eyes *and* my mind had surely been taken over by a form of mental torment that in this moment I called dementia.

And I stared.

Stared.

And I *stared.*

I took baby steps toward the window in frozen feet that did not wish to move, crystallized within a body that did not wish to respond, under the heavy scrutiny of eyes that had gone bad and a mind that had gone mother-loving mad.

I stood at the window as I had done so many times before, crying and begging, pleading and talking to God, asking for him to bring back Felicity from the dead and give her to me as his kindest act of mercy on behalf of humankind. I have stood for what seemed like half of my life, looking out of and *into* picture windows in search of something that would prove to me beyond all knowing that life goes on beyond the grave and that those whom we choose to love in life and in death go on.

I have called on God's grace and divinity with all that I am and ever would be in hopes that in between a single thread of fabric, in all of life's existence, that he would hear me and answer me back.

Tonight he did.

He answered me back by calling my name out loud as the woman who sat in the corner, dining on scrambled egg whites and slightly burnt toast for dinner, was no other than Felicity Hardaway herself!

I literally stood dumbfounded.

Amazed.

On the verge of passing out onto the concrete, melting and drizzling away down the street to pour into the city sewer for lack of something greater to do in this bizarre turn of events.

Felicity Hardaway?

For I thought with certainty I had done it—gone stark, raving, raging mad, staring at the woman at the table, who would briefly and intermittently reach across her plate to hold hands with a lover, until she looked up from her eggs and toast only to lock eyes with mine with a piercing green reflection. And it was here that I collapsed onto the concrete for a spell of time, but I was down no more than ten seconds, and before I could stand up, there was a gentleman who rushed to my side to assist me.

"Are you okay?" he asked with great concern.

"Yes," I said, a bit disheveled, "just . . . just . . ." I quickly rose to my feet, turning my attention back to the window, but she was gone. And I desperately plowed inside the restaurant as the man called after me, "You sure you okay?"

I didn't bother to answer, for there was no time when fate and destiny, hell and heaven, earth and all its inhabitants were calling out to me . . .

F-e-l-i-c-i-t-y

It was whispering in the wind; it was cutting through the air; it was the fragrance of the fresh flowers and the lilies of the field. I barged into the restaurant with a look of desperation, and all would turn their attention to me.

What in the hell? it seemed as though they said, but instead they opted for, "Can we help you, miss?"

"Where's . . . where's . . . Felicity?" I asked, barely able to breathe and mouth the words that were getting stuck on the roof of my tongue.

"Felicity!" I screamed aloud in the restaurant, making the customers stop and stare.

Fuck you all.

Eat your steak.

I've got things to do, I felt like saying, but I did not have time for such frivolous conversation when the most pressing urge, bending upon my chest, screamed, *Find her.*

"Where's your bathroom?" I asked in haste. They pointed and I was gone. I opened the bathroom and saw only empty stalls, and it would seem that I would search them one by one till turning in desperation to head out of the door, and *there she stood.*

And I stopped.

Speechless.

Horrified.

Scared of her almost.

A ghost?

Real?

Dead?

Alive?

She seemed as equally all of those things herself. Eternity slammed into time, and neither of us uttered a word for sixteen seconds, because I counted, and then from her vocal cords, a string of words would tear: "This is not a ghost you're looking at, girl, so ease up on the eyes."

I did not speak.

I did not smile.

I did not bend or cater to joy as though this were God's answered prayer on my desperate behalf. I would not surrender to great relief that the dead had arisen. I would not recount the story of Jesus Christ and wonder if this were a modern-day compliment to his own resurrection. No, instead I would rage with emotion—anger, and betrayal—teething with violence and hurt. And eventually, my first words to her in three long years would be, "I could kill you myself."

And just like that, she smiled and pulled out a cigarette. I could not BELIEVE her casual stance. She had raped me of a life belonging to love.

"That's all you got to say for yourself?" she asked, taking a hit of the cigarette and blowing the smoke directly in my face. In this moment, all of my love for her turned to vicious hate.

"I grieved for three years!" I said with anger and rage. "Three long years!"

Three mothafucking years!

Three years, Felicity!

"You shouldn't have wasted your tears, darling," she said with no remorse.

"You're a monster," I directly accused. "Who fucking pretends to be dead?"

"Somebody who doesn't want to be alive in the life they're living," she said very casually. It all seemed like play and games, shits and giggles. "I told you from the gate, Blaze, that somebody could get hurt."

"And I told you three years ago that somebody already had gotten hurt! How could you do that to another human being? Just up and die? Just fucking pretend to be . . . to be . . . you're fucking SICK—how could you do that to me when I loved you?"

She seemed unmoved as she took another hit off the cigarette.

"I loved you!" I screamed. "I couldn't breathe without you! I loved you!"

In that moment, the toilet flushed and I became consciously aware that we had not been alone in the bathroom. The woman who had dined with Felicity, a beautiful Latin woman, slowly exited her stall and walked to the sink and began to wash her hands. And this is where it all ended, life as I knew it when Humpty Dumpty would say good-bye at his final curtain call.

"I never loved you, Blaze," said Felicity Hardaway to my face for the very first time, "but I liked you a lot. I knew that you would *never* get on with your life as long I was in the picture. I didn't want that for you. I truly thought that out of all the scum in that miserable little town, that of all people, *you* deserved better." Then she glanced upon my shiny, bright, huge wedding ring that sparkled, and twinkled under the bathroom lighting. "And it looks like you got it," she said.

I stood in the middle of the floor flabbergasted beyond all description, for this is something words will never be able to convey, and there is no translation for the hole that had just been blown through my existence. And while desperately trying not to shake, weep, and melt upon the floor, I could barely get enough oxygen in my lungs to speak these words out loud. "You were never, ever in my picture, Felicity," I said. "You *were* my picture."

And with that, all the tears came, and the Latin woman washing her hands turned off the water and stepped around me, catching hands with Felicity. They stood as lovers, neither having the guts to look into my desperate eyes and see my broken heart bleeding from the creases of my stare.

"You deserved a better view," whispered Felicity as she and the Latin woman, in perfect synchronicity, turned to form a perfect circle, closing the widest gap of my life upon their exit. And I would stand in utter numbness knowing not what to say, do, or be.

I drove home in silence.

And stillness.

On automatic, barely remembering where I lived, unable to fathom what to do now with the rest of my life.

Life is a master game, and it is we who decide its outcome with every hand that we play. We are the chess pieces, and life is the sweeping motion that moves us across a checker board.

There are infinite outcomes, but only one eternal movement—
evolution.

Life goes on.

It can move with elegance or grace, or it can be blown and
ravaged by harsh winds.

It can die.

And obviously after tonight, I have seen that it can also come
back to motherfucking life.

It is the compliment of every choice we make.

Like for like.

No exceptions.

No rules.

Even when we're wrong, life will honor our mistakes and
make them rightly our own to bear the fruit of our decisions.
Life *is* the greatest audience of all, for it is always prepared to
give back to us an accurate reflection of the worlds we choose to
see beyond our windows.

It can be narrow.

Or grandiose.

It can be streaked with the strokes of sadness or brightened
by the colors of joy. It can be dirtied, it can be cleaned, it can be
cracked, even shattered, but always there is a window for our
viewing. And always, it will be our choice, of what we choose to
see beyond our skin.

By the time I arrived home, it was close to midnight, and I
would have no recollection of or accountability for the past four
hours of my life.

Nate was a tattered mess, and upon entry into our home, he
grabbed me into his arms and held me tight.

"Dear God," he cried out, "I thought something had happened to you."

I did not respond, just allowed myself to rest in his arms,
hoping that he would never remove himself from my counsel.

"I was afraid that you had died in an accident," he whispered,
weeping gently.

I pulled away and looked at him, this desperate man who
loved me so much, beside himself and run amuck by his affec-

tions. And for the first time, I saw *myself*. Nathaniel Wheaton
was me. He was just wearing a different body.

Same heart.

Same raging love.

Same desperate need.

Same deep longing for connection.

I was Nathaniel Wheaton.

"I could have," I whispered softly in his ear.

"What?" he asked, pulling me back, frightened.

"I could have died tonight," I said in a daze. "It would have
been . . . easy."

"What are you saying?" he asked, beginning a panicked inspection of my body with his eyes. "Are you hurt?"

I sat down in the middle of the floor, and I motioned for him
to sit down in front of me, which he did. I looked into his eyes
for the very first time and I saw a soul.

It was love.

It was compassion.

It was frail.

It was invincible.

It was a whisper.

A deafening thunder.

It was life.

All of life.

It was Nate and it was me.

I slowly began to unbutton his shirt and rub his chest gently
with my hands. He closed his eyes and clung to my touch, like
the dying reaching for their last breath. And I followed the
curves and dents of his chest, and massaged and caressed him as
though he were a work of art, all of life in motion, poured from
eternity into time.

In this moment, I began to think that there was no such
thing as gay, straight, or bisexual. There was no place called ho-
mosexual, and no destiny of heterosexual, and no lost island of
transsexual. There was no normal and no abnormal. There was
no acceptable and unacceptable. There was no perverted and
nonperverted expression. There were no hang-ups or put-downs.

There was nothing, nothing, NO-THING but love wrapped up in *skin*. As I rubbed his chest, I whispered into his ear on the edge of breaking down, "I want to tell you something."

"What baby?" he asked me, eager to hear.

"It's something that you should know," I whispered.

"Talk to me, baby. What is it?"

After a long, breathy pause, I finally spoke. And these words would close out the final chapter in the greatest love story never lived: "Felicity Hardaway is *dead*."

FINDING ME

Darnella Ford

The following questions are intended
to enhance your group's discussion
of this book.

Discussion Questions

1. What is the nature of Blaze and Aerial's relationship prior to the fire, and how does it change after the tragedy?

2. Do you agree with the manner in which the twins' mother, Aliyah James, separated the girls following the fire? Was there a more appropriate way in which to handle the situation in keeping the girls connected?

3. In your opinion, should Blaze have lived with Felicity Hardaway following the tragedy?

4. Do you feel that Felicity influenced Blaze in choosing the lifestyle of a lesbian?

5. In your opinion, is a woman *born* lesbian or is it nothing more than *learned* behavior? Is homosexuality "wrong"? Explore your ideas about Christianity and homosexuality.

6. Did Blaze resent Aliyah James when she became an adult? If so, why?

7. How did you feel about Felicity and Blaze's love affair? Should Felicity have prevented the relationship from occurring? Who was responsible, if anyone?

8. Explore your feelings about Felicity's "fake death" and its impact upon Blaze's life.

9. What was the nature of Blaze and Nathaniel's relationship and how did it change throughout the story, if ever?

10. What did Blaze learn by the story's end? What did you learn by story's end?

Enjoy the following excerpt from Darnella Ford's

NAKED LOVE

Available now wherever books are sold.

Prologue

A Suicide Note

I am a simple Midwesterner, who, on this beautiful autumn morning in downtown Chicago, made my way to the twenty-eighth floor of the Landmark II building, climbed twenty-eight flights of stairs, gained access to the roof, walked to the edge, and jumped.

This is the story of a dying woman who has twenty-eight floors, fifty-seven seconds to tell her side of the story, and not a moment more. Time is of the essence, so let us not waste a page, a splotch of ink, or a breath.

This is not a suicide note; this is a suicide novel, and once I hit the concrete, the rest of this story will be written in my blood. But do not be alarmed—it is a fascinating story, I promise.

Chapter 28

As I plummeted toward the ground from the twenty-eighth floor, I remembered Juno and the day he lost his virginity.

The less you know about me, the better, and it's not because I'm riddled with flaws but because my life span is grossly short. From this page forward, my life expectancy is fifty-seven seconds, so I implore you to reserve judgment till the end as we return to the beginning of time.

My name is Adrian Moses. In many ways I have always felt like the biblical Moses, wandering the wilderness, waiting to be delivered from *everything* breathing.

My skin and eyes are so translucent that if by chance you blink upon meeting me, I become invisible. I have been called "painfully beautiful" by many, and even I am amazed at how well God tended to the details while putting me together. My exterior is exquisite; however, do not be fooled by that, as my interior life reflects something entirely different.

I am thirteen today, but by tomorrow I will be thirty-one years old, because all you need to change time is a pen that doesn't erase.

I grew up in Saxon, Wisconsin, a small town two hours north of Milwaukee. My mother died of cancer when I was two, leaving me to be raised by my father, Juno. That's what he insisted that I call him: Juno.

Not Papa.

Not Daddy.

Not Father.

Not friend.

"Juno to you, my dear," he would often remind me. "Juno only."

Juno was his stage name. My father was an actor, brilliant and before his time. He had a theatrical production named after him, *Juno and the Temple of Gloom*. It was the longest-running one-man show in the history of Saxon.

Juno was funny, witty, articulate, and tortured.

"Juno, may I have another piece of toast?" I would ask each morning at the breakfast table.

He would giggle like a girl. "Why certainly, daughter, you can have another piece of toast and another after that."

"Another after that," I would mimic when he turned his back. "And another after that."

Juno was different from most of the fathers on the block. He would dance around the kitchen each morning like a schoolgirl, wearing an apron and fancy hairpins.

Juno was so feminine that I was never sure if that was just part of his act. "And another after that and another after that, daughter," he would mumble incessantly, trying so hard to please me. On many occasions, he would insist that I was his daughter but never that he was my father.

"You are my daughter," said Juno on one such day.

"And you are my f—" I would begin, but he'd cut me off.

"Ah," he scolded. "Bite your tongue."

"But why can't I say the word *father*?" I always asked.

"Because I am an *actor*—more specifically, Juno," he would declare. "And performers must be free to be . . ."

"Be what?" I challenged.

"To be whatever the script dictates," he said passionately. "For I am *created*."

When he said that, my eyes would roll back in my head. I wanted to mock him so badly, it was all I could do to control myself. "Juno, isn't that make-believe?" I asked him. And when he heard those words, he grabbed his chest dramatically. "Make-believe?" he squealed. "Make-believe?"

Oh Juno, I thought, *you're such a drama queen.*

"The only make-believe things in this world," he'd whisper in my ear, "are the phony lives we try to convince the rest of the world we are living. I, on the other hand, am very realistic about my fantasy world."

Juno was a combo of Pee-wee Herman and Mr. Rogers, and if that doesn't scare you, nothing will.

He was always running late, behind, or on empty. He was always catching his breath, wiping the sweat off his brow, trying to keep up and catch up. And perhaps the fact that his sperm took it upon themselves to reproduce and deliver him an off-spring was the greatest irony of all.

"What do you want to be, daughter?" he asked, usually every day.

"I want to be rich."

"That's nothing to aspire to," he said. "Who cares about riches?"

"I do," I would say. "I want to live in an ivory castle."

"Castles are overrated," he said.

"How do you know?"

"I was born in one in Milwaukee," he said. "Reva Joe Moses was the queen of the castle and I was her prince."

"Your mother was a queen?"

"Yes," he said, "so trust me when I tell you that castles are overrated."

"Okay," I said. "Then I want to be an artist."

"Oh," he would squeal with delight. "What kind?"

"I want to write the story of my life."

"But you're only a teenager," he said with a laugh. "You haven't lived enough life to make a very long story yet, eh?"

"I've lived long enough."

"Nonsense. There's a lot of living left to do," he would always say, while attaching an apron to the front of his feminine-looking pants.

After Mother died, Juno started wearing aprons, hairpins, and skirts, easing toward womanhood and a little farther away from manhood. At first, I thought he did it because he needed to protect himself from spilling biscuit flour all over him, but after a while I began to worry that it was more than that. He began to go through an identity crisis, changing from male to female in front of my eyes—at least that's what I gathered from the pre-death photos of him and my mother. As far as I was concerned, they both died back in the summer of '69. My father was never the same after my mother died. It was like he became someone else, lost in grief. It was as if he made a personal vow *never* to be normal again.

I used to have friends till the eighth grade, but then I came home early one day with playmates to find my beloved father scrambling eggs, wearing a skirt, high heels, and a pair of Hanes panty hose. He'd inserted tube socks under his shirt in place of breasts.

"Juno!" I screamed. "You're wearing a skirt!" He was so startled that he dropped a raw egg on the floor. I remember it bursting open, sunnyside out, raw and oozing.

The grits hit the fan.

The eggs hit the floor.

Juno is a boy who wants to be a girl.

Your father's posing for Cosmo *on his downtime.*

He's a girl on his off days and when no one's home, he's masturbating to the Julia Child cooking show.

Dear God, do away with me now!

He even shaved his legs and armpits. He had less body hair than I did.

Cold cream.

And mud masks.

Hair gels.

And manicures.

"Juno!" I shouted. "Why are you wearing an old lady's skirt?"

"This is not a skirt!" he insisted. "This is a kilt!" he said, trying to justify the absurdity. "And I'm wearing it for a role that I landed in the new town play!"

"What?" I asked him, horrified.

"I am a Scottish guard," he said, parading around the kitchen in front of my friends, who were giggling amongst themselves.

"Do guards wear lipstick and mascara?" I snapped, noticing his makeup.

My friends burst into laughter and ran out of our house. From that day on, I also became an absurdity, just like Juno. The world would define me in the same manner they defined him, so we *both* became outsiders.

I loved him because he was so beautifully unusual, and at the same time, I hated him because he was so ridiculously unusual.

I juggled both emotions emphatically and erratically, waiting for the moon to pull on the tide to ascertain exactly how it was that I felt about Juno.

Poignant.

That is the best description I could come up with.

I felt *poignant* about him.

"I'm having a crisis," I confided to him on the eve of my fourteenth birthday.

"Why?"

"Because I have these," I said, ripping open my shirt and exposing my breasts, which had grown rather large during the last year of my life.

Juno's eyes popped out of his head because he could not believe how gargantuan my breasts had become. Now, it may seem odd revealing my breasts to my father, but Juno was so feminine it was like showing them to a woman. No big whoop.

"Oh my," he said gently. "We'll have to upgrade your cup holders."

"My cup holders?" I asked, eyes wide.

"Yes," he replied flatly.

"You mean my *bra*?" I said loudly, pulling on the words for emphasis.

"Yes, yes," he replied briskly.

"Okay," I replied.

Tortured by reality and tormented by dreams, I often found him sitting on the bedroom floor, crying real tears for a life barely lived at all.

"Juno," I called gently. "Juno, are you unwell?" He wouldn't respond. He'd just sit with his back against the wall, eyes cast downward, spiraling out of control in silence.

"Shhh," he advised softly.

And I would stop speaking *and* breathing.

"Shhh," he would repeat. "Back up and give me space, daughter. Give me space to go."

"Where are you going?"

"Crazy," he'd say. And then water would begin to flow from his eyes.

Crazy.

I would crawl on all fours to sit beside him in silence. If he was really going crazy, I was destined to be an orphan before all was said and done.

"Why are you crying, Juno?"

"Because I am sad," he replied softly.

"Why are you sad?"

And that's where the conversation would end because Juno just stopped responding.

Why are you sad?

Why are you sad?

And why are you sad?

He never answered and I never knew. It felt like I spent my entire life reading Juno's emotional barometer. Loving and distant at the same time, he wasn't an authentic, active participant in my childhood. He was too busy chasing his own little boy *or* girl on stage three nights a week, and when the lights dropped low, Juno appeared center stage to deliver his monologue to the eager residents of Saxon and Milwaukee. He entertained the crowd with theatrics and dramatics as I sat in the front row applauding. Every night he got a standing ovation from the tiny audience of twenty people or so—we would rise to our feet to pay homage to a man who was truly one of God's unique creations.

I was human till the age of fourteen—then I became something else. I woke up one night after having a nightmare, hoping to sneak into Juno's room and steal a space on the floor for comfort. But upon entry, I found him on his knees in a submissive position, sucking a gentleman's *wee wee* like a lollipop.

Oh, dear God!

I screamed.

Juno screamed and so did his companion. All three of us sounded like adolescent girls, but in truth, only one of us was.

Me.

Not them.

Me.

I quickly tore out of the room while Juno yelled something inaudible to his male companion, some sort of indecipherable gibberish or code.

I ran back into my bedroom and locked the door. This was beyond any nightmare a fourteen-year-old girl could ever have on her own.

God, can you please take me now? I collapsed face first into my pillows and sobbed, while Juno struggled with damage control on the other side of the door.

"Daughter!" he called. "Daughter, let me in!"

I did not respond because I did not think he was worthy of a reply.

"Daughter!" he called in panic. "Daughter, let me in!"

Knock forever, Juno, but I'll never let you in.

Knock again.

And again.

But I'll never let you in.

I'll just lie here until I rot, waiting for God to deliver me, just like Moses did.

"Daughter!" he yelled.

"Daughter!"

The next day I finally unlocked my bedroom door and stepped

outside. There lay Juno, face pressed against my bedroom wall where he had fallen asleep mid-knock at midnight.

"Juno," I said, shaking his sleeping body. "It's time to get up off the floor." Slowly, he opened his eyes, which were blanketed by shame and humiliation. "It's time to get up off the floor," I repeated as I walked away. "You're not a virgin anymore."